I0729370

Strong Women Series, Book 3

Thecla, the First Woman Evangelist

Mary Jo Nickum

Saguaro Books, LLC
SB
Arizona

Saguaro Books, LLC
16845 E. Avenue of the Fountains, Ste. 325
Fountain Hills, AZ 85268
www.saguarobooks.com

ISBN: 978-1-7366967-2-9
Library of Congress Cataloging Number
LCCN: 2022933329
Printed in the United States of America
First Edition

Dedication

This book is dedicated to those who are willing to walk in the footprints of biblical characters who preached about and brought people to Jesus. What was life like for an evangelist in those days, especially a woman? Were they thinking much the same as we do today? What were their challenges? Did they love, preach and bleed as many dedicated evangelists have done through the ages?

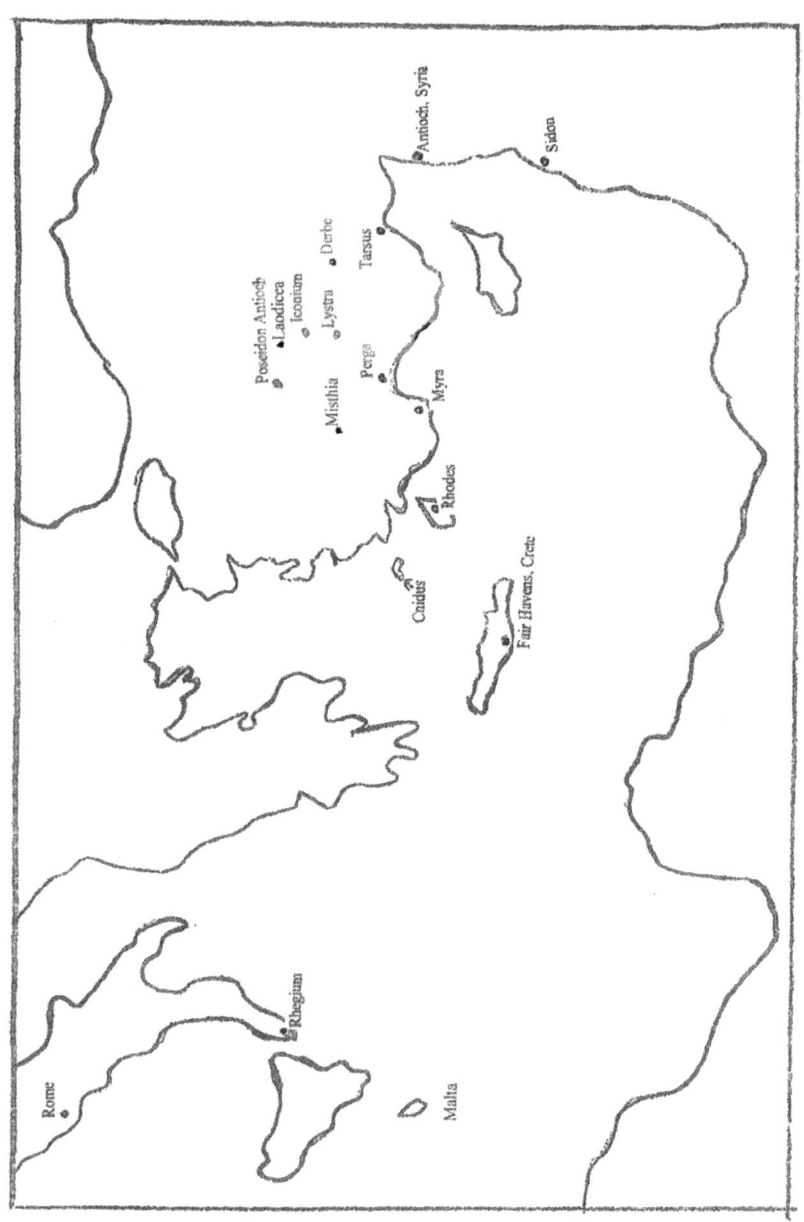

Places and towns where Thecla traveled

Prologue

Paul prophesies Thecla's eventual status as an apostle: "Go and teach the word, and complete the evangelical course, and share with me the zeal for Christ. For this reason Christ has chosen you through me, so that he may draw you to the apostolic office (eis apostolē̄n) *and entrust to you some of the still uninstructed cities"*

The story of Thecla is a legend. There is no unshakable proof she existed. There were many women and men in the early church who believed she did exist. Her life story developed from *The Acts of Paul and Thecla*, a non-canonical work read widely in the first century. Let us, then, suppose she did exist. How would her life have unfolded?

Iconium (modern Konya) is located 150 mi. south of Ankara and about 100 mi. east of Pisidian Antioch—via the road system. Paul and Barnabas visited the city on Paul's first missionary journey (Acts 13:51–14:7). Here they preached in the synagogue then the city. After about three months the opposition became so great they had to flee for their lives to Lystra and Derbe. Paul revisited the city on his second (Acts 16:2) and probably third journeys.

Iconium is situated at the western edge of the great Anatolian plateau at an elevation of 3,600 feet and roads from the east, especially from Cilicia (Tarsus) gather to it. From Iconium, there is a pass through the mountains to the west — as the road heads toward Pisidian Antioch. In Paul's day, the prosperous city of Iconium was a Roman colony.

From her early years in Iconium, to her captivation with Paul's teachings, Thecla was devoted to God. At first, she'd heard other traveling ministers, preaching "The Word". They hadn't struck her as having anything to offer in faith, until she heard Paul. She thought Paul was the most beautiful human being she'd ever seen. Sure, he walked with a slight limp, but that made him even more interesting. His voice though was captivating. He spoke loud enough for everyone gathered in the street to hear him. His voice was that of someone self-assured, someone who knew he was right. His message made sense. The subject, of course, was God and His everlasting goodness. Thecla was in love, she thought, but not sure if it was God she loved or Paul, or both. The seed of admiration was planted.

The next day, Paul came back to the street to speak again. Thecla ventured down the steps of her family home to listen. She stood in the back of the gathering, watching the reaction of those close to her as she glimpsed Paul past the heads of the taller, surrounding listeners. Paul was calling those who believed his message to come forward and follow him to a lake outside of town for baptism. She wanted to follow to see what this baptism involved but didn't think she was ready to be baptized yet. Several of those around her mumbled in the affirmative but many shrank back and began to walk away. At that point, she heard her mother calling her back inside the house. She returned.

Thecla had few encounters with Paul after that for some years. Thecla was of Egyptian descent, via her mother, with caramel colored skin, black hair and eyes. She continued to grow and mature until she was sixteen, her beauty undeniable. Her mother found a man and had Thecla betrothed. Thecla was not happy but there wasn't anything she could do, or was there? After all, it was customary. Her mother began to prepare for the eventual wedding. Thecla was not included nor did she want to be. She felt her life was about to take another path and it would involve Paul.

Chapter 1. Thecla's Early Years

A loud rumble echoed off the walls. The house shook. People were running in the street. Thecla and her mother were not overly alarmed. Earthquakes were not unusual. They occurred every two or three years. This one, though, seemed more violent, closer, with more damage. That's when her brother, Leos, called that a wall had cracked and in danger of collapse. Thecla and her mother, Theoclia, hurried to the steps to the back entrance to answer Leos' call.

"What has happened?" Theoclia asked.

"There is a large crack in the north wall, just above the steps," Leos reported.

"Do you think it will hold?"

"It's hard to say. It doesn't show on the outside, so it might not have gone completely through."

"That's possible. We'll try to get Alexander, the stone mason to look at it later today or tomorrow. Will you please try to find him and ask when he can look at it?"

"Yes, Mother, I'll start searching for him now. He'll probably be busy."

"Yes, I'm sure he will be. I wonder how many other homes have been damaged."

"Probably several, so I might be gone for a while."

"Yes, please be careful,"

Theoclia and Thecla returned to the living quarters and returned to their needlework. Sewing and weaving took many hours of their days. The material was woven in long sheets to be cut and sewn into robes for everyday wear. A loom took at least half the space of one room, positioned near a window to provide light and ample, air movement for the comfort of the weaver. Theoclia was an accomplished weaver, Thecla was learning. She studied and practiced weaving every day. It was an important craft to learn to make her a good wife, along with cooking.

"I hope Leos will be able to find Alexander," Theoclia commented to Thecla.

"I'm sure he will, if he doesn't stop to help people who are having worse problems than us," Thecla replied.

"Yes, he's learned well. He should try to help others but, right now, we need help too."

"Agreed. He'll do his best, I think."

Silence ensued as both women went back to work. The slap, bump, slap of the loom made the only noise in the house. Voices could be heard from the street, with an occasional scream or yelp.

Thecla and her mother put down their weaving and sewing tasks to begin to make dinner. They baked bread in the outdoor oven in the back of the house. Thecla proceeded to mix the dough and knead it for baking. She formed a perfect round ball, flattened it somewhat and slid it into the oven. She proceeded to watch the oven to maintain the even heat and time it so as not to overbake it. In the meantime, Theoclia prepared the olives, nuts and fruit to accompany the meal. It was nearly meal time and Leos had not arrived.

Theoclia called out to Thecla, "Do you see Leos anywhere?"

"No, Mother, I was wondering about him too."

"I hope he's all right. How is the bread?"

"It will be done soon, Mother. Should we eat or wait for Leos?"

"I think we should eat, he'll be along and, if he hasn't already eaten, he can eat when he gets back."

"All right, the bread is done. I'm bringing it in."

Both women sat to eat. The bread was hot and filling, the olives were tasty, the fruit was sweet. They'd just finished eating when Leos bounded up the back stairs to the kitchen.

"Sorry, Mother, I've been all over most of the town. There is a large amount of damage. I found Alexander. He said he'd come over tomorrow to look at our damage. Then I stopped to listen to two men preaching about God. I think their names were Paul and Barnabas, or something like that. They seemed so intent on spreading their word, I just couldn't walk away."

"I understand, Leos. We were beginning to worry. You had been gone so long," said Theoclia.

I wonder who the new preachers are, thought Thecla. *I've not heard those names before. Maybe they'll come by our street and I'll hear them. I've been wanting to hear about this new religion with only one God for everything. The Roman gods sound confusing and silly. I just can't make myself believe in them.*

"What did these preachers look like?" Thecla asked.

"They'd been traveling. They were dusty and needed a bath, a change of clothes and some water to drink. Their voices were a little hard to hear," Leos said.

"What colors were their robes?" Thecla asked.

"I'm not sure. I think brown not red, though. They weren't Romans, if that's what you're worried about," Leos said.

"No, they probably weren't Romans if they were talking about one God," Thecla reasoned.

"What does it matter?" Theoclia said. "There are always various kinds of preachers coming through here, Thecla; I'm wondering why you're so interested."

"Because I like the 'one God' approach to religion," Thecla stated.

"Well, here we go again. You know that's against Caesar. You'll get us all in trouble if you keep that up," Theoclia stated.

"Yes," Leos piped up. "That might even make trouble for Father in the Roman army. He's trying to earn a Centurion position, remember."

"Yes, it could spell trouble for your father, if word gets out, which it surely will; and Leos wants to follow in his father's footsteps in another few years," Theoclia said.

That won't stop me from learning as much as I can about the 'one God'. Maybe I'll follow the preachers too. The Romans will never know. They don't know who I am nor do they care. It's not going to be a problem for Father or Leos, Thecla thought.

Some days later, Thecla sat by the window busily engaged on a sewing task. She listened to the hub bub on the street below. Suddenly, the sounds changed, voices softened and two men approached the steps to the fountain. One appeared to walk with a limp, maybe slightly disfigured. The other one was older, robust and helped the one who limped climb the steps. They stood, looking at the crowd and the crowd hushed.

"That's them," Leos said, as he stood behind Thecla.

Startled, she said, "Who?"

"The ones I told you about last night."

"Go find something to do while I listen to them."

"Why do you want to listen to them? It might be considered treason."

"Oh, hush. Go away."

"I'm going to get Mother."

"She went out. Leave her out of this. Now, go."

Leos shuffled out of the room. Thecla was able to settle in the window to listen.

Chapter 2. Thecla Hears Paul

Seated comfortably in the window, sewing forgotten, Thecla listened as Barnabas spoke first. He gathered the crowd to face the speakers and began a prayer to God: "Our Father, who art in Heaven..." he intoned. Some of the crowd recognized the prayer and joined him. Other stood respectfully quiet. Barnabas stepped back and Paul introduced himself. Most recognized him and applauded, some whooping. Paul thanked them, blessed them and proceeded to preach.

"We gather today in praise of our Lord God and Jesus, our Savior. Men of Israel and you Gentiles who fear God, listen to me! The God of the people of Israel chose our fathers. He made them into a great people during their stay in Egypt, and with an uplifted arm He led them out of that land. He endured their conduct for about forty years in the wilderness and, having vanquished seven nations in Canaan, He gave their land to His people as an inheritance. All this took about 450 years.

After this, God gave them judges until the time of Samuel the prophet. Then the people asked for a king, and God gave them forty years under Saul son of Kish, from the tribe of Benjamin. After removing Saul, He raised up David as their king and testified about him: 'I have found David son of Jesse a man after My own heart; he will carry out My will in its entirety.'

From the descendants of this man, God has brought to Israel the Savior Jesus, as He promised. Before the arrival of Jesus, John preached a baptism of repentance to all the people of Israel. As John was completing his course, he said, 'Who do you suppose I am? I am not that One. But He is coming after me whose sandals I am not worthy to untie.'

Brothers, children of Abraham, and you Gentiles who fear God, it is to us that this message of salvation has been sent. The people of Jerusalem and their rulers did not recognize Jesus, yet in condemning Him they fulfilled the words of the prophets that are read every Sabbath. And though they found no ground for a death sentence, they asked Pilate to have Him executed.

When they had carried out all that was written about Him, they took Him down from the tree and laid Him in a tomb. But God raised Him from the dead, and for many days He was seen by those who had accompanied Him from Galilee to Jerusalem. They are now His witnesses to our people.

And now we proclaim to you the good news: What God promised our fathers He has fulfilled for us, their children, by raising up Jesus. As it is written in the second Psalm:

'You are My Son; today I have become Your Father.'

In fact, God raised Him from the dead, never to see decay. As He has said:

'I will give you the holy and sure blessings promised to David.'

So also, He says in another Psalm:

'You will not let Your Holy One see decay.'

For when David had served God's purpose in his own generation, he fell asleep. His body was buried with his fathers and saw decay. But the One whom God raised from the dead did not see decay.

Therefore let it be known to you, brothers, that through Jesus the forgiveness of sins is proclaimed to you. Through Him everyone who believes is justified from everything you could not be justified from by the Law of Moses. Watch out, then, that what was spoken by the prophets does not happen to you:

'Look, you scoffers, wonder and perish!

For I am doing a work in your days that you would never believe, even if someone told you.'" [1]

Thecla closed her mouth, as she found it open when she returned to the present. She was absolutely enthralled by Paul's message. His voice thrilled her. She wanted to continue to hear his voice. Thecla moved away from the window, closed her eyes and listened to him in her head.

'You are My Son; today I have become Your Father.' In fact, God raised Him from the dead, never to see decay. As He has said:
'I will give you the holy and sure blessings promised to David.' So also, He says in another Psalm:
'You will not let Your Holy One see decay.'

Thecla listened to it repeatedly in her head. Finally, unwillingly, her attention was drawn away by the appearance of her mother.

"My goodness, Thecla, what or who were you dreaming about? You looked miles away when I came in here."

"I was right here. I was just thinking about what I heard from speakers across the street at the fountain."

"And who were they?"

"Paul and Barnabas, the same ones Leos heard yesterday."

"What did they say? Oh, forget that. I don't want to hear it and I don't want you listening to that babble."

"Mother. It was a beautiful message."

"Quiet. I'll hear no more. I explained last night what the dangers are. I don't want you listening to that tripe any more. Stay away from that window."

"I need to sit at the window to sew. You know I need the light."

"No more arguing with me. Bake the bread for dinner."

Thecla rose and left to bake the bread.

"What happened? Mother found out about your listening to those ministers, didn't she?" Leos asked, with a smirk.

"Yes. It isn't funny either. The message was clear. Paul is a rapturous speaker," answered Thecla, as she prepared the bread.

"Yeah, you were raptured because he's a man," Leos teased.

"Oh, stop it, Leos. You should listen to them both. Maybe you'd learn something."

"Naw, I already know how to capture a woman's attention."

"Stop it. Go away. You are being evil."

Thecla slipped the bread in the oven and shut the oven door harder than she intended, making a loud banging sound. Her mother came to the door looked out but said nothing, returning to her work on the meal.

Several days later, Leos boastingly teased Thecla, "Paul and his friend are going to preach in the Synagogue. They won't be in the street or at the fountain anymore. What are you going to do? You aren't Jewish so you probably won't be able to get in. Oh, what will you do?"

"I'll go to hear him at the Synagogue. That's why he's not been back to the fountain. The crowd has grown too large. You see, little brother, there are many who are listening and believing."

"Stop calling me 'little brother'. I'm enlisting in the Roman army soon then you'll see me in red with a helmet and a sword, same as Father," Leos said, as he retreated to the back of the house to continue his swordsmanship practice.

I must go to the Synagogue. I need to hear Paul and see him. I had better leave now, while Mother is out. Leos is sure to tell her where I've gone and she'll be angry but I can deal with her.

Thecla readied herself and left the house through the front door. She was feeling exhilarated with a strange sense of freedom. She had made a decision, not realizing it was a life changing decision. As she approached the Synagogue, she viewed a large crowd milling about. At that point, doors opened and people pushed and jostled to get in. Thecla was in the back of the crowd and the seating was almost completely filled when she entered. She spied one seat in the front row and almost ran to take it before another man was able to get to it. This meant she was only a few feet from Paul and Barnabas. She was pleased with herself, as she waited for the opening prayer.

Barnabas finished the opening prayer and turned the meeting over to Paul. Thecla waited for Paul to begin. He welcomed the crowd and began to teach. He talked of the love of our Everlasting God, of the death and resurrection of Jesus and of the miracles of Jesus. The crowd stood hooting and yelling in belief. Paul suggested those who wanted baptism to follow him to the river outside of the city. Paul and Barnabas exited, with the crowd following close behind. Thecla did not follow; she wanted to watch the baptism ritual but didn't feel she was ready to make the commitment. She still wasn't sure if it were Paul she loved or God or both. Until that decision was clear in her mind, she didn't think baptism was the next step.

Thecla decided it was time to go home and face her mother, who, she was sure, would be irate at her following Paul to the Synagogue. As she opened the door at the top of the steps, she called, "I'm home, Mother."

"Did you enjoy your visit to the Synagogue?" her mother asked, in a stiff tone.

"Yes, I did. As a matter of fact, there was a huge crowd that filled the Synagogue."

"Well, isn't that wonderful? You sound proud of yourself to be a part of such a crowd. You know that will goad the Romans."

"I don't think so, Mother. A part of the crowd followed Paul and Barnabas to the river to be baptized."

"Did you go?"

"No, I don't think I'm ready."

"You better not be. I've already explained to you why you should not be following these strange, fringe ministers with their words. The Romans are sure to arrest these ministers sooner rather than later. I don't want you mixed up with that. Think about your father, in the army, and brother, soon to be in the army. Don't you see how it could be bad for them?"

"I don't think they'll be arrested. They haven't done anything wrong."

"Honestly, Thecla, how can you be so naïve? Of course, they're doing wrong. They're preaching against the Roman gods. Caesar is bound to hear of unrest in Iconium and the general will be commanded to end the affair."

"Oh, Mother, you worry so."

"Yes, I do; for good reason. I've seen these things happen before. I love my family and I don't want to see harm come to them," Theoclia was sounding close to tears now.

"All right, Mother, I'll stay home now." Thecla kissed her mother and went to her room.

Chapter 3. Thecla Is Betrothed

Thecla had resisted the urge to go back to the Synagogue, which continued to draw full capacity crowds. The people came from miles around. The merchants were pleased and the city prospered. Theoclia continued to worry, though. She expressed concern repeatedly to Leos and Thecla that all of this activity would draw attention from Rome.

Theoclia decided it was time to contact the family of the man she'd chosen for Thecla. *I've probably put it off too long now. If I don't get her betrothed, she might run after this Paul, she's so entranced by. Her father will lose patience with me and her. He's already given me a directive to approach his family. I'll approach them tomorrow morning, early. Thamyris will be perfect for her and the family is well to do and well respected.*

The next morning, bright and early, Theoclia left the house to meet Thamyris' family. They were several streets away from Theoclia's house, so she looked a bit disheveled and out of breath when she arrived. She had walked faster than she'd intended so anxious she was to complete this betrothal. Thamyris' mother answered the door and invited her in, offering her a cup of water because of her appearance. Theoclia did not want to waste time on niceties; she wanted the betrothal to happen now. She explained the situation to Thamyris' mother, who, predictably, called in Thamyris' father. Theoclia explained the situation again and produced a signed sheet of parchment containing Theoclia and her husband's names. Thamyris' parents agreed and called Thamyris in to discuss their decision. Theoclia was amazed at Thamyris' poise, as if he had been hoping for such a match for some time. Theoclia thanked them and left, carrying the precious signed document in the case attached to her belt.

When Theoclia arrived home, she immediately called Thecla to the kitchen. Leos was already seated, finishing his morning repast. "Sit down, Thecla. I have some important, wonderful news for you." Thecla took a seat, wondering why her mother was so excited. Theoclia retrieved the parchment sheet from its case and pushed it toward Thecla. Leos craned his neck to glimpse at the heading. "There, Thecla, your father and I have procured Thamyris for your betrothal. I will begin the wedding plans this day. The wedding will take place six months from now, at the winter solstice."

Leos snickered but said nothing. Thecla was aghast. She could think of nothing to say. She knew it would do no good to object; it was tradition. She sat, staring at the document with all the signatures. Theoclia finally said, "Thamyris is a handsome man. He is well respected in the community and will inherit his father's business when his father grows too old to work. Your life will be safe and comfortable. Hopefully, you'll have many children."

At this, Thecla rose quickly from the table and left the kitchen. She went directly to her room, slamming the door. Theoclia rose to follow but stopped at the slam of the door. She heard muffled sobbing coming from the room and commented to Leos, "Thecla is crying, she's so happy. This was a welcome surprise to her."

"No, Mother, I don't think she's crying out of happiness. I think you just shattered the world she envisions for herself. She's in love with Paul. Haven't you noticed?"

"Of course I have. That's why I decided to seal the betrothal now, before she gets further involved with this 'minister'."

"I understand your concern but I don't think the tactic will dissuade her from following Paul. It might make her more determined to follow him."

"Will you help me try to keep her home and away from Paul and this Barnabas?"

"Mother, you know I'll be leaving for the army post in a few days. I won't be able to watch her all the time. You won't be able to hold her against her will. You know how determined she can be."

"Yes, what you say is true. I will appeal to her love and loyalty to family. With Father gone, what more can I do?"

"Nothing, Mother. Father couldn't do anything either, just forbid her to leave. If she's determined to leave and follow Paul, there's nothing any of us can do. She has a mind of her own."

Leos left the kitchen then to practice with his sword. Theoclia sat at the table, her head in her hands and wept. Nothing good would come of this, she realized.

Thecla stayed in her room, declining all meals for three days. She'd heard Leos depart for his army posting but did not emerge from her room to bid him farewell. She did not want to face her mother nor did she want to meet Thamyris. The thought of having his children sickened her and sent her again into paroxysms of sobbing.

Finally on day four, with no tears left, she emerged from her room. Theoclia greeted her, "Feel better, daughter?"

"No, Mother, I'll never feel better."

"You better get over it and prepare yourself to take up the life of a respectable woman in Iconium. You have much to offer and a good future with Thamyris."

"That might sound good to you but it sounds unlivable to me. Through his sermons, Paul has convinced me to live a life of celibacy. The end is near and having children doesn't make sense under those conditions."

"I knew those ministers were filling your mind with treachery. I did not realize it had gotten that bad. Now, you are betrothed and there is nothing you can do about it."

Thecla did not continue the debate; instead, she ate her morning meal and sank deep into thought, *No, I'll not marry Thamyris and I don't want his children. I want to spend the rest of my life listening to Paul. I would marry him and have his children happily, if he wanted to marry. The best I can do is to follow him, yes, follow him. He is an itinerant minister, spreading the Word of God to everyone. He has a group of followers; I'll join them. This is exciting, it's what I want and, I think, what God wants. Now, to get out of the house...*

Theoclia spoke and jarred Thecla out of her reverie, "I'm going out to the market. Stay right here. I want you here doing the sewing we need to be done. I'll be back before noon. Be here."

Thecla said nothing, making no promises. She did not want to disobey her mother; in fact, Paul said it was a sin. She felt her mother was committing a bigger sin by forbidding her to hear the Word of God. Thecla decided to leave to hear Paul, once again, in the Synagogue.

The crowd had already begun to gather as Thecla approached the Synagogue. These people, she learned were Paul's followers. Some said they'd been baptized in Antioch and planned to follow him on to Tarsus. Thecla took up a conversation with a young woman named Zaortha. "My name is Thecla. I've just begun to hear Paul's message. Have you followed him long?"

"Yes," replied Zaortha, "I believe everything he says. He has the Word of God on his lips and tongue."

"I feel the same. I feel liberated when I hear him speak."

"I am committed to follow him and seek none other."

"My mother has betrothed me to a man I refuse to marry. She's trying to keep me away from Paul."

"Join us on the way to Tarsus. We are baptized followers. I am committed to a life of celibacy, as Paul teaches."

"Yes, I know that is what he teaches and I am committed to that way of life too, unless Paul changes that. I'd be willing to marry him."

"Many women have said that. He'll not change his mind. I'm convinced of that."

"It sounds as if you've thought of it too.

"I have and it's not part of Paul. He says it's impure to consider coupling with another. These are the end times and having children will send us to perdition."

"Oh, my, those are strong words. He'll not have any woman then." *A strange man, indeed,* Thecla thought.

Then, the doors to the Synagogue opened and the crowd entered. Thecla took her usual seat in the front row. She felt the anticipation rising in her mind, as she waited for the first glimpse of Paul. Not to be disappointed, Paul and Barnabas entered and a hush came over the crowd almost immediately. Barnabas performed the usual welcome and opening prayer then took his seat and Paul stood. He spoke for several hours telling the people of God's power and love, of Jesus' life on earth, his parables and miracles. As he was completing his description of the meaning of Jesus' crucifixion and death, a disturbance began at the side door of the Synagogue.

Roman soldiers marched directly to Paul and Barnabas and grasped them roughly, binding their hands behind their backs. Thecla was astounded. Many of the crowd came forward to defend Paul but were pushed back and directed to leave or be arrested. Thecla couldn't move if she'd wanted too. She was mesmerized and shocked at the same time. Her brother, Leos, was one of the soldiers shackling Paul and Barnabas. *How can he be part of this? He's heard Paul too, didn't he believe? Maybe I should call his name. Would he acknowledge me? Would he arrest me, too; his own sister? Quite likely...he's a Roman now, just like Father. I'll not give him the chance.*

The Romans cleared the Synagogue and sent the people away. Paul's followers melted into the surrounding community; Zaortha was nowhere to be seen. Thecla decided to go home and deal with her mother. As she trudged up the steps to the front door, her mother rushed out the door to confront her. "Why did you go out? I told you to stay here. Why did you disobey me?" Theoclia shouted.

"I went to hear Paul. He was arrested and Leos was one of the arresting soldiers."

"That's good news. Now get in the house and get to work."

Thecla entered the house and her mother shut the door.

"Now, girl, did you speak to Leos?"

"No, he was busy doing his duty. I thought about calling out his name but I was afraid he'd arrest me too."

"He might have and you would have deserved it."

"Mother, you don't mean that. Why are you being so vindictive?"

"Vindictive? Thecla, you are being difficult. You are about to be a married woman; married to a wholesome, successful young man. What do you think his family would think if you were arrested? Don't you think of the rest of us?"

"Of course I think of the rest of our family that's why I didn't call out his name. I covered my face so he couldn't recognize me."

"And you didn't think of Thamyris' family?"

"Of course not, why should I? I don't plan to marry him."

"It doesn't matter if you plan to marry him, you will marry him."

No I won't. I'll join the traveling group as soon as they gather again. I'll find Zaortha. She has already invited me to join their troupe. I will walk alongside her. We are of the same mind, dedicated to Paul and God.

That night, Thecla couldn't sleep. She kept envisioning Paul in prison, wondering if he were being tortured. She'd heard of that in the Roman prisons. *I'll take some money out of the family treasure box in the hall, go to the prison, bribe a guard and visit Paul. I'll leave out the back door now that Leos is gone; otherwise he'd hear me and wake Mother. This will be easier now.* Thecla dressed and quietly walked to the treasure box, opened the lid, grabbed a small sack of coins and closed the lid quietly. She exited the house and walked swiftly toward the prison. The night was not quiet. The merchants were receiving carts of merchandise to sell in their shops. As in the majority of Roman colonies, the streets were left open to the people for commerce during the day and used at night for carts and wagons to supply the shops.

Thecla arrived at the prison almost an hour later. She was met by a door keeper who asked her business. She stated she wanted to visit a prisoner, as she gently shook the small bag of coins. The door keeper understood her intent and said he'd get the guard. Thecla waited patiently for what seemed an hour. Finally, the guard appeared.

"You wish to visit a prisoner in the middle of the night?" the guard asked.

"Yes," Thecla stated.

"Is this person someone important to you; a relative, a lover?"

"Yes."

"Yes, what?"

"A lover. His name is Paul. He was arrested yesterday in the Synagogue," she said, rattling the coins softly.

"All right, I understand." He held out his hand and she relinquished the bag of coins.

The guard opened the bag to see they were legitimate Roman coins, slid the bag into his uniform pouch and motioned her forward. They entered the prison, walked down the hall past cells of many sleeping inmates then the guard opened a door and they descended a flight of stairs only to enter another long hallway of cells. About halfway down the hall, they stopped and the guard said this is the man you wanted to see. The guard opened the cell and, as she entered, he said, "You have an hour. Better make it quick." The guard slammed the cell door shut, locked it and left.

Thecla immediately ran to Paul. She fell to her knees and grasped his legs. "Oh, Paul, I was in the Synagogue, in the front row, I saw them arrest you."

The moonlight coming through an opening above the cell illuminated her face. "I remember your face. I saw you sitting there, anxiously absorbing my words. What brings you here?"

"I want to hear you again. I want to hear more of your words. I want to be baptized."

"Sweet child of God, calm yourself, all in due time. There is much yet for you to learn and absorb."

"You were about to tell us of Jesus' passion and death and what that means to us. Tell me this now, while I sit at your feet to listen."

While Thecla listened, Paul began the story of Jesus' arrival in Jerusalem, riding an ass, His arrest, torture, crucifixion and death. Each event was explained and the meaning to believers presented in detail. Finally, late in the night Paul told her of Jesus' resurrection, its importance to believers and, finally, His ascension into heaven. Thecla started to cry in appreciation and an outlet of devotion. She was struggling with the thoughts of going back to her mother and staying with Paul.

Thecla begged Paul again for baptism. He relented and reached for his water bowl. He poured some of the water from the bowl onto her head saying the words of baptism. Then they prayed together for a while longer. Daylight was beginning to stream in through the small opening above the cell. A guard came by, stopped and asked Thecla how she got into the cell and she'd have to leave.

"No," Thecla said. "The guard last night said I could stay with my lover." She heard Paul gasp at that but he said nothing. The guard winked at Paul and left.

"What did the guard mean?" Paul asked, as soon as the guard left.

"I told the guard last night you were my lover. I didn't say my 'spiritual' lover."

"I see. Well the 'spiritual' lover would have been a better description." Paul said, laughing. Thecla realized that was the first time she'd heard Paul laugh.

Two guards suddenly approached the cell, keys jingling. Barnabas was with them.

"We have been directed to bring you to the Governor for trial," one of the guards said.

"Me too?" Thecla asked.

"Yes, you and your lover," the guard said, with a smirk.

Looking at Paul, he said, "Hope she was good." Paul said nothing.

Barnabas and Paul exchanged glances, communicating nothing. Barnabas probably had questions about the guard's revelation but chose not to ask them. The prisoners and the guards made their way to the court of the Governor. Thecla was surprised to see Theoclia and Thamyris in the court room. Both peered at her as she was brought in shackled as were Paul and Barnabas. Everyone was ordered to stand as Governor Castellius entered. The governor sat as did the others.

"Now, I have before me three prisoners and two family members. I understand the prisoners are accused of upsetting the function of the city by attracting huge crowds, causing losses by shopkeepers and other businesses. What do you say for yourselves in defense?"

Paul spoke in defense, "We have drawn crowds to hear the Word of God, of which I relate. The people choose to follow. We do not pay them or incite violence. We are a peaceful gathering."

"Yes, there are many of your kind and there seems to be no uprising fomented by your gatherings," said Castellius. "Whoever has brought this charge, please come forward."

Theoclia and Thamyris stood before the governor. "We brought this matter to your attention because sales for my company have fallen drastically since these gatherings in the Synagogue," Thamyris testified.

"Do you have proof of this effect on your business?" asked the governor.

"Yes," Thamyris answered. He handed a scroll to the guard, who passed it to the governor.

The governor took the scroll, read its account balances and looking directly at Thamyris said, "This tells me nothing. I must see what your shop had been getting to see where your losses are."

"I don't have that information. My father will not disclose that to me. I work for him," Thamyris answered.

"Sounds as if he doesn't trust you," the governor said.

Theoclia spoke up, unrecognized by the governor, "Governor, you have to do something with these prisoners. Flog them and make them suffer. My daughter is betrothed to Thamyris and we want our family's name restored."

"You have spoken out of turn. I don't care about your family's name. That's your problem," the governor retorted.

Thamyris spoke up in Theoclia's defense, "Thecla is my bride to be. I want her unshackled and returned to her mother and our family."

At this point, Governor Castellius started to laugh, "Your bride to be just spent the night in the cell with the prisoner and you want her back? What kind of a man are you?"

Thamyris and Theoclia were dumbstruck.

"Take your seats. I will pass sentence now," Governor Castellius said. "The prisoners are expelled from Iconium and the surrounding area. They have twenty-four hours to gather their belonging and leave. Guard, unshackle the prisoners so they may leave."

The guard promptly obeyed the governor and unshackled all three prisoners. Theoclia started toward Thecla but was stopped by the guard. The governor admonished Theoclia, "Sit. Your daughter is directed to leave Iconium with the other prisoners. She is no longer under your roof."

"But she is betrothed to Thamyris," argued Theoclia.

"You argue with the Provincial Governor? asked Governor Castellius.

Theoclia hung her head, sat with her head in her hands, crying softly. She'd been reprimanded by the governor and was now fearful and embarrassed.

Unshackled, Thecla took Paul's hands and kissed his wrists where the shackles had caused the skin to break and begin to bleed. Paul saw the marks disappear after her kisses and knew Thecla was favored by God.

The governor rose to leave. The guard stepped forward and announced, "This session of the court has ended. Clear the courtroom now." With that, the guard led the prisoners out the side door to commence their preparations for departure.

Thecla did not see her mother again nor did she want to see her or Thamyris. She had won her freedom. She was now free to follow Paul and hear him preach and teach.

Chapter 4. Thecla Follows Paul

Word of Paul's release from prison traveled quickly throughout the city. His followers emerged from the homes in which they'd stayed. Thecla found Zaortha. They hugged and laughed together. "Yes, we're free to leave. I'm no longer bound to Thamyris or my mother," said Thecla.

"I understand you're happy to be relieved of the betrothal but you have been exiled. You have no home now. Your reputation is smudged and you cannot live here any longer," Zaortha said.

"I know all that. I don't want to live here anymore. I only want to follow Paul and learn as much as I can from him."

"You will learn how to wander. We were exiled from Antioch now Iconium. I wonder what will be next. Perhaps we'll stay in Tarsus for a long while."

"I don't know what Paul's plans are."

"I'm not sure he has any, just go from town to town and preach and baptize."

"That suits me so long as I can listen to him preach and teach."

"You don't realize how far we've walked and how much farther we will have to walk. The dust and carrying packs of food in the heat is trying."

"I'll not mind doing all that for Paul."

"I heard you spent the night in the prison cell with Paul, did he make it worth your while?"

"Yes, I was baptized."

Zaortha turned away at this, stifling a laugh. After she recovered, she turned back to Thecla saying, "Baptized. That's wonderful."

Thecla realized Zaortha wasn't taking her seriously. "Zaortha, you sound as if you don't believe me."

"Prison is a strange place to be baptized. How did you get into his cell and why did you spend the night. Don't you understand how that sounds?"

"Of course I do but I went to hear more about Jesus' death and resurrection and ascension into heaven. I bribed a guard to let me in."

"All right, that's starting to make sense. How did he get the water to baptize you?

"He used some of the water from his water bowl to pour on my head and say the words."

"Now, I believe you. You are blessed. I understand why you want to follow Paul. He is your spiritual mentor."

"Yes, I have much more to learn and I can only learn by listening to him and following him."

"I thought you just wanted to get away from your betrothal situation."

"Yes, that was part of it. I don't want to marry anyone. I want to live a life of celibacy."

"Yes, Paul says that is the way to heaven."

"Yes, I understand and agree with him. I'm not interested in a comfortable life with money from a husband. I want to hear of God and, perhaps, teach and baptize too."

"Those are high aspirations for a woman. I've never heard of a woman preacher and teacher, much less a woman baptizer."

"Nor have I. I have not told anyone else about my desire. It's not a plan. I just want to spread the word."

"I'll not mention this to anyone. We'll see how and if it comes about. How do you think Paul would take such an idea?"

"I'm not sure. I don't think he's ready for it and I know I'm not ready for it, either. I have much to learn before such an undertaking could come to be."

"Let's walk together; both of us have much to learn. I want to hear what you have learned and, maybe, I can fill a few gaps for you."

"That will be good. It sounds as if we're moving to the edge of the city. Perhaps Paul will speak to us and tell us when we're moving out and where we're heading."

"That's usually what he does when we're wandering. I'm sure he has a town picked out between here and Tarsus."

"I hope so, Tarsus is a long walk."

"Yes, we would definitely need more supplies before that."

Thecla and Zaortha joined the rest of the followers and walked behind Paul and Barnabas. More followers from Iconium joined the troupe but Thecla did not know these people. Carts and supply wagons joined the followers, making the trip better supplied and raised the morale of the entire group.

When they were comfortably outside Iconium, Paul stopped the group. A large group, numbering over 200 at this point, took some time to stop and find appropriate places to sit. All situated, Barnabas began to speak, "Welcome all who follow. We were instructed by the governor to leave Iconium and our ministry there. This is not unusual in that it also happened in Pisidian Antioch, as well. We now must decide where our next place of preaching will be. Paul has decided to strike for Tarsus, his home city. Along the way, there is Lystra and Derbe. What say you we stop at both? There is not much between Derbe and Tarsus, which will be the longest part of the journey.

Finally, a young man asked, "Will we find many Jews along the route or are most of them Greeks?"

"It is a mixture as in Iconium but in smaller numbers," answered Paul. "There are several preaching the word of God. Some are confused and some accuse us of spreading false words.

We must be careful not to antagonize them but also not stop preaching the Word."

"How do we handle those who accuse us?" asked another.

"Say nothing. Point them out to me, I will speak to them," said Paul.

"What if they throw rocks or grab our women?" asked a woman.

"Throw nothing. Women try to stay within the group and inform me, though these incidents would be quite unusual," said Paul. "I do not expect any harm to come to this group along the way."

Paul began to preach the words of Jesus, asking people to love one another. After he'd concluded his words of teaching and the sun was low in the sky, the people ate their evening meal, after which they laid out their bedding for the night.

The next morning, the followers rose, prepared and ate their morning meal and, after a blessing from Paul, resumed their walk to Lystra, the next city of size beyond Iconium. Because the road was rutted from much wagon and cart traffic and the surrounding countryside was level, the group swelled to the sides, making walking easier. The group could separate to the sides easily to accommodate other traffic, while their wagons and carts could travel the road with ease.

Thecla and Zaortha walked side by side as planned.

"Have you experienced stone throwing or grabbing in your travel so far?" asked Thecla.

"No, but I've heard of it from others who've walked farther," answered Zaortha.

"The woman who asked the question sounded quite alarmed."

"Yes, I think she's worried for her daughter. She's a comely one and a bit flirtatious. I don't mean to gossip."

"I understand. I'll say no more about it. And stone throwing, has anyone been hurt?"

"I don't know about that at all. I don't spend any time listening to the men."

"That's wise. We'll just have to wait and see what, if anything happens and what Paul expects," said Thecla.

They walked on together. The crowd grew quieter as the temperature rose. The wind came off the land this day so they were not cooled by the breeze off the Great Sea. They stopped for a water break then on until stopping for a mid-day meal of bread, fruit and water. At the end of the break, Paul blessed the crowd again and the walk resumed.

A little after mid-day, from ahead, there came a rumble and the sound of a trumpet. Everyone moved to one side of the road, further from the road than Thecla expected.

"What's going on?" Thecla asked Zaortha.

"I don't know. The trumpet sounded Roman. Maybe the governor is making trouble after all," Zaortha said.

"I doubt it. He would have done it while we were there. Why would he send the army to track us down?"

"I don't know. It might not be the army, just a centurion and some soldiers. Who can understand the Romans? I don't trust them."

"My father is a soldier hoping to be a centurion and my brother just joined the army. So, yes, I trust them."

"They're not all similar to your father and brother. Believe me, some are killers. Remember what happened to Jesus."

"Yes, but that was a long time ago and in Rome."

"It wasn't that long ago and it doesn't matter whether it was in Rome or where it was, the Romans can't be trusted."

"The governor just expelled us from Iconium; he didn't imprison us or have us stoned."

"No, because he was so tired hearing from your betrothed and your mother, he just wanted to be done with the whole problem."

"Yes, I should thank Mother and Thamyris, I guess."

"Don't get carried away. Let's just change the subject."

Changing the subject was easy at that point. A Roman army in full battle gear was marching six abreast down the road. A sea of red passed them by and all anybody did was gawk. No one spoke nor attempted to ask to where they were marching or where the battle would take place. The crowd knew there would be no friendly answer, if there was an answer at all. Paul blessed the soldiers as they marched past but the soldiers looked only straight ahead, never looking to the sides.

After the last century passed, the crowd moved to the road again. Paul asked the crowd to move to the countryside above the road for a message and water. Everyone partook of water and sat to listen to Paul's message. Paul spoke of the wisdom of living with oppressors as Jesus had done. He also spoke of peace and the coming of peace when we are admitted into our heavenly home. It was almost sundown when he finished his message. He blessed the crowd, bid them eat their evening meal and settle for the night.

Late the next day as the sun was setting, they arrived in Lystra. They camped outside of the city. Paul and Barnabas sought out five of the most devout followers to accompany them into the city in the morning. Thecla, Zaortha, Benjamin, Atreus and Jason were chosen to assist Paul and Barnabas to begin gathering the inhabitants. Paul led prayers and a short discussion of tomorrow's plans.

"Barnabas and I and five of my most fervent followers will enter the city by the main gate to meet the city leaders and begin to draw the inhabitants," Paul began, after concluding prayers. "In the past, we have found this to be the most effective way to introduce ourselves and make our message known."

"Does anyone have any questions?" Barnabas asked.

"Have either of you been to Lystra before?" a follower asked.

Barnabas looked at Paul. "Not in many years," Paul said. "I grew up in Tarsus and accompanied my father and uncle here a few times but never with a message."

"Then we don't know how the people will react, they might be hostile," the follower stated.

"This is certain, we don't know how they will react that is why we're not going into the city in mass. We'll approach their leadership first, if we get their approval, we will more likely be accepted," Barnabas said.

"Will we be able to go into the city to shop?" a woman asked.

Barnabas took a moment to answer as he stifled a chuckle, "Yes, as soon as we are granted acceptance, everyone will be brought into the city. Please though, be mindful, this is a mission with a conversion message, not a shopping trip."

Several of the males guffawed. The woman resumed her seat, her face reddened beneath the dust. Several women approached the supply wagon for water to distribute to the followers for washing. After everyone was cleaned, the evening meal was served. After the meal, some chose to visit while others unrolled their sleeping mats.

Zaortha and Thecla remained seated for a time. "I am surprised Paul singled us out to go into Lystra with him," Thecla said.

"I think he has seen promise in you. I'm just surprised he asked me too," Zaortha said.

"I think he sees us both as possible teachers."

"You think? I think Paul sees us together all the time and he didn't want to hurt my feelings."

"Would he have?"

"No, silly, you are the one who wants to have a ministry."

"Shhhhh, don't let that get out. Remember that's our little secret. No one must know."

"Sorry, I tend to talk too loud. I'll be more careful."

"Please do. I really don't want Paul to hear it from some woman or man in the group. He might ask us to leave."

"Yes, the same as that woman who wants to go shopping. She was so embarrassed when she sat down she might want to shift the embarrassment to someone else. That's the way some people act when they don't know how else to cope."

"You know a lot about how people behave. How did you learn that?"

"My father worked for a Greek physician who observed human behavior and wrote texts about it."

"That's fascinating. Did you learn to read then?"

"Yes, my father taught me but I never read his writings, just overheard him talking to the physician when he visited us."

"That is so interesting." Thecla lowered her voice almost to a whisper, "Because you have some understanding of human nature, you could help me with my ministry, just as Barnabas helps and travels with Paul."

"Oh my, are you sure? That's a big and important job. I'm not sure I'm the one for it."

"Oh, Zaortha, you have an understanding of people I don't have. I think you would be the best travelling companion. Please think about it. It will be a while yet, so you don't have to make up your mind right now."

"All right, I'll think about it. I'm so pleased you want me by your side."

"I honestly do, Zaortha. We'd make fabulous partners in a ministry."

"All right, but you'd have to be the teacher, like Paul."

"Yes, then you'd be like Barnabas, huh?"

"I probably could," Zaortha said, noticeably warming to the idea.

"Let's get our bed rolls out and get some sleep, so we're fresh to go with Paul and the others into Lystra tomorrow morning," said Thecla.

"That sounds good. I am tired."

"Me too. Good night."

"Good night."

Paul and Barnabas were up early, as the sun was just making its shadowy appearance. They spoke in hushed tones, so as not to unnecessarily awaken the troupe.

"I'll see who the mayor is and how he acts, if he's welcoming or standoffish," Paul said.

"All right, I'll watch the other officials to see if they don't seem to be fomenting trouble." Barnabas said.

"I'll ask if we can use a large building. I'll point out to him it's safer and less trouble to have a crowd there than in the streets, as we found in Iconium."

"I'm concerned the word from Iconium could have reached them here before us."

"Of course, that's possible. We were slowed by that Roman army marching by."

"Yes, I wonder where they were going."

"Maybe to Iconium or maybe all the way to Pisidian Antioch."

"They looked as if they were going to put down a rebellion.

"Could be; there's always a rebellion in these parts."

"Are we ready to get our little group together and depart for Lystra?"

"Yes, and let's try to be quiet about it."

Paul and Barnabas gathered the five chosen members of the party and left the camp.

They entered Lystra at the main city gate, asking the gate guard the way to the city offices.

"What is your business here?" the gate guard asked.

"We've come to speak to the mayor," answered Paul.

"And the nature of your visit?" asked the gate guard.

"We wish to preach God's Word and bring salvation and truth to the people," said Paul.

"Is that your crowd outside the city walls?" asked the gate keeper.

"Yes, they are believers who've followed us to continue to learn as we preach," Paul said.

"I will send a slave to get the city officials, if they wish to hear your words. Wait by the wall for word." The gate keeper called the slave and sent him to the city offices.

Later in the morning, the slave arrived, leading two officials. Paul and Barnabas introduced themselves and the officials introduced themselves as Cestus, the vice-mayor and Amatol, the recorder.

Paul opened the conversation saying, "We have arrived to preach the everlasting Word of God to those in Lystra who want to hear and know the truth."

"You are not the first to come by with God's word. What makes your message unique?" Cestus asked.

"We have brought a following of about 200 people who will attest to the value of the teachings and help to spread the word on a personal level," Paul answered.

During this exchange, Amatol steadily scribbled notes on his wax tablet. Barnabas, though standing quietly observed the body language of Cestus and Amatol, noting the clenching and unclenching of Cestus' toes in his sandals. *What could that mean?* Barnabas wondered. *Is he normally a nervous man or is Paul making him nervous? I wonder why the mayor didn't come. Maybe there are other ministers here or maybe they left a bad impression. I need to speak to Paul about this.*

"I will discuss this with the mayor and give you our decision tomorrow morning early here at the gate," Cestus said and departed with Amatol in tow.

Paul, Barnabas and the select group returned to the camp outside the city. Barnabas and Paul retreated to their tent where Barnabas related his observations to Paul. Paul was not alarmed but thanked Barnabas and asked him to continue his observance tomorrow,

Thecla and Zaortha were wondering why they were asked to accompany Paul.

"I am not sure why we went along with Paul and Barnabas," Thecla said.

"Paul wanted us to go with them so we could see how to begin a mission in a city. I think we were being taught," Zaortha said.

"Do you really think Paul sees us as missionaries?"

"Oh yes, I do. He keeps us close, giving us little chores and visits with him."

"I know he's giving us extra lessons but I thought it was because he knows how hungry we are for truth."

"Yes, of course that's part of it but observation of how he goes about these tasks is important, too; how he manages a crowd not only of the followers but those who gather to hear him for the first time."

"You are astute, Zaortha. I had not figured that all out. Again, you do know and understand people."

"You are a better speaker and teacher. We'll make a good team."

"Yes, we will." *Then it's settled, I understand she's decided to join me on my missions. I'll not mention it to her. She thinks that is enough of a clue. I'll just go ahead and assume she'll join me.*

Paul, Barnabas and the five designated followers arrived at the Lystra city gate early the next morning as directed by Cestus. They did not have long to wait this time. Cestus and Amatol arrived and notified Paul and followers, "You may preach to our residents your good words. We want them to be peaceful. Any disturbance and you will be driven from the city immediately. Is that clear?"

"Yes. Is there a preferred place where we can accommodate a crowd?"

"You may use the amphitheater."

"That will work well. Thank you. We will bring in our followers and they will spread the word of our intended teaching."

"Make sure your people are peaceful."

"They will be. The Word of God is peace and love."

Shaking their heads and smirking, Cestus and Amatol left the gate. Paul and his group left the city and returned to the waiting followers.

Paul and Barnabas got everyone's attention and began the instruction to the followers. Paul opened the lecture, "We have been invited to preach and teach in the city of Lystra. This invitation was not granted quickly without forethought. The vice-mayor presented the invitation with a strict augmentation. Our visit must be peaceful. Do not in any way antagonize the citizens of the city. You must spread the word of our intendent preaching with peaceful persuasion. We will have our first meeting this afternoon. Those who are interested are invited. No one will be strong-armed. We will go now, spread the word and meet late this afternoon at the amphitheater. Proceed to the city. The gates are open."

The followers were ready and began to enter the city as soon as Paul finished talking. The carts and wagons and drivers would re-supply their loads while inviting those with whom they came in contact. Most of the women gravitated to the shops and market areas, while the men went to stables, taverns and other establishments.

Thecla and Zaortha decided to visit the brothels. They knew some men would probably go there but not to invite the prostitutes. Zaortha, always aware of the people, suggested to Thecla, "We should go to the brothels and invite the women to hear Paul."

"I think that is an excellent idea, Zaortha. We must not let the other women in our group see us."

"Yes, we should hang back and approach the city last. Let the others go their ways and we'll go to the brothels unseen."

"Yes, that should work. We'll spend extra time helping others who haven't packed completely then we'll pack our own things and go into the city."

By the time Thecla and Zaortha arrived in the city, it was nearly mid-day. They headed to the fountain to sit and enjoy their meager lunch of bread and fruit. They knew brothels were usually in the lower areas of town, away from the 'higher class' living areas and businesses.

"Let's go down the hill toward what looks like a stream running along the bottom of the hill. There may be brothels in that direction," Zaortha suggested.

"That sounds to be a good idea. Everyone who came with us seems well out of sight," Thecla agreed.

They finished eating and started to walk down the hill. They had just started down the hill when a woman came running up to them saying, "Girls, don't go that way. Nice girls don't want to be seen down there."

"Why?" Thecla asked, as she felt Zaortha's elbow forcefully poke her ribs.

"There're brothels down there. Nice girls don't go there, unless you two are looking for work." She sniffed and quickly walked off.

"Well, that's an introduction we didn't need. At least we know we're going in the right direction," Thecla said.

"Yes. I hope none of our people go in this direction. She'd probably tell them about us. She knows we're new to Lystra. That type of woman knows all the residents and watches the streets as a hawk. The local gossiper, I'd bet," said Zaortha.

As they moved down the streets, the buildings became more rundown and shabby. They passed several taverns before finding the first brothel. A sign saying **Penny's Pussies** in bold red letters was nailed above the door.

"That's so disgusting," Thecla said.

"Careful, Thecla, we must not act judgmental. Remember what Jesus said, 'We are all God's children'," Zaortha, admonished gently.

"That's right, Zaortha."

They entered the establishment and Penny introduced herself. "Hello, may I help you? I am Penny, the owner of this establishment. Are you two seeking work or some comfort?"

"Neither," Zaortha spoke up because Thecla was tongue-tied at the moment.

"We've come to tell you and your girls about Paul who has come to preach the Word of our true and everlasting God," Thecla said, recovering from her momentary lapse.

"I'm not sure anyone wants to hear a wondering preacher, unless he's in need of a woman after his travels," Penny said.

"Paul is not in need of a woman. He is celibate and wants only to share his message with those who have not heard. He is preaching the Word of God this afternoon in the amphitheater. We want you and your girls to hear him. Please come and hear him and decide for yourselves after that," Thecla said.

"You are very persuasive. I think I'll come and I'll ask the girls to see if any of them want to join me," Penny said.

"Thank you. We look forward to this afternoon," Thecla said, as they turned to leave.

"That was an extraordinary meeting," said Zaortha. "You did so well taking over the conversation. I thought you'd lost your voice for a few seconds."

"I did," admitted Thecla. "Penny was dressed so elegantly, I was staring at her attire."

"Yes, they seem to have money, doing well for themselves."

"We'd better move along so we can get back in time to hear Paul," said Thecla.

They stopped at two more brothels. One would not let them in or talk to them. They refused to hear the Word of God. The last one on the street was **Mathilda's.** Mathilda welcomed Thecla and Zaortha in and asked her girls, four of them, to hear Thecla, who gave them the same information she'd given Penny. Mathilda, speaking for all, said they'd think about it and ushered them out.

"It's time to head back to the amphitheater," Thecla said.

"Yes it is. Let's go back the way we came so maybe no one will see us," Zaortha said.

That sounded to be the best idea so Thecla agreed and they set out. They were nearing the top of the hill when the same woman came from nowhere laughing, saying, "You didn't last long. Must've been good though, you both look spent but smiling. I've heard those girls can take care of women, as well as men."

Zaortha and Thecla tried to ignore her but she wouldn't give up. "What's the matter? You don't want to tell me so I can pass it on to other women; they don't know what they're missing?"

Zaortha decided to invite her. "We are followers of the minister, Paul. He has come to teach the Word of God. Why don't you get some of your friends and come to the amphitheater in about a half hour to hear him. That will give you something to talk about."

"I might just do that. Nothing happens around here I don't know about."

"Come to the amphitheater then," repeated Zaortha as they walked on.

A sizeable crowd milled outside the amphitheater when Thecla and Zaortha arrived. Two men were carrying a third on a makeshift litter. Others seemed to be encircling him to protect him and move the crowd away. The doors opened and the crowd began to shuffle in. Paul and Barnabas were already on the dais in front of the seating. Thecla noticed the lame man was brought to the front and set on the floor in front of the dais. Barnabas opened the meeting with a prayer as he always did. Paul rose and immediately walked to the corner of the dais closest to the man on the floor. Paul, looking closely at him and seeing there was saving faith in him said aloud, "Stand upright on your feet." At that, the man sprang up and began to walk.

The crowd, seeing what Paul had done, cried out in the Lycaonian dialect, "It is the gods, who have come down to us in human shape." They called Barnabas Jupiter and Paul Mercury, because he was the chief speaker and the priest of Jupiter. The defender of the Lystra brought out bulls and wreaths to the gates, eager, as was the crowd, to do sacrifice.

The followers tore their garments in horror when they heard it and Barnabas and Paul ran out among the crowd, crying, "Why are you doing all this? We too are mortal men as yourselves; the whole burden of our preaching is that you must turn away from follies, such as this to the worship of the living God, who made sky, earth, sea and all that is in them. In the ages past, he has allowed Gentile folk everywhere to follow their own devices; yet even so he has not left us without some proof of what he is. It is his bounty that grants us rain from heaven and the seasons which give birth to our crops, so that we have nourishment and comfort to our heart's desire." With words such as this, they persuaded the people, with some difficulty, to refrain from offering sacrifice to them.

The crowd quieted and Paul began his preaching. It was nearly dark when he finished and the crowd dispersed. Before Paul, Barnabas and some of the followers could return to the camp outside the city, some of the Jews from Antioch and Iconium were in the group of followers of Paul. These followers had won over many Lystrans to their side. While following Paul and Barnabas outside, they grabbed stones and began throwing them at Paul. Barnabas tried to protect Paul but the borage of stones prevented him from getting close to Paul. The crowd stoned Paul and dragged him out of the city, leaving him there for dead. Thecla and Zaortha were horrified as were many of the other followers. The crowd was so frightened and shocked; in fact, they didn't react, just stood dumbfounded. Regaining some faculties, Barnabas and the select five, including Jamel, who Thecla had converted on the way to the amphitheater, formed a ring around Paul, in protection.

In time, Paul regained consciousness and sat up, rubbing his eyes and head. "Why did they do that?" he asked.

Barnabas answered, "Some of the followers from Antioch and Iconium were Jews who did not believe but convinced Jews and some others here to silence you."

"But why would they? I only speak the truth," Paul said.

"That's true," Thecla said, "but some are not ready for the truth."

"Then we must go back to the city to show them they have not killed me," Paul said.

The group, with Paul in the lead went back into the city. The angry crowd had dispersed by then so they left the city to join their followers in their camp. It was evening by now and Paul addressed the followers, "I have made a decision. We will leave this city and go to Derbe. We cannot accomplish more here."

"Does that mean he's giving up?" Jamel asked.

"No," Thecla said, "he doesn't give up. He'll be back when things have quieted, probably on his next mission."

"All right, because I'm sure there are people here who will be converted," Jamel said.

"All in due time, according to God's Will, he would say," Zaortha added.

"Yes," agreed Thecla.

The next day the followers left Lystra with Paul and Barnabas, for Derbe.

Derbe was about sixty miles from Lystra. The followers loaded the largest items into the wagon and on the carts. These conveyances held food supplies for the entire troupe and a few tents so there wasn't much available space for personal items. The people shouldered their bags and a day's supply of water and food and began the trek. Paul and Barnabas led the group with Thecla, Zaortha and the three young men walked directly behind Paul and Barnabas. The others followed in a long line. The group had shrunk by about fifty to sixty followers. Those had been arrested by the Romans safeguarding the peace in Lystra. Five days later at nearly sunset, the troupe arrived outside Derbe. Dragging with fatigue, they set up camp and prepared a meagre meal. Barnabas led them in prayer and Paul spoke briefly. "Rest here this night. My select group and I will approach the city officials at the gate tomorrow morning to seek admittance to the city."

Thecla had begged Paul to add Jamel to the select group. Some saw the new member and were not pleased. "Why does a new member of the group get to go instead of one of us who have been following since Antioch?" a woman asked.

This question prompted Paul to teach a lesson on jealousy and sharing. "Jealousy at its core is discontent and selfishness. Left to grow, it becomes hatred and can result in so many horrible acts. Genesis 37:4 says, '*When his brothers saw that their father loved him more than all his brothers, they hated him and could not speak peacefully to him.*' This was the beginning of the jealousy that would ruin their relationship with each other and their father. After Joseph continued in favor with his father and with God, his brothers, were jealous of him'. And soon, Joseph was sold into slavery by his own brothers.

"God loves those who willingly share their goods or place with others. You may not know why someone is chosen before you only that the one is. That should be enough, accept God's Will and rejoice."

"How do we know it's God's Will?"

"God has spoken to me and directed me to spread His Word," Paul said.

The woman had no response and Paul led the group in prayer.

The next morning the select group followed Paul. Today, Barnabas stayed in the camp to help the followers and nurse his sore feet. The walk had been purpose driven, partly because of the stoning in Lystra and partly to arrive in Derbe as quickly as possible. Also, there might be more dissention brewing in the followers, based on the woman's question last night. Barnabas was to work with the various people, especially the women, so as to hear what they were saying and find what the sources of disagreement were. If there were none, they would all go into the city.

The next morning, Paul and the five were admitted to the city and met with the city officials. They were welcomed to Derbe. There was no large building in which Paul could preach. The city officials said the followers would be welcome to stay with city residents when they heard Paul had arrived. This came as a surprise to Paul. He thanked the city officials, saying he would return to the city tomorrow with his followers.

Paul and his group walked out the city gates but, before returning to the followers, he stopped the little group.

"I am gratified they welcomed us so. God is making it possible to fulfill our mission here," Paul said.

"That is what we saw. We've experienced God's Will today," Thecla said.

"Now we must tell the followers we are blessed without bragging. Thecla, please plan a message to the followers regarding today's welcoming then I will discuss with Barnabas and inform them of their staying with city residents," Paul said.

"Paul, with God's help, I will construct the message in my mind to be given to the followers," Thecla declared. *Now I've received my first assignment from Paul. I'll talk to Zaortha and prepare the talk to be given later this afternoon.* They ate the bread and fruit presented to them by the city officials and returned to the camp.

The group arrived in the camp where all the followers were busy cleaning, stitching torn garments, feeding the mules and asses and various and sundry jobs needing work. Paul sought Barnabas and they went into Paul's tent to, perhaps, strategize. Thecla, Jamel and Zaortha walked to the edge of the camp and sat on the mats they'd brought.

"How do we proceed to spread the word?" asked Jamel.

"Zaortha and I went to the brothels to spread the word in Lystra," Thecla said.

"We could still do that. Would you want to join us, Jamel?" Zaortha asked.

"I will go with you because that is a dangerous part of town. We should look for a place to stay that is not in the tavern and brothel area," Jamel stated.

"You are right, Jamel. We need to be more careful. The stoning Paul experienced could happen to us if we are considered dangerous to the citizens of this city," Thecla said.

"Let's find a place to stay first then begin our missionary work," Jamel suggested.

"I agree," Thecla said, "we will attempt to find the brothels after we settle. We should not have too much trouble finding them."

With that, they moved back to their part of the camp to prepare for entering the city in the morning. Paul and Barnabas called the attention of the group to notify them of their first mission was to find a house in which to stay. The city officials had welcomed them and the residents agreed to open their homes to them. When approaching the residents, they must tell the resident they are followers of Paul and their mission is to spread God's Holy Word. If they are admitted, they must be gracious and responsible. If they are refused, they must be thankful and move on to the next abode. "In seeking this place, you are doing God's work," Paul finished, with a blessing.

The next morning the group arose, picked up their meagre belongings and walked to the city gate. They were admitted immediately and dispersed to find lodging. Thecla, Zaortha and Jamel stayed together to seek a place to stay. They headed in the direction of homes that looked poorer but with some outbuildings. The others appeared to be going to the larger homes. The three stopped at the first house, knocked at the door and were met by an old woman, who told them she was unable to accommodate them but was interested in their message. Thecla assured her they would return and they left. The next house appeared slightly larger and better kept. A man answered the knock and welcomed them in doors. "My name is Thaddeus and my wife is Janis. Our house is your house. My wife and I welcome you and are interested to hear your message. Please settle here and join us for dinner tonight. We can begin to hear your message then," he told them.

"Thank you. You are doing God's will and we will be glad to begin teaching at dinner tonight," Thecla said. "These are my fellow teachers, Jamel and Zaortha."

"Please come with me and I will show you to your rooms. Our children are grown now so we have many more rooms than we need. I am so happy to be able to provide a place for you to sleep," Janis said. She showed a larger room with two beds to Thecla and Zaortha and a smaller room with one bed to Jamel.

"Thank you for your willingness to share your home and provide us this comfort. God will bless you both," Thecla said.

Janis left and the followers unpacked their small packs of belongings. "It was easier to find lodging than I thought it would be," Zaortha said.

"Yes, it was easy but we are doing God's work and He's making it easy for us this time. It won't always be easy, as He showed us with Paul's stoning in Lystra," replied Thecla.

"Yes, thank you, Thecla. I wasn't giving God the credit for our good fortune."

"Yes, Zaortha, it's easy to accept good fortune without giving praise to the One who blesses us. I know you did not mean to miss attributing our success to God."

"No problem, Thecla. I just forgot myself. You are the teacher."

"Who's teaching?" Jamel asked, smiling as he approached the women's room.

"Thecla was reminding me of God's help in finding our lodging," Zaortha said.

"In deed He did. Let's all offer a prayer now," Jamel said.

They closed the door and prayed to God in thanksgiving for their lodging.

In the afternoon, the three emerged from the house and walked to survey the city.

"Which is the best direction to go first?" asked Zaortha.

"Because you want to find the brothels, we need to find the taverns and the bawdy side of town," Jamel said.

"I'm guessing that area is below the hill similar to the area in Lystra," Thecla suggested.

"Yes," Zaortha and Jamel said in unison.

"We'll head down that way and see," Thecla said, motioning with her chin..

"All right, you two go to the brothels, which will be close to the taverns I'll visit," Jamel said.

They walked on for several blocks and heard increasing joviality. This, they knew, meant they were heading in the right direction. Zaortha called Thecla's attention to the sign over a door across the street. It said **Women, Cheap**. "That looks like our first stop," Thecla said. Shortly after they knocked, a woman came to the door in full make-up and a short dress.

"Who have we here?" she asked. "Looking for work?"

"No. We are missionaries with Paul and we are spreading God's Word," said Thecla.

"Oh, I heard he was here. Going to preach at the fountain in the middle of the city, right?" the woman asked.

"Yes, we have come to invite you and your women to come to listen to the Word of God tomorrow afternoon," Thecla said.

"I'm not sure Paul or God would want us there. We were told by other missionaries we are a house of iniquity and must repent," the woman said.

"I'm not sure what the other missionaries told you but you should come to hear Paul's word. He has seen God and will give you the word straight from God," said Thecla. "God requires your cooperation but he is a forgiving and loving God. Please come to hear it directly from Paul."

"Thank you. I'll talk to my girls and see if any are interested," the woman said.

"We hope to see you at the fountain tomorrow afternoon" Thecla said.

Zaortha and Thecla walked further down the street when Thecla saw a sign **Women Abound**. "Here's our next stop, Zaortha," Thecla said.

Their knock on the door was met by a rotund man who asked their business. "People don't usually knock on this door before entering," he said.

"We are followers of Paul. He has arrived in town and will preach tomorrow afternoon at the fountain. We are inviting you to come to hear God's word," Thecla said.

"Yes, I've heard of him. He got knocked off his horse, right? Hit his head and saw God?" the man asked, laughing at his own joke.

"Sir, your joke is not humorous. Paul saw God and has converted many followers. It is God's Holy Will that we spread the message of a loving, forgiving, God," Thecla stated, being careful not to sound as if it were a retort.

"Forgive me, I see you are serious and I have offended you," the man said, trying to be humble.

"Offending me is not the problem, it is almighty God who you must try not to offend," Thecla responded.

"I will ask to see if anyone is interested in going to the fountain tomorrow afternoon," the man said, sheepishly.

"Thank you for your time, sir," Thecla said, as Zaortha and Thecla turned to leave.

At this point, Thecla and Zaortha heard someone running behind them, breathlessly. It was Jamel. "I finally found you," Jamel said, breathlessly.

"Why were you running so hard?" Zaortha asked.

After he'd caught his breath and looked over his shoulder more than once, he said "I tried to invite the bartender and customers to the fountain. One of the customers took offense and came at me with a sword. The bartender made us go outside. The man came at me again and I ran. I kept running until I found you."

"Where is the man now?" Thecla asked.

"I don't know. I don't think he could run far. He was portly and didn't look or act fleet of foot," Jamel said.

"Well, let's move on and we'll watch for more places as we go," Thecla said.

They continued walking. Jamel stopped at a few taverns and Thecla and Zaortha visited two more brothels. At this stage, they decided to begin their walk back to their lodging.

"We should stop by the woman in the house where we first stopped this morning. She was interested in our mission," Thecla said.

"That's a great idea, Thecla; a good way to end the afternoon," Zaortha said.

"That's true, Zaortha, but we won't be ending the afternoon. We still have to teach Thaddeus and Janis at dinner," Jamel said, with a smile.

"That's true but I wasn't counting dinner; just while we're walking," Zaortha said, laughing.

They knocked at the woman's door and she answered quickly. "Well, you came back, I see," she said. "My name is Margot. I am widowed and anxious to learn about Paul's teaching."

"Margot, we're pleased to meet you. This is Zaortha, and Jamel and I am Thecla," said Thecla. "We are committed to spread the word about Paul's teaching tomorrow afternoon at the fountain."

"Please come inside, sit and tell me about Paul's teaching and what to expect tomorrow afternoon," Margot said.

They entered, sat and began to teach. They spent two hours with Margot after which, they bade her farewell with the promise to walk with her to the Fountain tomorrow. They could see Margot might have trouble walking that far; so, after they left her, Jamel said he would try to find a cart and driver to carry Margot to the fountain and home again. "That's a good idea, Jamel," said Thecla.

"I'll see if Thaddeus knows anyone who might be interested in going and has a cart," Jamel said.

"I'm sure there is. Even if Thaddeus doesn't know anyone, you can probably find one tomorrow morning," said Thecla.

"I'll help find one," Zaortha said.

"Great, you and Jamel can look for a cart and driver while spreading the word," Thecla said. "I'd like some time with Janis. I think she has some questions she wants to ask, personally.

They were at the door and knocked respectfully before entering. The meal smelled delicious and Janis had the table already set for the meal. The missionaries had only a short time to wash and get ready to be seated at dinner.

The next morning, Thaddeus, Jamel and Zaortha went in search of a conveyance for Margot. They found one on the street corner as Thaddeus said they would. The cart driver planned to go to hear Paul and was happy to take Margot to the meeting and home afterward.

In the meantime, Thecla and Janis had time to themselves as they discussed Paul's probable teachings. Thecla was uplifted by Janis' understanding and desire to learn more. She was anxious for baptism and wondered if Paul would be baptizing. "I'm sure he will. The fountain will be a good place for baptisms," Thecla reassured her.

Soon it was time to go to the fountain. Margot, seated on the cart, Thaddeus, Janis, Jamel, Thecla and Zaortha started toward the fountain. The day was hot and the party moved slowly as the cart bumped over the cobblestoned street. Margot, though, treated it as a welcome outing. Thecla and Zaortha were amazed at Margot's resilience. She never once complained of the bumps. They acknowledged to one another she will be a stalwart Christian. The crowd grew larger as they neared the fountain. The cart driver found a place to park the cart so that Margot could remain sitting in the cart to listen to Paul. He would unhitch the ass and move to another location. Janis and Thaddeus stayed beside Margot. Jamel, Thecla and Zaortha moved to the front of the crowd to be as close to Paul as possible.

The crowd numbered nearly 500 people as Barnabas opened the meeting with the now traditional welcome and prayer. Paul stood on the raised platform for that purpose. He, too, opened with a brief welcome and prayer. He began to teach and preach about the loving God, Jesus, our Savior and that Jesus is also God. This took much time to instruct the people that there is only one God; Jesus is not a separate god but part of the one God.

He preached for nearly four hours. A few at the back of the crowd drifted away but most stayed. At the end, Paul asked those who wanted baptism to come forward. He and Barnabas began the baptisms. Margot wanted baptism but was unsure of walking in line to be baptized. The cart driver was nowhere to be seen. Thaddeus tried to find him but couldn't. Thaddeus and Janis agreed to walk with her between them to support her in line. By the time Margot stood before Paul to be baptized, her legs gave way and she fell to her knees. Paul baptized her and lifter her. She walked away as if she were a young woman. "I'll not need the cart for the ride home. I will walk," she told Thaddeus and Janis. They were astounded but happily agreed. Thaddeus went to inform Jamel then Margot, Janis and Thaddeus left for home.

Jamel searched for the cart driver, he could not find him so Thecla, Zaortha and he left to go back to Thaddeus' house. When they arrived at Thaddeus' abode, they immediately began to discuss the miracle of Margot's walking home. "We were amazed, almost frightened," Janis said.

"It happened so quickly but no bolts of lightning or voices, she just got up and walked," Thaddeus said.

"That was the first miracle we've ever witnessed," Janis said.

"Paul has worked miracles, not often, though. This happened to a woman who was exceptionally desirous of baptism, enough to walk and stand in line beyond her level of endurance," Thecla said.

"Yes, I see your point. We were all desirous of baptism but not exhibiting effort beyond our natural ability," Janis said.

"That makes some sense but there must be more to it," Thaddeus said.

"Of course there is. We don't know what kind of past life, trials and tribulations Margot has overcome. She was probably tested by God many times in her past life," Thecla said.

"Margot has never told us of her past life. She's quite a private person," Janis said.

"Yes, I'm sure she is guarded because she wishes not to be bragging about her successes or appear to be seeking sympathy," Thecla said. "Those are attributes proclaimed by Paul as holy and pleasing to God.

"She appears to be living a simple life, requiring no help from others," Thaddeus said.

"Margot was so appreciative of the cart and everyone's turning out to accompany her. She was heartily surprised," Jamel said.

"And she was surprised when she could stay in the cart to hear Paul," Zaortha added.

"Yes, and she volunteered to walk when the driver couldn't be found, though she knew it would be nearly impossible for her," Janis said.

At this, Thecla suggested they all pray before dinner to thank God for Paul's miracle.

Many more days pasted before Paul spread the word to the followers they would be leaving Derbe and to meet outside the city gates tomorrow morning. Of course, some from Derbe decided to follow. Margot did not decide to follow and Thecla, Zaortha and Jamel were thankful to God for her foresight as the trip would be demanding. Paul and Barnabas had preached and made many disciples.

Chapter 5. Thecla becomes an Evangelist

The followers met outside the gates the next morning full of anticipation. They were well rested and had plenty to eat. The supply wagon and carts were loaded and all preparations had been made. Then Paul made his announcement, "I have decided not to go to Tarsus. We will return to Iconium and Antioch to fortify the churches that have already been started. We will detour around Lystra so they will not be alarmed by our passing too close to their city."

"What about Iconium and Antioch?" a man asked "We were run out of them too."

"More time has passed since we were in Iconium and Antioch. They will have had time to see our churches at work and see we are no harm to them," Paul answered.

Paul blessed the followers and they began the long trek to Iconium.

Nearly two weeks later Paul, Barnabas and the group of about 150 people of all ages arrived on the outside of Iconium. "We have arrived at our chosen destination. We'll set up camp here before entering Iconium tomorrow. Make yourselves comfortable tonight and tomorrow we'll seek rest in the homes of those who will welcome our arrival," said Paul. "Let us pray to God in thanksgiving for our safe arrival and beg for welcome into Iconium." Paul then led the prayer, blessed the crowd and they proceeded to prepare their evening meal.

The next morning, they arrived at the city gate and were admitted to seek shelter and food. Thecla did not visit her mother as one might expect. The attempt at betrothal was too fresh in Thecla's mind and her mother's, Thecla feared. *Better to avoid an altercation*, Thecla thought. Thecla and Zaortha sought shelter at an inn near the center of the city. Jamel joined other males who found shelter in another part of town. Paul and Barnabas returned to their friend, Onesiphorus', home. Paul, Barnabas, Thecla and Zaortha sought the heads of the church Paul had left in Iconium. Abril and Jonas were immediately available as they were still engaged in building the physical church they'd begun in the city. Abril reported "We've secured enough donations from rich converts to build the church as soon as possible."

"Was this a requirement of the donated sums?" Paul asked.

"No," Abril said, "we wanted to show them how we spent much of the money."

"Would it not have been better to spend it on apostatizing now and erecting a church building later?" Paul asked, trying not to sound critical.

"We wanted to show new members the church they would be joining," Jonas said.

"But the church is more than a building," Barnabas said.

"That's right," Paul said, employing his teaching voice. "New members must first feel the community of believers. They should follow you for more teaching before baptism. Becoming a church member is a process. It must not be embarked upon too soon. Believers must be given time to assimilate the truth and, perhaps, tested to find their true fervor."

"But how can we test them? We don't want to torture or humiliate them," Abril said.

"That is true," Paul said. "No, by testing, we mean give the potential new members time to follow before baptism. Make sure they are ready. Do not baptize too quickly. Some may plead they are ready but it is the overwhelming feeling of discovering the truth. Can these people abide by the truth and all its facets? Remember your following before baptism. You spent much time before baptism, following from Pisidian Antioch to Iconium.”

“Yes, we remember,” Jonas said, Abril shaking his head in agreement.

“Now, we’d like to see your plans for the building then we’ll set up a time for my preaching to the new members and others who wish to hear,” Paul said.

“Very well, please join us at a table outside the building where the plans are laid out on parchment sheets,” Abril said.

They moved to the table, sat on the benches and looked over the plans for the new building. Satisfied, Paul said, “The church building will more than suffice to house the community you are building. Now, as to my preaching, where is the best place to preach to a crowd without alarming city officials, especially the governor?”

“The governor position has changed,” Abril said. “Shortly after you left, a large contingent of the army came here to quell an uprising begun by the Jews. In the process, the governor was replaced by an Iconium man, who has been much easier with whom to work.”

“We wondered why it was so easy to approach the city,” Barnabas said.

“That is why,” Jonas said. “The governor now wants to encourage commerce from other cities to build businesses here in Iconium.”

“Does the new governor have ties to Rome?” Barnabas asked.

“Yes, his wife is related in some way to Caesar,” Jonas said.

“That explains his appointment,” said Barnabas.

“Good, now back to my preaching, where is a good place and when?” Paul asked.

“Let’s use the public gardens near the governor’s mansion at a little past mid-day,” Abril suggested.

"That sounds appropriate. I will preach and see if some are ready for baptism," Paul said. "Thecla and Zaortha will spread the word and the other followers will, in turn, spread the word about time and place."

Thecla and Zaortha knew their role and left immediately to find the others, especially Jamel and his friends.

"That was an interesting meeting with Abril and Jonas," Zaortha said, as soon as she and Thecla were beyond earshot of the group.

"Yes, it was" Thecla agreed. "I see we have much to learn about a ministry. Paul's statements about baptizing too soon, registered with me. I begged him to baptize me long before he did then not in public."

"I followed Paul from Pisidian Antioch to here before I was baptized," Zaortha agreed. "Now I know why."

"It's interesting how we continue to learn from Paul, long after we think we know all there is to know," Thecla said.

"Hello," Zaortha shouted, waving her hands at an oncoming group of young men.

"Oh, I see now, that is Jamel and his group. You have better eyesight than I do," remarked Thecla.

They met the group, told of the time and place of Paul's scheduled preaching engagement and they were tasked with joining the other followers in spreading the word. The group set out to find the others and spread the word.

The next day, about noon, Thecla and Zaortha met Jamel and his group at the inn for a noon meal. As they talked, Thecla talked again about Paul's talk with Abril and Jonas, "I think he wants to teach the people but not in the mode of immediate baptism. He wants to spread God's Word and have people think about it and believe. He doesn't think 'spur-of-the-moment' acceptance of the Word and belief are the same thing."

"How can we know when believers are ready for baptism?" Jamel asked.

"When they have followed, heard much teaching and 'suffered' privations of the walk, I think," Zaortha said.

"That means only the literal followers can be baptized?" asked another in the group.

"No, I don't think so," Thecla responded. "He has baptized people here without their walking with us. I pleaded for baptism several times and he said 'No, you're not ready. You still have much to learn' then he finally baptized me when he was in prison."

"Did you have much to learn?" Jamel asked.

"Yes, I did and I'm still learning but I must have reached a point where he thought I was ready," Thecla said.

"That still doesn't answer the question, 'How will we know'?" persisted the man in the group.

"I think Paul will teach that when he chooses and anoints new ministers. Not everyone is or will be a minister; therefore not everyone will baptize. If we are not ministers, the question is mute," Thecla stated.

With the conversation ended, they rose to go out and seek more people to attend the gathering. Thecla and Zaortha performed their usual task of inviting women from the brothels. Jamel and his friends canvassed the taverns and inns to notify proprietors and customers of the upcoming meeting at the garden. Other followers had visited neighbors of the houses in which they stayed. By the appointed time for Paul to speak, a substantial crowd had arrived in the garden and either stood or found seating on the lawn to listen to Paul, in comfort.

Barnabas opened the session with the predictable welcome and prayer then introduced Paul. Paul rose to the makeshift dais and again welcomed the crowd and offered a prayer. The subject of this lesson was about salvation, Jesus' sacrifice and their sacrifice if they chose to follow Jesus. He taught about how to follow Jesus, what it meant, how to go about it in their lives and what the rewards would be in the hereafter, Heaven. This was much for people to absorb and understand. Some in the crowd grumbled; others were deep in thought, formulating questions, perhaps. When the afternoon sun was setting, Paul blessed the crowd and finished. Paul, Barnabas, Abril and Jonas worked through the crowd answering questions and discussing the meaning in some of the teachings.

Suddenly, there were loud voices and what seemed to be a scuffle beginning in a corner of the garden. Everyone looked in that direction. The governor's mansion guards were beating several of the people who had listened to Paul. Several men and women were involved. Thecla and Zaortha heard remnants of the shouting, "Paul is right..."; "He said..."; "He hates Caesar"; "No, he...". Whether it was the guards talking or the followers shouting, they could not tell. Finally, the guards came for Paul and Barnabas. "Those followers of yours say 'He hates Caesar', pointing at you," the first guard said.

"That is not true. That follower must have misunderstood," Paul contended.

"We talked of Jesus Christ as our savior," Barnabas said, trying to defend Paul.

"You both know Christ was condemned to death. He defied Roman law and was crucified as are most common criminals. If you continue to promote that criminal as a savior of our people, we will imprison you again," said the guard.

"The governor invited us to speak and use his park," Paul said.

"We were sent by the governor," the guard said.

"Then Barnabas and I and three of my select followers will be glad to appear before him and settle this issue, Paul said.

"You and your select followers will appear before him tomorrow morning. You and your followers will spend tonight in prison," the guard said.

The guard then turned to the other three guards telling them, "Bring the arrested, book them into prison on a separate floor and return to the governor's estate."

Paul, Barnabas, Thecla, Zaortha and Jamel were shackled and led to the prison by the guard. As they walked, Jamel whispered to Thecla, "Why us? We weren't speaking."

"I think we're learning something," Thecla whispered back.

"No talking," said the guard, in a loud voice, giving Jamel a shove.

Zaortha looked at Jamel and Thecla, pursing her lips; clearly, she was sending a message to be quiet.

They arrived at the prison and were booked in and shone to their cells in a brusque manner. They realized they were in cells facing each other across a narrow aisle. When they heard the door slam at the end of the hall, they knew the guards were gone. Paul led them in prayer and began to teach about when and how to resist authority and when to politely voice your case. "We know we have done nothing wrong; however, the guards and the governor are pointing to the case of Jesus Christ and his crucifixion. Are they wrong?" Paul asked and the others nodded, yes. "Not entirely," Paul said, as the others stood, open-mouthed.

"How can you say that?" Jamel asked.

"Jesus preached about a King of the Jews, which infuriated Pontius Pilate, the governor of Judea. The Romans saw this as treason. That is a high crime in Roman Law, as it is in all kingdoms," Paul said. "When we preach about Jesus Christ and, indeed, glorify him, we are, in the eyes of Rome, saying we defy Caesar."

"How do we counter such an attitude?" asked Jamel.

"We will counter this Roman attitude by telling the truth. We will appear before the governor with head held high, not as criminals. I will speak when asked as will any of you, always answering truthfully without fear. We will take any punishment the governor meats out as followers of Jesus. Now we must pray, rest and wait for our meeting with the governor tomorrow," Paul said. He blessed them and retreated to the inner wall of the cell.

The next day, the guard came to get the group saying, "The governor will hear your case now." They marched unceremoniously down the long hall, all still shackled. They entered the room and saw the group of followers who had started the fracas. None of Paul's group recognized them. *They must not be true followers. They must have heard from someone Paul was going to be in the Park. They just wanted to start trouble*, thought Thecla.

"I've never seen them before," muttered Barnabas to Paul.

"Nor have I. I wonder what they're up to," whispered Paul.

"I think we're about to find out," whispered Barnabas, as the guard announced the governor's entrance.

"Governor Captilan. Please take your seats," the guard announced, stiffly.

"I have come to hear a case against these men, supposed followers of Paul. Paul, do you know any of the accused?"

"No, I do not. I don't know all of my followers," Paul said.

"I suppose you don't. There are many and you're always moving around. Did you personally invite them to the meeting in my garden yesterday?" the governor asked.

"No, I did not. My followers were charged to spread the word about the time and place of the meeting. They could have heard it from many people, including followers, shopkeepers, or just someone on the street," Paul said.

"All right. I'll ask them. From whom did you learn about the meeting in the garden yesterday?" the governor asked the accused.

The one who acted as leader spoke, "We heard it in the tavern from him," pointing at Jamel.

Looking at Jamel, the governor asked "Did you speak to these men at the tavern to invite them to the meeting?"

Jamel stood, licking his lips nervously, replied, "No, not personally. We stopped at several taverns and invited the customers and proprietor in a loud voice."

"I see, so they heard a generalized announcement. Is that it?" asked the governor.

"Yes, sir," Jamel replied and took his seat.

"I want to hear from you five, what got the fracas started in my garden yesterday?" asked Captilan.

"We were standing near the fence when the minister started praying or something. He was acting like he thought he was God or something. Pretty soon we started mimicking him and some of his followers told us to leave. That made us mad so we decided to get him in trouble," the leader said.

"Then somebody called the guards and they started hitting us with sticks and we struck back. We were protecting ourselves," another one spoke up.

"We didn't mean anything, just saying Paul hates Caesar because he was talking about Jesus, who was a criminal," the third man said.

"All right, that sheds some light on the matter," said the governor. "How does your group respond, Paul?"

Paul nodded at Thecla and she stood to speak, "Governor, we appreciate your asking us for a rebuttal. These men were in the far corner of the garden, among the fruit trees. They were too far away to hear Paul clearly. I think they heard snippets of Paul's teaching and reacted to his words out of context. Paul talked about Jesus as our savior in the context of the church we are striving to build. We ask only those who are actually interested in hearing the truth of the one, true God to attend. Paul is not running some kind of show for entertainment. We will not exclude any who truly wish to hear Paul and make up their mind whether or not to follow him. If these fellows found Paul's message not to their liking or offensive to their sensibilities, they were free to leave. Paul preaches the truth and the followers seek more truths."

"Very interesting and well spoken," the governor said. "I will give this more thought and make a ruling tomorrow morning. Paul and his group are free to leave now. The accused are to return to the prison. Everyone be here tomorrow morning at sun up."

Paul and his group left the building. Paul walked close to Thecla so the other could not hear their conversation. "Thecla, you laid out our defense expertly. I'm proud of you and may God bless you. I believe your unflinching grasp of the situation and your presentation of it, set well with the governor. I think that is why he set us free tonight."

"I think he might rule in our favor," Thecla said.

"Indeed he might, Thecla, but the governor will think on it and we'll find out for sure tomorrow," Paul said.

"Yes, I must not think too far ahead," Thecla said.

Thecla and Paul went to the tavern in the inn and each enjoyed a glass of wine and relaxed.

The next morning, Paul and his group made their way to the governor's room, where he heard cases. The arrested group arrived at about the same time, under guard. The governor was already in the room so he started the court immediately.

"Good morning," he said. "I have studied the backgrounds of all of you. You all seem to have had experience with the court and the governors before. I will discuss each group and give you my determination. This will not take long. Guard, please bring the perpetrators forward."

Paul's group watched the accused group shuffle forward. Their shackles emitted a clanking noise as they walked.

Finally, when they stood before the governor, he looked up at each of them. "All of you have been here before. You and you," he said, looking directly at the leader and the one standing next to him, "have been here several times. You are troublemakers. Will you never learn?" The two prisoners shuffled, as if they wanted to run. The governor continued, "I am putting you both in prison and you will work in the mines." This caused howls and moans from both. "There will be no mercy for either of you. Guards, remove them." Two guards came into the room and took the prisoners out.

After the room settled, the governor said "Now, you three have only been here once. You have been keeping bad company. I just sent the two you were following to the mines. Is that where you wish to go? If so, I can do that and save you and me much time."

"No," the three almost shouted in unison.

"No what?" the governor asked in a patient voice.

"No, we don't want to go to the mines. Please have mercy," they all said, more or less in unison.

"All right then," the governor said, "you will go to prison until I'm convinced you've learned your lesson. Guard, please remove these to the prison."

After they'd shuffled out, the governor asked Paul's group to come forward.

"Paul, Barnabas and Thecla, you have all been here before. Thecla, you provided an excellent defensive statement yesterday. You should consider being a lawyer instead of a missionary," Governor Captilan said, with a smile.

With a straightened face, the governor began again. "Paul, you and your group may leave but, in the future, please look for a way to attract good people to your meetings so this kind of rabble-rousing doesn't occur again."

"Yes, governor. Thank you and God bless you," said Paul.

"Yes, yes. Thank you," the governor said, rose and left the room.

Paul and his group left the governor's house and returned to the group of followers waiting at the fountain. A hush came over the group as they waited to hear Paul's description of the situation. Paul began with a blessing then launched into a summary of the proceeding before the governor, "We were brought before the governor and presented our case as did the accused. Thecla provided a well-spoken defense of our cause and reason to be here. The governor took the statements from both sides to conjugate overnight. He definitely did his research. He called us all to return in the morning for his decision. He found the two leaders had been in much trouble before. He sentenced them to prison and the mines. He gave the remaining three lighter prison sentences. For us, he told us to be more careful how and to whom we disseminate the call to come to our teachings. Then he told us we were free to leave."

"How can we know who is a troublemaker and who is not?" asked one man.

"That is hard to know," admitted Paul. "One way would be to talk to individuals. Invite them as friends only if you would invite them to your house."

"We've had people ask us when Paul is going to speak. They've heard of you and already have been touched by the Spirit," said Zaortha.

"Yes, we've been in Iconium before and some of you live in this city, so we can be more careful here. My advice is to speak more carefully and not to just make a generalized invitation to a crowd in a tavern or inn."

After Paul indicated he was finished, the followers began to talk to each other in small groups. Many wanted to speak to Paul and Barnabas, others singled out Zaortha, Thecla and Jamel to try to get more details. Jamel sought out Paul and admitted to him he had made a generalized appeal in a tavern to all customers about Paul's teaching in the garden. Paul thanked him for his honesty, blessed him and asked him to continue spreading the word with care. Then the crowd broke up and moved off to find their mid-day meal.

In mid-afternoon, the crowd gathered again at the fountain. Paul began to speak as soon as the crowd of followers settled. "I have made a decision. We will leave here at the end of this week, in two days, for Pisidian Antioch. There, I will visit my churches and preach to new members and baptize some who are ready. Those who decide to stay here may go with my blessing, all who wish to continue to follow must be ready to leave. I will finish my work here and ask those who stay to live as examples of our faith, serve others and continue to speak about our faith to those who have not yet heard." He blessed them and sat near the fountain, looking exhausted.

Thecla and Zaortha went to him, concerned about his appearance. "Are you unwell?" Zaortha asked Paul.

"No," Paul said, "just tired. I must meet again with Abril and Jonas to secure the church here. Then we can move on to the churches in Antioch."

"Please try to rest before we leave again," Thecla said. "We need you to lead us and to fill our hearts with the Spirit."

"Thecla, no, you don't need me anymore. You must go on after Antioch and lead your own ministry." Paul said.

Thecla, caught short, gasped, "Paul, what are you saying? I must lead a group of my own followers? How could I do such a thing? Who would follow me? How would I lead?"

"Thecla we've discussed these things in general terms. Did you think I was just talking? Did you not realize I was teaching you?"

"Yes, Paul we did speak of these things but, no, I did not realize you were preparing me for a ministry," said Thecla, in a subdued voice.

"I've selected you, Zaortha and Jamel to accompany me on these various situations so you could learn the practice of ministry. I want you to lead and Zaortha and Jamel to accompany and help you," said Paul. "Please do not mention this to the other followers. I will make it public in Antioch."

"Must we go to Antioch?" Jamel asked.

"Yes," said Paul, "Antioch is fertile ground for conversions. There are several churches there and more to be started. We were expelled from Antioch so going back requires some skill. I want to show you again, how to re-enter a city that has closed its doors to us in the past. In Iconium, we were fortunate. The change of governors worked for us. Entering Iconium could have been difficult but it was not. I chose not to re-enter Lystra because our expulsion had been too recent. It would only have resulted in more strife."

"We understand," Thecla said, politely taking a leadership role.

Two days later, Paul, Barnabas and the followers left for Pisidian Antioch. The day was warm, not yet hot, and the followers were rested. Spirits were high. Many of the Iconium followers chose to stay home and travel no further. Paul's followers numbered under 100, on leaving Iconium. In some ways, it made the walk easier and allowed the followers to become acquainted; however, it also meant fewer supplies could be carried, limiting the amount and variety of food available, water was at a premium. Medical supplies were non-existent. The walk would take at least six days.

Paul and his followers arrived in Pisidian Antioch dusty, thirsty and hungry. Some were limping, nursing sore feet. Paul instructed them to find what shelter they could, preferably with existing church members. Barnabas escorted the followers to visit Tatin, a church leader. They would be directed to homes by Tatin. Thecla and Zaortha remained with Paul. Jamel had joined with Barnabas. Paul, Thecla and Zaortha went to the house of Paul's friends, Charis and Delva. This couple knew Paul well and had a large home with a veranda as well as several rooms on the inside. They were wealthy and supported Paul and his mission anyway they could. They welcomed the three and showed them to their rooms, pointing out the bath for their use.

After Paul, Thecla and Zaortha had finished bathing and changed clothes, they were ready to enjoy dinner with their hosts. Charis and Delva welcomed them to the table.

"Have a seat," Charis said, "we are anxious to hear of your travels and successes."

"First, I want to formally introduce my most avid followers, Thecla and Zaortha," Paul said.

Charis nodded to each of the women and Delva said, "Welcome, we are always happy to meet Paul's followers. Have you been following Paul long?"

"I have followed Paul since he was here in Antioch last," Zaortha said.

"So you were part of the group that had to leave suddenly?" asked Delva. She received a sideways glance from Charis.

"Yes, we went directly to Iconium," said Zaortha, "which is where I met Thecla."

"Zaortha and I have become fast friends. We travel well together and have many of the same interests," said Thecla.

"We are glad to have you visit us," Delva said.

Paul and Charis had been carrying on a conversation about the Antioch churches in low tones while Delva spoke to the women.

"I was hoping the churches would have grown larger in my absence," Paul said as Delva finished her conversation with the women.

"I think some of the new converts are waiting for you for baptism," Delva said.

"Well, I can't be everywhere," Paul said, with a chuckle.

"That is true," Charis said, "but confidence must be bolstered and only your preaching can do that for a fledgling church."

"Then I will plan the first preaching tomorrow mid-day. We must get word to Tatin, Barnabas and the other followers to spread the word to other congregants. Do you have a messenger?"

"Yes, we have a dependable messenger we can call on." With that, Charis left the room to call the messenger. When the messenger arrived a few minutes later, Paul repeated the message to him and expressed urgency. The messenger left immediately and everyone at table settled to consume their evening meal.

Thecla and Zaortha accompanied Paul to visit the city magistrate, Alexander. Alexander fell in love instantly with Thecla. She paid him no attention. Thecla and Zaortha went out into the street to find Barnabas, Jamel and the followers. Paul remained in discussion with Alexander.

"I will give you gifts of gold, silver and gems, if you will give me Thecla," Alexander said, finally.

"I do not know the woman of whom you speak, nor does she belong to me," Paul said.

Paul and Alexander left the city building and walked a distance down the street. Alexander spotted Thecla in the distance, left Paul and hurried toward her. Alexander rushed to Thecla and kissed her. Thecla reacted in a loud voice, "Force me not, who am a stranger; force me not, who am a servant of God; I am one of the principal persons of Iconium and was obliged to leave that city because I would not be married to Thamyris. I will have no man."

Alexander made another move toward her. Thecla stood her ground, staring at him. He saw her eyes change from deep brown to icey blue and felt a sharp pain in his chest, as if he were pierced by a knife. He crumpled to the ground. Capital guards arrested Thecla and led her to the governor. The governor ordered his men to check the health of the magistrate. Alexander had recovered partially and no marks of any instrument could be found. The governor refused to hear anything more about the case and released Thecla to Paul.

Paul and Thecla hurried to his preaching place in Tatin's church. There Barnabas and the followers, including Zaortha and Jamel relaxed at the sight of Paul and Thecla. "We have come to speak the Word of God once more and baptize those who sincerely believe. Thecla has performed another miracle and I am introducing her to preach some of the Word, also," Paul began. Paul continued to preach after Barnabas offered the prayer.

Midway through the afternoon, Paul called upon Thecla to preach about her commitment to God. Thecla took the dais with confidence; Zaortha stood slightly behind her and to her right.

"I am pleased to come before you to speak the Word of God. God has blessed me and all of you in so many ways. First, you have heard the Word from Paul, the very best preacher of God's Holy Word." Here she was interrupted by loud applause and shouts. "I am blessed to have my very best friend, Zaortha, to share ideas, travels and trials with me. I have decided to be celibate in God's honor. I pray daily for God's help to be chaste, honest and loving to all God's children. I pray for all new believers that they feel the commitment to God through baptism. I am witnessing to you the power of baptism. After baptism, you will feel the will of God in your daily life. You will feel the urge to spread the Word, not necessarily to preach, but to tell others of the power of His Word. God will reward you and ask more of you. He will ask you to honor only Him, forsake all other gods and live according to his commandments. In short 'Love your neighbor as yourself. Do onto others as you would want done onto you'."

The crowd was in quiet awe. They had never heard a woman preach before. The simplicity of her words was breathtaking. Thecla spoke in a loud, clear, confident manner, as if she'd practiced and preached many times before, which she had not. Paul stood once more, blessed Thecla and Zaortha, after which he directed those to be baptized to the fountain outside the church. Baptisms took place, administered by Paul and Barnabas, until sunset. The sky darkened and night approached as Paul, Thecla and Zaortha made their way to Charis and Delva's home.

Chapter 6. Thecla has her own ministry

The next morning after they'd broken their fast, Paul motioned Thecla aside. "Let us meet by the large, old olive tree in the park in an hour. Bring Zaortha and I'll try to get Barnabas to join us."

"What do you have in mind?" Thecla asked.

"I need to tell you all a few decisions I have made," said Paul.

"All right, we'll meet you under the old olive tree in an hour," agreed Thecla.

An hour later, Thecla, Zaortha, Jamel and Barnabas settled under the tree. Paul stood and began to speak, "Thanks for coming on short notice. I have made several decisions that will affect you all. First of all, I have decided to go from here to Syrian Antioch by way of Perga to Antioch then to Salamis and Paphos Cyprus and back here in about a year. I do not expect you, Thecla, Zaortha and Jamel to follow. I hereby anoint Thecla as a minister of God's Holy Word. Thecla, you must take your followers and spread the Word of God to places where we have not visited. There are many who have not yet heard the Word." With these words, Thecla went to her knees and Paul blessed her and anointed her with a small drop of sacred oil.

In so doing, Paul instructed Thecla to "Go and teach the word. You have completed the evangelical course and shared with me the zeal for Christ. For this reason, Christ has chosen you through me, so that he may draw you to the apostolic office and entrust to you some of the still uninstructed cities."

Thecla was overwhelmed, as was Zaortha and Jamel, who wept for joy. Jamel was the first to recover, stood and helped Zaortha and Thecla to their feet. Thecla said to Paul, "I accept the honor Christ has bestowed upon me through you. I will seek those who wish to follow and leave directly for Iconium. I will go from there into the countryside and to smaller cities who want to hear the Word."

Paul blessed the small group and they left to assemble those who chose to follow Thecla. Thecla led the group a short way into the city and stopped under a yew tree. "Let us sit for a short time and try to develop a plan for this ministry," she said.

"Who do you think will want to follow us?" Jamel asked.

"I am not sure," answered Thecla, "I'm not comfortable taking Paul's followers away from him."

"I don't think he's worried about that," Zaortha said. "He just wants us to preach to those who have not yet heard."

"Thank you, Zaortha, that makes me feel better. We do need to plan our ministry and find what followers we can. I've thought about going back to Iconium first. There are surrounding villages and farmers who have not heard Paul. I also plan to visit my mother and speak God's Word to her."

"That sounds like a plan to me," Jamel said.

"I have to confess this to the two of you. I've wanted a ministry for so long. Now that it's happened, I'm nervous and somewhat unsure of myself."

"I think that's normal," Zaortha said. "You have to pray for guidance and we will help find those who are interested in following."

"I will stay beneath this tree and pray. You and Jamel find what followers wish to travel and bring them back here," Thecla said.

Zaortha and Jamel decided to go in different directions to find followers. Jamel decided to talk to Tatin to see if his church members might be interested in following. Zaortha planned to contact followers of Paul who were mainly concentrated in Antioch proper. After sunset and dusk took hold, Zaortha and Jamel brought about thirty followers to Thecla.

"We have found thirty followers for you, Thecla" announced Zaortha.

"You both have done well. Let us bless them and say a prayer of thanksgiving," Thecla said.

She turned to the assembled group of followers, blessed them and prayed a short prayer of thanksgiving, "God bless you all for agreeing to follow and support me. Thank you, Lord God, for inspiring these people to help spread Your Holy Word."

With that they sat, opened their provision packs and ate an evening meal. Some talked among themselves but the meal was somber. After they finished eating, Thecla outlined the simple travel plan she had discussed earlier with Zaortha and Jamel. When Thecla finished, she bade them to return to their respective lodgings and prepare to leave from this place tomorrow morning. Thecla, Zaortha and Jamel went to Charis and Delva's home to rest and prepare for tomorrow.

As Thecla and Zaortha prepared to leave and, during final goodbyes, Delva presented Thecla and Zaortha with large sacks of provisions and a sack of coins, several denarii. Charis provided Jamel with the same farewell package. The three left their lodging and made for the yew tree. Everyone sat under the tree, quiet for a few moments. "That was quite a farewell," said Zaortha.

"I was astounded," Jamel added.

"I was surprised too but grateful for their support," said Thecla, trying to bring their surprise to a practical level. "We will survive and preach only with like support from future believers."

"That is how Paul was able to preach and travel," Zaortha said.

"Now we must prepare to move on from here. I plan to go first to Iconium. My mother is there and I want to try to convert her to the Word of God. While there, you both can find any followers who are willing to travel with us to the countryside," Thecla said.

"Zaortha and I will find our followers here and tell them we are ready to leave," Jamel said.

"Yes, we will leave from here in an hour," Thecla stated.

In slightly more than an hour, all who chose to follow Thecla were assembled and ready to begin the trek to Iconium. One brought an ass and cart which allowed most to place their packs on the cart. Some, including Thecla, chose to carry their packs as an outward sign of humility. *Practice what you preach*, Thecla thought.

Five days later, Iconium was in view from a hilltop north of the city. "That is where our mission begins," Thecla said. "We will find shelter there among the believers of the church Paul began. Be courteous and patient and our needs will be met."

From there, they strode into the city. Jamel and Zaortha led the group of followers to seek shelter among Paul's believers; Thecla went directly to her mother's home. Upon arriving at the front door, Thecla knocked firmly. Her mother, Theoclia, answered the door and was dumbstruck. For a moment, Theoclia could not find her voice. Finally, she said, "Thecla, you are here. What brings you to my door?"

"Mother, I've come to visit you. Are you not glad to see me? Will you welcome me?" Thecla asked.

"Yes, of course. What brings you here? I thought you'd gone forever."

"No, not forever; I joined Paul to hear more of his word."

"You chose to join that cripple worth nothing and jilted Thamyris. Are you satisfied with yourself?"

"Of course not, Mother. I am sorry about Thamyris. Is he still in town?"

"He died as did his father. Both killed in an accident with runaway horses and a wagon."

"I'm sorry to hear that."

"You should be. If you'd have married him, you would be rich now, inherited all the family wealth."

"I am not interested in their wealth. I am preaching God's Word now."

"There sure is no wealth in that. You've decided to be poor all your life. Why?"

"Because truth needs to reach as many people as possible," Thecla answered. "These are the end times and there is no time to spare."

"Did you get those crazy words from your Paul?"

"Yes. They are not 'crazy' words and he's not 'my' Paul."

"Denial is not an answer to an argument. Tell me again why you are here."

"I have come to enlighten you to the Word of God. I want to tell you why I believe in Paul's teachings and what he taught so you, too, can understand the teachings of the one, true God."

"I don't understand how you can accept there is only one God when our ancestors and the Romans all have many gods to rule the heavens and the earth. Are you saying our family and government are wrong?"

"Yes, and here is why..." Thecla launched into a sermon of three hours, during which her mother cooled off and went to sleep.

Upon awakening, Theoclia said she did not believe a word of what Thecla had said and banished Thecla from the house. Thecla was shocked and hurt, emotionally and physically. She left the house blinded by tears, stumbling down the steps. She picked herself up, bleeding from scratched and scrapped knees and elbows. She also limped from a possible broken ankle.

Thecla made her way to Daphne's home, a believer and follower of Paul. Zaortha was also there. When they saw Thecla bleeding and in pain at the door, they helped her in the house and bade her sit. Then she began to tell them of her visit to her mother. She was more distraught than either Zaortha or Daphne had seen her. Thecla could only talk between sobs so the two women were not sure of the whole story.

Daphne worked to determine the extent of injury to Thecla's ankle while Zaortha washed and bandaged Thecla's arms and knees. Thecla sobbed in the pain her mother's rejection had caused her emotionally. Thecla looked to Zaortha for support. Zaortha put her hand on Thecla's heaving shoulder, attempting to sooth and quiet her. Daphne determined the ankle was broken and called a physician, a member of the church, to assist in setting it. In the meantime, they helped Thecla to Zaortha's room which had two beds. Thecla lay on the bed to wait for the physician. The two women left Thecla, closing the door. They had told her to rest and talk only when she felt like it.

By the time the physician arrived, Thecla had recovered enough to describe the injury coherently. She described being banished from her mother's home, her teary decent down the steps and stumbling. She described remembering turning her ankle on a lower step but only thought she'd sprained it so she'd limped to Daphne's house, the closest church member she knew. "That's a good description. It helps me," the physician said. "Walking on it probably made it worse but you needed help."

"Yes, I am grateful for Daphne and Zaortha," Thecla said.

"As I set to fix and wrap this ankle it will hurt. Please bear with me as best you can," the physician said.

"That will be easy. I will only concentrate on Jesus' suffering," Thecla said.

"You are a saint," the physician said, as he went to work.

Thecla emitted a few groans and deep sighs but no cries of pain, which she most assuredly must have felt. Daphne saw the physician out while Zaortha came into the room to see Thecla. "You made it through without crying out," Zaortha said.

"It was a true trial but I concentrated on the sufferings of our Savior as Paul preached," Thecla said.

"You are definitely equipped to preach the Word. You are inspired."

"I think I'm lacking. I failed to convert my mother. She drove me away."

"I don't think because you failed to convert one person, you are a failure."

"She is my mother. She must be saved. I must save her," Thecla said, close to tears again.

"As you saw from following Paul, some refuse baptism and, thus, being saved," Zaortha reasoned.

"Yes, of course you are right but she is my mother. I care about her eternal life."

"Of course you do but a person must want to be saved."

"That is true and that is what Paul would say but how can she be convinced to want to be saved?" Thecla was blubbering by this time.

"Perhaps, approach her one more time, when you've recovered and see if she will listen to you," Zaortha suggested.

"All right. Will you come with me?"

"Yes, Thecla, if you think it will help."

"I do and maybe Daphne too?"

"We'll wait to see how long it takes for you to recover and whether or not Daphne wants to join us. Now you must rest. I'll bring your dinner in a few hours," Zaortha said.

Zaortha left Thecla crying softly and feeling quite low. She was at a loss as to how to raise Thecla's spirits and went to talk with Daphne and to help with meal preparations.

"Daphne, Thecla is still quite distraught. I can't think of any way to help her," Zaortha said.

"I am not sure. I'd like to make a special tea for her. It's been known to help others."

"It's worth a try. She's resting now. Let's give it to her at the evening meal."

At that point, they moved to the kitchen to prepare the meal with two other kitchen helpers.

The sun was setting as the evening meal hour approached. Dishes rattled and the smell of cooked meat permeated the house. Zaortha prepared a tray of roast mutton, vegetable and tea. She carried the tray to the room where Thecla was resting. Zaortha rapped on the door politely and entered. Thecla's eyes were red and her hair disheveled. She looked hurt and in pain.

"Did you get any rest?" Zaortha asked.

"No, I cried myself to sleep but I still feel the pain of my mother's rejection. Why won't she listen to me?" Thecla said, as she dissolved into another round of tears.

"Now, now, Thecla. Crying won't help. Please eat from the tray I brought and drink this special tea Daphne made for you."

"All right," Thecla said, drying her eyes. "It is so pleasing to have a loyal friend in you."

"I want to help. I just don't know quite how."

"Please sit with me and we can talk while I eat."

Zaortha sat on the other bed, her bed, while Thecla ate. She ate quickly and Zaortha could see she was ravenous from not having eaten all day.

"This tea is wonderful. What is in it?" Thecla asked. "It's so soothing."

"I don't know how it's made. Daphne said it has worked for others," Zaortha said. "You will feel better in time."

"I'm feeling better already."

"That's great. You'd better get more sleep after you finish eating."

"Yes, I'm feeling sleepy now."

"Perhaps the tea is helping to relax you."

Thecla finished eating, lay back in bed and was asleep before Zaortha finished gathering the tray. She slipped out the door, shutting it quietly.

Three weeks later, Thecla felt healed and decided to head back to her mother's house again. Zaortha accompanied her this time. They did not invite Daphne because they were unsure of the reception they would receive. Thecla rapped loudly on the door. Both women waited for a response. Finally, the door opened.

"Oh, it's you," Theoclia said.

"Yes, Mother and this is my friend, Zaortha," Thecla said.

All three women stood, staring at each other. Thecla finally broke the impasse.

"May we come in?" Thecla asked.

"Why, only to preach at me?" her mother asked.

"I hoped we could have a friendly conversation," said Thecla.

"All right, come in," Theoclia said.

The women took seats and looked at each other. Now it was up to Thecla to begin the conversation. "How are Father and Leos doing?" Thecla asked.

"The last I heard they are doing well. I only hear from either of them every two to three months," Theoclia said.

"Has father received his promotion to Centurion?" Thecla asked.

"Yes and Leos is now the *decanus* of his *Contubernium*," Theoclia said, proudly. "I'm sure he will continue to rise in stature in the army."

"I am happy for him," Thecla said.

"Where are they stationed?" Zaortha asked.

"Both are in Rome, currently but my husband will be going to Alexandria soon," Theoclia said.

"Is there trouble there?" Thecla asked.

"No, I don't think so. It's some kind of force to keep the religious strife quiet," Theoclia said.

"Religious strife could mean war," Zaortha stated.

With that comment, conversation lagged and Theoclia left the room to get fruit drinks for everyone. "I must try to start teaching again. That's why we're here," Thecla whispered to Zaortha.

Zaortha nodded her head and prepared herself for the barrage she knew would come. "All right, if you're ready," Zaortha said.

"Yes, I'm as ready as I'll ever be," Thecla said, quietly.

Theoclia brought the fruit drinks in, served them and sat. "Now why did you really come?" she asked.

After a long drink, Thecla started to answer, "Mother, I've come to talk to you again about the one, true God."

"And I have told you I am not interested," Theoclia said.

"I would like to know why you are not interested," Zaortha said.

"The old gods have served us well. It is Caesar's desire that we only worship the Roman gods," Theoclia said.

"Are these the old gods of which you speak?" Zaortha asked.

"No, we worshiped gods of our ancestors," Theoclia said.

"And you had no trouble converting to the Roman gods?" Zaortha asked.

"Some, but the governor was assigned by Rome and he oversaw our mass conversion. We didn't really have a choice," Theoclia explained.

"Now that you have a choice to hear about the one, true God, you are choosing not to listen?" Zaortha asked.

"I would not have accepted the Roman gods, if I'd had a choice," Theoclia said.

"I see, to convert, you must be forced?" Zaortha asked.

"I can be converted without believing," Theoclia said.

Zaortha could see her line of questioning was taking them down a blind alley. She looked at Thecla, who nodded her assent to pick up the conversation.

"Mother, we are asking you to open your mind and heart to listen about God and our savior who died for our sins to open the gates of Heaven to us when we die," Thecla said.

"Thecla, I've heard this from you before. I told you I don't want to hear this nonsense. If you want to spill this to those poor, witless farmers go ahead but don't speak to me about it again. Now, I ask you both to leave," Theoclia said.

"Mother, I beg you to listen," Thecla said.

"Leave," Theoclia shouted.

Zaortha and Thecla grabbed their packs and exited the house. Theoclia slammed the door after they stepped outside.

"I must give up trying to convert my mother," Thecla said.

"I think she's made up her mind, Thecla," Zaortha said.

"Yes, let's seek out Jamel and his friends. We need to talk about this difficulty. We could be facing a similar mindset with other listeners," Thecla said.

"Yes, I was thinking that, too."

"I wonder what Paul would say or do?" Thecla said, thinking aloud.

"I think he would say 'patience and prayer', if I were to guess," Zaortha said.

"I think you're right. Let's see what Jamel thinks," Thecla concluded.

An hour later, the two women found Jamel, Tatin and another friend in a café near the church. Tatin invited the women to sit with them and eat a mid-day meal. Orders taken and the meal served, Thecla was hesitant to open the subject of her mother's rejection of the Truth but Zaortha launched into a description of their visit to Theoclia immediately. The three men listened to her as she described her questioning.

Upon finishing, Tatin said, "She might say she believes to keep you from preaching to her but you wouldn't want to baptize such a person."

"She didn't even say she believed, just for us to leave. She was screaming when we left," Thecla said.

"That is painful," Jamel said.

"What am I doing wrong? I can't even convert my own mother. What kind of an evangelist am I?" Thecla asked, close to tears again.

Zaortha took her hand, attempting to bolster her confidence.

"You are a good teacher. Paul thinks you have the gift from God to teach His Word. Paul blessed you and gave you this ministry. He did not guarantee you would convert every person to whom you preached," Jamel said.

"Thank you, Jamel. That was well stated. See, Thecla, you are punishing yourself needlessly. Please relax and enjoy your meal. We can talk more later," Zaortha said, hugging Thecla.

Tatin and the other man rose to leave, saying they must return to oversee work on the church building. Jamel, Zaortha and Thecla remained seated. "Where do we go from here?" Jamel asked.

"I'm not sure. What do you think, Thecla?"

"We should leave Iconium and take our ministry to the countryside," Thecla said, half-heartedly.

"Oh, Thecla, please don't let the experience with your mother darken your path forever," Jamel said.

"Yes," Zaortha added, "we need you to lead us to your next town. Please don't let one set-back destroy your mission."

"Remember how Paul didn't let it stop him when he was driven out of cities often," Jamel said.

Taking a deep breath, Thecla said, "You are right, Jamel, Paul didn't let set-backs stop him. He just kept pushing on. We'll do the same. I'm planning to head for towns and villages, such as Misthia, Amblada or Umanada."

"That sounds promising," Zaortha said. "They're smaller and have not heard the message of the one, true God."

"Is your ankle up to the journey?" asked Jamel.

"Thecla, I think you should rest at Daphne's the rest of this week and head out on our mission next week. This is the first time you have walked on it for any distance, after all," Zaortha cautioned.

"All right, I'll do as you suggest, Zaortha," Thecla said.

With that, they parted from Jamel, who said he would return to the church. Zaortha and Thecla returned to Daphne's home, where Thecla went to the room to rest immediately on their arrival.

"I can't believe how tired I got from that little bit of walking. How am I ever going to travel to those villages?" Thecla asked.

"You will get stronger every day. We should walk about town as you can every day. You'll be surprised how quickly your strength will return," Zaortha said.

"I'm sure you are right. Now I just need to rest."

"Yes, I'll see if I can help Daphne with anything. Rest easy, Thecla."

The week passed and Thecla was again ready to leave Iconium for Misthia. All was packed. Jamel had acquired an ass and cart, which freed everyone from carrying heavy packs of provisions and water. Thecla had acquired a following of about twenty men, women and a few children. They were in high spirits as they began the trek. Misthia was about four days walking from Iconium. They knew the ass and cart would slow them but their bundles were lighter so walking on the cart track road was not difficult. The Romans had built roads and tracks that were easy to follow. As they walked, Thecla, Zaortha and Jamel talked to the others about what they planned to accomplish, how, what and where they intended to preach. There was no group of believers on whom to rely in Misthia, therefore, Thecla declared to the group they would make camp outside Misthia.

Four days later, Thecla and her followers arrived at the gates of Misthia. Following Paul's example, she and Zaortha decided to try to enter the city. Jamel would stay with the followers and direct the establishment of the camp. Though late in the day, Thecla decided to approach the city gates. Accompanied by Zaortha, Thecla got the guard's attention.

"Who goes there?" the guard bellowed.

"Thecla of Iconium and Zaortha," Thecla answered.

"What is your business?"

"We wish to speak with the city leaders." Thecla kept her voice strong, though she was nervous.

"It is late in the day; no one may be willing to talk to you."

"Please send a messenger to ask if anyone will talk to us."

The guard turned to speak to others and a slave was sent with the message.

"Wait outside the gate until the slave returns."

Thecla and Zaortha found stones on which to sit, while they waited.

Nearly an hour later, the slave returned with a lesser city official. The guard introduced the official as Tortus to Thecla and Zaortha.

"Why have you interrupted my leisure time? What business could two women have that is so important that I must talk to you?"

Thecla could tell, by his tone, this conversation would need to be opened with care. "I am Thecla of Iconium and this is my friend, Zaortha. We are approaching your city with twenty of my followers to preach the Word of the one, true God. Perhaps you've heard of Paul? I have been a follower of him. He has blessed me as a minister of The Word."

"That's much information for me to digest. No, I never heard of this Paul. Do you want to move into my city?"

"No, we are prepared to camp outside the city gates. We only need a place in your city that would accommodate a crowd of at least fifty people," Thecla said.

"Woh-hoh, you expect that big a crowd to hear you speak about some god?"

"This is not just some god," Zaortha chimed in. "This is the one, true God, who sent his son, Jesus, to die for our sins."

"Yes, I heard about that debacle from the Romans," Tortus said.

"Now, may we enter the city tomorrow morning to find any residents who want to hear what we have come to say?" Thecla asked, sensing the conversation could go wrong if she didn't change its direction.

"Because I want to get back to my house and not spend all night listening to you, I'll grant your entrance tomorrow morning. If you manage to gather any listeners, you may speak at the fountain at the city square. Absolutely no disturbance or you and your followers will be chased from the city immediately."

"That is understood and we thank you for your cooperation," Thecla said, sweetly, though thinking *grudging cooperation*. Thecla and Zaortha bowed deeply and left for their encampment.

When both women arrived at the camp, they called a meeting and the discussion with and direction from Tortus was detailed. Thecla emphasized they had to be peaceful. No one must let tempers flare, no matter what is said. She tried to use Paul's admonishments as they applied to this occasion. Thecla, Zaortha and Jamel had witnessed, first hand, how quickly a group could be run from a city. The camp was bade rest for the morrow and the necessary work it would entail.

The next morning, all broke their fast, received further instructions on notifying people of the preaching. She also reiterated where and not to locate possible people who might be interested. "No one must approach the taverns or brothels," Thecla declared. "Though they too may be interested, they could cause trouble. At this time, we will only approach households."

The adults prepared to go into the city. Two women were left behind to care for the children. Every man and woman who followed Thecla was excited to approach new members but somewhat apprehensive about addressing them.

"These people may never have heard of Paul or the Christian message," one follower said to Thecla

"Will they be interested or will they react in anger?" asked another.

Thecla stopped everyone and announced, "I have decided two followers should approach each residence. Do not overwhelm a listener. Be prepared to answer questions as well as you can. Decide which person will talk and who will support. Remember Zaortha's and Jamel's words last night."

This quieted the followers and made them more comfortable. They began to walk again and were soon at the city gate. The entourage was admitted readily to the city. Each pair chose a street where they began knocking on doors. All was quiet for some time until a disturbance erupted from the neighborhood chosen by Jamel and his fellow believer. Thecla was on the next street away and wondered what the problem was. *I've not heard such a commotion before when we were speaking to potential listeners. What could the problem be? That is Jamel's street. He can handle it.* She willed herself to let it pass until she heard running footsteps behind her.

"Thecla, Jamel is hurt. He's lying in the street," said the man who had paired with Jamel.

"What happened?" Thecla asked, as she turned to speak to him.

"We stopped at this house and the man who answered the door was real mean. I think he was drunk."

"Did Jamel try to talk to him?"

"He didn't have a chance. The man came out of the house yelling obscenities then he hit Jamel with a club."

Thecla found Jamel on the ground bleeding from a serious head wound and, perhaps, a broken arm. Jamel was still unconscious.

"Please run to find some of the men to help lift Jamel from the street. We'll stay here with him to be sure he is not run over by a cart," Thecla said. The man left as he was bid to find help.

"Jamel could not have expected such an outburst from this neighborhood yet we never know what is on the other side of the door," Thecla said.

At that point, Zaortha arrived and ran directly to Jamel. She brushed her hand softly across his forehead. He moaned. "Oh, Jamel, it's me, Zaortha. I'll get some help. We need to get you out of the street," Zaortha said, as comfortingly as possible.

Finally three men approached and looked at Jamel. They shook their heads and one asked the women, "To move him, we need a large piece of cloth, a wrap. Will any of you women be able to sacrifice a wrap?"

"I will," Zaortha volunteered as soon as he finished talking, handing him the material.

"That should work," the man said.

All hands worked to move Jamel onto the cloth. The men took up the ends of the cloth and carried Jamel to the side of the street, laying him gently on the ground. "Now, we have to get him to a place where we can treat him," Thecla said.

"We could go back to camp and get the mule and the wagon," suggested one of the men.

"I don't think we have a choice," Thecla said. "It will take some time. Perhaps, Jamel will come around and we can assess more accurately his injuries."

"I'll go with them to get supplies and freshwater to clean his wounds," Zaortha said.

Thecla heard the wagon and the mule coming as it turned the corner to enter the street. "We have help coming, Jamel" Thecla told Jamel, who moaned on hearing her words.

The driver stopped the wagon close to Jamel. "We have a broad board to place Jamel on to lift him into the wagon," the driver said.

The men unloaded the board and lifted Jamel onto it and loaded him into the wagon. Thecla and Zaortha climbed aboard the wagon and began to wash Jamel's wounded head then bandage it. The wagon progressed back to the camp with all of Thecla's followers close behind. *I want to tell the gate guard about this incident but I don't think he'll do anything about it. He might even say we started it*, Thecla thought.

By the time they arrived at the camp, Jamel had lost consciousness again. The men carried him from the wagon to the campfire, where there was sufficient light for Zaortha to assess his injuries. She set to work immediately by removing the wrapping on his head, washing the injury again and re-wrapping it. Then Zaortha checked his arm. She felt a break in his upper arm. This, she determined, would need a splint to heal properly. "I need two slim boards to use for a splint. Can you make them?" she called.

"We'll look but may have to make them," one of the men called.

"Please hurry. I want to set the arm while he is unconscious," Zaortha replied.

Several minutes, it seemed hours, later, the man brought the splints to Zaortha. He helped her set the arm and bind it securely. Zaortha took another piece of cloth and fashioned a sling for Jamel's arm. She found several large bruises on his hip and leg but thought they did not require treatment. Finishing her perusal, she stated, "Now, we should try to wake him gently. I must speak to him to be sure he can tell me his name and where we are."

"What can that tell you?" the man asked.

"If he can answer quickly, without much thought, it means his head injury is less severe. If he cannot answer those questions, his head injury is severe and he will have to rest much longer," Zaortha said.

"You are a healer. I didn't know we had a healer among us," the man said.

"I learned much from my mother and other women in the city," Zaortha said.

"What city?"

"Pisidian Antioch."

"Oh, that city," the man said, as he turned to wander back to the group of men.

I wonder what he meant by 'that city'. He's probably heard of Paul's misadventure in Antioch and thinks it is a dangerous city. He's from Iconium and the gossipers are plentiful there. It's too bad he feels that way. I will ask Thecla if she knows him. Perhaps, she will talk to him. It would be best if those negative feelings can be blunted immediately, before trouble arises, Zaortha thought.

Zaortha bent over to begin the process of waking Jamel. He answered her groggily. She continued to talk softly to him until he was fully awake. She asked him the questions and he answered them clearly and correctly. Now she was relieved and asked if he was thirsty. He was so she procured a cup of fresh, cool water. She made sure he was comfortable and joined the women to report on Jamel's injuries. Everyone sat around the fire for the late evening meal. After she finished eating, she approached Jamel, offering him a cup of broth held out from the soup from the evening meal. He agreed to the cup of broth then said he needed to go back to sleep; Zaortha agreed.

Zaortha sought Thecla to speak with her about the man who seemed to take umbrage at Zaortha's being from Pisidian Antioch. She also wanted to consult with Thecla about Jamel's status. Thecla agreed Zaortha should stay in camp with Jamel for the next day. Thecla wanted Zaortha at the fountain for the teaching. They would select another person to stay with Jamel for that time.

The next morning, after breaking their fast, Thecla gathered the group and discussed the day's work ahead. "We will continue where we left off yesterday. We must invite as many as will hear us. Again we will go in pairs. Do not let Jamel's experience yesterday frighten you but be aware there is a possibility of negative behavior. We will teach tomorrow, mid-afternoon at the city square and fountain. Let us go now with God and do the work we have chosen," Thecla instructed.

The group walked to the city gate and dispersed to the streets to carry on the word of Thecla's impending sermon at the fountain tomorrow. The day went on without incident. Many, especially women, responded encouragingly, planning to attend. By late afternoon, they reached the lower area consisting of poor hovels, taverns and brothels. The group met in the lower district and Thecla addressed the group, "We will not visit these places tonight. It is too risky. We'll go back to camp and decide what to do tomorrow morning."

"There will be more men in the taverns tonight. We might be able to find listeners," one man said.

"That is true," Thecla said, "but the risk of danger outweighs the likelihood of getting more listeners. We will return to camp now."

Most returning to camp were happy but tired; a few were sullen and miffed at Thecla for cutting the day short. *I'm not sure why I feel a discord among the followers. Did they really want to visit the taverns and brothels to spread the word or for other purposes. I need to talk to them individually to discern the growing problem,* thought Thecla. *I'll talk to Zaortha after the evening meal to see if she has gleaned any information.*

During the evening meal, Yaco, the wagon master requested time to go into the city to procure supplies, to which Thecla agreed, readily. Sitting beside Zaortha and a little away from the rest, Thecla decided to present her query to Zaortha. "I detect unrest in a small segment of the group. Have you heard any complaints?" Thecla asked.

"Nothing in words but raised eyebrows and smirks when you give instructions," Zaortha replied. "I don't think it will cause disruption. I've seen the same in Paul's followers from time to time."

"I'm just trying to avoid problems. The problem Paul had in Lystra keeps coming to mind."

"I'm sure we don't have anyone that perverse. It is possible they are expressing doubt about your being a woman leader. Do you sense it especially among the men?"

"Yes, especially since Jamel is injured and can't lead the men."

"Is there another one we could choose?"

"I can't think of one right now."

"How about Yaco? He seems level headed and pleased to help."

"That's true. I hadn't thought of him. I'll think about it and decide tomorrow morning."

"I think he'll be honored. I know he'd like to contribute more."

"I don't want to overburden him. He's such a friendly, likeable person."

"Yes, present it to him as a need; a contribution of his time until Jamel heals, not forever."

"Good idea. I'll speak to him tomorrow morning. Now, I'm planning to speak to the ones who I noticed to be sullen on our way back to camp this afternoon."

"Will you also talk to the man I found to be less than happy about my being from Antioch?"

"I will talk to him first."

Thecla and Zaortha parted ways after the meal; Thecla to talk to selected followers, Zaortha to help Jamel with his meal.

The day of Thecla's first teaching in Misthia dawned and she was ready to see how many would turn out at the fountain. She was following Paul's plan as close as she could but she was not completely confident she could draw a crowd of listeners. She had taken care of the internal problems; Yaco agreed heartily to help and all was set for the sermon at the fountain.

They branched out in the morning to get more listeners and returned to camp mid-day. Thecla thanked Yaco and asked him to remain with Jamel for the afternoon. Yaco agreed and said he and Jamel would play a board game in the afternoon. Thecla moved on to speak with Zaortha about the afternoon and the sermon.

"Zaortha," Thecla called, "I need to talk to you for a minute."

"I'll be right there," Zaortha said.

When Zaortha walked over, Thecla said, "Zaortha, Yaco will stay with Jamel this afternoon while you accompany us to the fountain."

"All right, Thecla. Jamel will enjoy spending time with Yaco. He plays a board game with Yaco. Jamel has mentioned it several times."

"Now, we must leave for the fountain. We need to be there early so we're there before anyone else arrives. We'll follow Paul and Barnabas' routine. You'll start with a brief welcome and a short prayer then introduce me."

"That should work. It worked well for Paul and Barnabas. "Will there be any baptisms?"

"No, not yet. We'll give people more time to learn and ask questions. Paul always said we have to let them think it over for a while, not baptize in the heat of first hearing."

"We'll be here for some days then?"

"Oh, yes, maybe a month or two, depending on our success."

"Maybe we'll be invited to stay with some of the believers?"

"I hope that will be the case, especially for Jamel. Healing will be easier if he can be more comfortable. First, though, we have to make some conversions.'

"Quite true. Let's get to work"

Thecla and Zaortha called the followers together and left camp for the fountain.

They arrived at the fountain before anyone else. Thecla decided on a place to stand to preach so the listeners were not facing the sun. Soon after all decisions were made, listeners began to arrive. As mid-afternoon approached and a crowd of nearly40 people sat waiting, the chief city manager, Tortus and several council members entered the town square. Thecla swallowed hard. *What could be the meaning of this?* she wondered. *Are they going to expel us? Will they cause trouble?* Thecla turned to Zaortha and whispered a concern, "Why are they here? What do you think?"

"I am not sure. Let's start and see what happens," Zaortha whispered back.

Thecla sat at the edge of the fountain and Zaortha stood to begin the welcome. "Welcome friends. Thanks for joining us to hear the Word of the one, true God. May God bless this meeting and its attendees. Please place your Words in our mouths so we can tell these people of your love and power." She continued by introducing Thecla then took a seat at the edge of the fountain.

Thecla stood and addressed the crowd for nearly three hours. No one left nor did they interrupt her teaching. As she finished, she delivered a prayer that each person think through what they'd heard and return for the next teaching in a few days' time. Many approached Thecla or several of her followers with questions and observations. The crowd had dissipated when Thecla noticed the city officials still standing on the periphery of the fountain area. Zaortha stood with her as Tortus and the other officials walked toward them.

"Here they come. Relax, Thecla," Zaortha said.

"Greetings, Tortus," Thecla said. "Who accompanies you?"

"We came to hear your teaching and are quite overwhelmed. This is our City Chief, Lexus and six city council members."

"I, for one, am quite taken by your teaching and want to hear more from you," Lexus said.

"That goes for the rest of us, too," one of the council members said, as the other stood nodding.

Thecla took a minute or two to speak. She, too, was overwhelmed. "Thank you so much. Were you contacted by members of our group?"

"No, we heard about you from our wives and our neighbors. They said it would be worth our time and they were right," Lexus said.

"We are pleased you found our teaching something on which you will think and discuss," Zaortha said, in formal speech.

"Oh, yes, I'm looking forward to discussing it with my wife and the neighbors," Lexus said. "We appreciate your teaching. We will return to our work. Rest well this evening," Lexus said, turning to leave with his entourage.

Word spread quickly through the group of followers. Thecla and Zaortha walked together discussing the city officials' acceptance of their speech.

"I was so surprised, my mouth was dry, I couldn't answer him," Thecla said.

"I could tell. I was afraid you'd offend him," Zaortha said.

"I wasn't expecting such friendly words. I thought we were going to be arrested."

"I wasn't sure how they were going to act, either. There were no Romans in the crowd. I haven't seen any in the city; but they still could have been bothered by our preaching something so far removed from their Roman gods or traditional beliefs."

"That's what worried me. I'm thinking we should talk to all the followers when we arrive at camp, asking them if they observed any signs of incredulity, shock or uncomfortable shifting in their seats, head shaking or whispers."

Zaortha and Thecla were the last to arrive in camp that evening. Yaco and Jamel heard about the city officials' attendance from the first arriving followers. Thecla and Zaortha called the followers to a brief meeting.

"Welcome back," Thecla began. "We had a welcome surprise today. I am heartened by the attendance of the city officials. We must not, however, consider our work here complete or easy. Many residents were either not contacted or were not interested. What, then, must we do to encourage others to attend the meetings and to forsake their false gods?"

"That is the question we must answer among ourselves. I offer, first, continue to talk to residents without becoming obtrusive. They must want to join us. We must encourage those who attended to visit with their friends and neighbors to carry the words they heard to help others to understand and desire to attend future meetings. Last, we must continue to visit more households to invite more listeners," Zaortha said.

"While we eat our evening meal and after, let's discuss this plan for future meetings," said Thecla.

Several weeks past, as Thecla and the followers worked to acquire believers. Jamel had healed and joined his fellow followers to invite new listeners. The city square was now filled with listeners. Thecla held the first baptism. Zaortha and Jamel assisted by helping people form a line for baptism. They talked to those in line, answering questions and helping the infirm.

As Thecla stood by the fountain and prepared to pour water on the head of the first receiver, a man arose in the crowd, saying, "How can a woman baptize? That is a man's place." More rose to this statement, agreeing in loud voices. "Women can't baptize." "This baptism is not good." "We can't have this." Even some of the women joined this group. As this group yelled, a dark cloud moved over the sun. The crowd heard rumbles of thunder.

Thecla stopped and addressed the troublemakers, "I have been chosen by God, through Paul, to speak His word and baptize believers. If you do not believe in my baptizing, you speak against the one, true God." The cloud dissipated and the sun shone. The people understood the event as a sign from God and became quiet. Many baptisms took place that day and in future days.

When about two months had passed, Thecla announced their work in Misthia was finished and they would move on. Lexus and Tortus, city officials, agreed to start a church in Misthia. They were instructed by Thecla, with Paul's experience in mind, to first build a community of believers then, if funds were available and the community of believers was too large to meet in members' homes, choose a location and build a church building where all could meet to honor God.

Thecla, Zaortha and Jamel decided to return to Iconium and, from there, go to the cities to the north. They decided to go by way of Iconium to return some followers to their homes and to stock up on necessary supplies. Thecla decided not to visit her mother again, for she realized her mother was not interested in conversion. Instead, they would visit Daphne and Jamel would contact church members. The day arrived to pack the camp and say their farewells to Misthia. Thecla and Zaortha made a brief visit to the city officials, gave last blessings to Tortus and Lexus and were off. The group left Misthia mid-day and stopped for the night at the base of the mountains. The trip through the mountains would take three days and another day to Iconium.

They arrived in Iconium late in the afternoon. Zaortha went immediately to Daphne's home. Jamel went to seek lodging with church friends and Thecla said farewell to her followers as they set out to their houses. Alone at last, Thecla sat to think about her first mission trip. *The trip was long and tiring. Many things happened good and bad. I must not focus on the bad, other than to learn from it, as Paul did, and make changes where necessary. The acceptance of the Word by the city officials and the desire by Tortus and Lexus to start a church were the two most surprising and fulfilling events.*

The minor disturbance at the first baptism was overcome by an act of God, to whom I am ever thankful. I did not anticipate that reaction by believers, though, as a woman, I should have. I wish I could ask Paul for his advice but he is far away, so I'm on my own. I'll talk it over with Zaortha to see what she advises; maybe Jamel too, though he is often reticent on such topics.

I feel a need to go to a place of quiet where I can contemplate and pray. Someday I'll do just that, maybe in the mountains, in a cave.

Zaortha arrived and brought Thecla out of her momentary contemplation. "Daphne welcomes us. She is preparing the evening meal and is ready for us," Zaortha said.

"That's wonderful, Zaortha. Thank you and God Bless Daphne," Thecla said, in the feeling she'd attained during her brief contemplation.

They walked slowly to Daphne's home. Upon arrival, Daphne met them and showed them to their room, the same one in which they'd stayed before. Thecla recognized the room immediately and remembered her broken ankle and how and why it had occurred. These thoughts flashed through her mind as she smiled and thanked Daphne. Thecla unpacked their bags. Zaortha left to help Daphne in the kitchen. They both bathed before the evening meal.

This time, Daphne's husband, Orel, was home for a brief time. He was an interesting man, an employee of the Roman government. He was also an unbaptized believer. This led to a deep discussion by him and Thecla. Zaortha talked to Daphne loud enough so Daphne's attention would not wander to Thecla and Orel's discussion. Zaortha described the visitation and baptism of the Misthia city officials. Daphne was equally surprised and wanted Orel to hear of it. Zaortha assured Daphne Thecla would surely tell him. The evening ended in amicable regard for each other. Thecla and Zaortha said their farewells, as Orel would be leaving early the next morning.

Thecla directed Zaortha and Jamel to find any locals who wished to follow, to meet at the fountain at mid-day. Both disciples took to the streets of Iconium to deliver Thecla's call for followers. Thecla was pleased when she saw Zaortha and Jamel had gathered about forty adults willing to follow Thecla wherever she planned to preach. As before, women outnumbered men but not by a large proportion; approximately 60 percent women, 40 percent men. Of course, the women brought children and babies. Though this complicated travel, all were welcome.

Thecla rose and started to outline her plan for this mission. "We will travel north to Laodicea. We will follow the main road, which will allow us to take the wagon for supplies. The trek north will take about fourteen days. There are warm and cool springs there so baths should be readily available. We walked to the west of there on our way to Iconium from Antioch and Paul did not stop there either. We will go there now and, if we can make conversions, we'll stay there for a time," Thecla said.

"If you wish to join us pack food, clothing and other necessary items and we'll load them on the wagon tomorrow morning. Yaco will be our wagon master again. Meet us here at sunrise tomorrow morning," instructed Zaortha. Jamel and Yaco nodded in agreement.

The next morning Thecla and her followers began the trek to Laodicea. The day was bright and spirits were high. The road led through valleys in the mountains, which allowed the people, mules and wagon to traverse the mountains with comparative ease. At last, the gates of Laodicea were in sight. It was late in the day so Thecla decided they would set up camp outside the city and go in the next morning. The city was of commercial importance so the gates would open early. Tents, food and cooking utensils were procured from the wagon. Yaco oversaw the distribution of belongings to the people and cared for the mules. Several women cooked the communal evening meal.

At dawn, women prepared a meal to break their fast. Thecla called a meeting of the followers and, after blessing them, launched into her usual assignment to the followers. "We must approach the city magistrate and proceed as always to invite residents to a teaching to be held in an area of choice. Wait here while Zaortha, Jamel and I make our presence known to the city officials. We will return with the information then we will approach city residents to invite them to the teaching," Thecla said.

In the morning, Thecla, Zaortha and Jamel met with the city officials. The city magistrate welcomed them and gave them permission to meet and teach in the Amphitheater. Thanking them graciously, Thecla, Zaortha and Jamel returned to the camp with the news. "We are set to visit city residents and invite them to the Amphitheater at mid-day tomorrow for a meeting and teaching. Discuss with them about our teachings of the one, true God. Do not be disheartened if some refuse to listen; instead, politely move on to the next house. Those who seem unlikely to hear the word now may discuss it with friends and join us later," instructed Thecla. With that, she called them to prayer and they departed for the city.

The next day and many days thereafter, Thecla preached while Zaortha and Jamel assisted. The crowd of listeners increased to thousands. Finally, Thecla decided it was time for baptism. Those who wanted baptism numbered about 2,000. Thecla instructed them to meet at the cold spring at the edge of the city. There she baptized residents for two days. When she completed the first baptism, she returned to camp and rested. Zaortha wanted to stay with her but she refused and told Zaortha to continue visiting new believers. Thecla intended to pray and contemplate her success in preaching.

As the days shortened and winter was arriving, Jamel came to Thecla to introduce Epaphras to her. "Thecla, please meet Epaphras. He wishes to speak to you about starting a church," Jamel said.

Almost overwhelmed, Thecla cleared her throat and acknowledged Epaphras with a smile and a nod. "Very well," she said, "we welcome believers such as you. By starting a church, exactly what do you envision?"

"I want to gather those who believe together for regular prayer and rituals associated with Jesus Christ's teachings, in other words, the mass."

"Yes, the church is a collection of believers who wish to praise the one, true, God and care for each other," Thecla said.

"We will begin to meet in members' houses but will eventually I hope to erect a church building," Epaphras said.

"You have my blessing to begin. Jamel, who is experienced in this, will help as much as you need him," Thecla said.

Epaphras said his thanks and left with Jamel to inform members of the beginning of a church in Laodicea.

I've dreamed of and prayed for the beginnings of a church. This is the fulfillment of my preaching and teaching ministry. I pray and hope for many more, Thecla thought. With these thoughts of the first glimmer of success, she lapsed into thoughts of Paul. *Oh, Paul, my guiding light, how I wish you were here to share this moment with me. I know you'd smile at me but caution me not to become overly exuberant. 'Forming the church will take a long time, much work and may never actually come to be.' You, Paul, are my rock. You bring reality to a situation by your thinking and experience. How I long to listen to you and hear your words.*

Chapter 7. Thecla Leaves Her Ministry and Retires to a Cave

Spring blossomed and Thecla announced they would be moving to their next mission.

"Where will our next mission be?" Jonas asked. Jonas was a new follower and not attuned to waiting for an explanation. Others nearby looked at him and smiled and twittered a bit.

"Thecla will explain as soon as all arrangements have been made," answered Zaortha. Jonas stomped off. *We better watch Jonas, either he is nervous or, worse, overly committed too soon. Either way, travelling with him may be a cause for concern. I'll talk to Jamel about him,* thought Zaortha.

Thecla continued to assign tasks to pack and break camp. Jamel was directed to oversee the packing and loading of the tents onto the wagon. All heavier items, including large cooking pots were to be loaded on a cart pulled by an ox. Thecla knew it would take at least a day to securely pack and load the camp items.

As late afternoon approached, Thecla called her inner circle to meet a short way from the group. When Jamel, Zaortha, Yaco, were seated, Thecla began the discussion. I want to move our mission to Sabatra," Thecla stated.

"Why Sabatra?" Zaortha asked.

"It is a smaller town away from Paul's travels. I doubt they've heard The Word." Thecla said. She had adopted the moniker "The Word" to describe her mission.

"That makes sense," Jamel said, "but do we know much about it?"

"No, but we haven't known much about other towns we've visited either. We'll learn when we get there," Thecla said.

"I've been there once, some year ago. Kind of a backward place then but I don't know how it is now. It's all desert to get there but there's the Roman road to follow that would take us near there," Yaco said.

"That's good news, Yaco. Can you provide any more information?" Thecla asked.

"Not really," he said. "When I go into town to get supplies for the trip, I'll talk to other wagon masters and try to obtain more details."

"That would be very helpful, Yaco" Thecla said. This is the reason I didn't want to announce the place yet. We'll make a final decision tomorrow after Yaco returns."

"Are there other places you're thinking about?" asked Zaortha.

"Yes, I also want to take the mission to Seleucia," Thecla said.

"That could be a dangerous place," Zaortha warned.

"There has been an uprising recently," Jamel added.

"All the more reason they need to hear The Word," Thecla countered.

Zaortha and Jamel nodded. "So be it," they both muttered as they returned to packing.

The next morning, they met with Yaco. He seemed in good spirits but became less talkative when Thecla opened the subject of Sabatra. What have you learned, Yaco?" she asked.

"Not what I expected," he said. "The city has grown. It thrives now as a trading center because of the Roman road."

"That should be good," Jamel interrupted.

"Not there. According to the wagon masters it is dangerous because of bandits on the road," Yaco said.

"But there's always bandits," Jamel argued.

"Let him tell his story," Thecla countered, nodding to Yaco.

"These bandits are in large groups, unlike the usual two or three. These bandits kill the wagon master and anyone else in the group then steal the contents of the wagons. Galatian and Roman authorities don't seem to do anything about it. Some think the local authorities are involved in these activities. I was warned to not go there or to have an armed escort if we did."

"That's amazing," Thecla said. "I'll give it more thought and decide tomorrow morning. Thank you, Yaco."

"For now, Yaco and Jamel, ask the people to stall the packing and prepare to spend another night here," Thecla stated.

"Zaortha, stay with me for a while," Thecla said, turning to Zaortha.

Zaortha knew Thecla needed to think aloud. She often mulled things over to Zaortha. *I wonder what she's thinking. I know she wants to go but the news is frightening. We should go down to the river, away from anyone so she can speak her mind...*

"Zaortha, let's go a ways from here so we can speak in absolute privacy," Thecla said.

"I was thinking we should go by the river," Zaortha said.

"That will work well," Thecla agreed.

They hastened to the Lycus River and chose rocks on which to sit, facing each other.

"I don't know what to think," Thecla said, with a slight tremble in her voice.

"It is a disappointing revelation Yaco brought back," Zaortha said, in a soothing voice.

"I want to go and the people need to hear The Word, maybe more so now."

"Yes, they've probably not heard any missionaries in some time, if ever."

"But I don't want to endanger the followers."

"Where would we get armed guards?"

"Maybe from this city but I really dislike the idea of an armed guard escorting a mission."

"Yes, it seems counter to The Word."

"And the ideals we're preaching…love, peace, and concern for our fellow man."

"Mmmm…" they both said and lapsed into quiet thought, as the river flowed quietly on its way to a larger water body.

Sometime later, Thecla opened her eyes and resumed thinking aloud. "What would Paul do?"

Zaortha opened her eyes with a start. She knew the question would come. "I don't really know. You worked with him closer than I did. What do you think he'd say or do?"

"He would go, beyond a doubt. He would warn the followers to be alert but he would go."

"Then you have decided to go?" Zaortha asked, knowing the answer.

"Yes, I think we must. I'll explain the danger or ask Yaco to tell them. Then I'll excuse anyone who wishes not to follow us to Sabatra," Thecla said.

"Will you ask for an armed guard?"

"No, that is counter to our mission. Paul never sought one."

"Quite true. It is decided then."

"Yes, go to Jamel and Yaco and explain to them in private. I will join you at the evening meal then speak to the followers. Now, I need some time for prayer."

"I will do that and wait for you to come to us this evening," Zaortha said, as she rose to leave.

The sun was receding in the west and the time of the evening meal approached. Thecla walked slowly toward the group of followers, who were helping Zaortha prepare the meal. Zaortha saw her out of the corner of her eye and set the dish down, waiting for her to approach.

"Thecla, we're almost ready to eat. Everyone is gathered and waiting to hear from you," Zaortha said.

"We'll eat then I'll talk. I think I have it worked out," Thecla said.

"All right, sit and we'll finish putting the food out," Zaortha said.

When the evening meal was concluded, Thecla rose to address the followers.

"My brothers and sisters," she began, "we will make the trek to Sabatra beginning tomorrow at first light. The people there are under rulers who are overtaken by greed. The city is a successful commercial site but the people worship the old gods or the Roman ones but have never heard The Word. Our mission is to bring the message to the people.

"It will not be easy and could be dangerous. Yaco has brought a message from other wagon masters of the proliferation of bandits along the road. These are not the usual sort. These bandits are larger, more brutal groups. The rulers of the city may also be hostile to our message; but we have to try. Spreading the one, true God's message is not for the faint of heart…"

"Why are we going to such a dangerous place?" interrupted Jonas. "I doubt they want to hear The Word," Jonas spit 'The Word' out with a sneer. Everyone around him could be heard catching their breath.

"Let me continue, Jonas. I will address your concern in a few minutes," said Thecla.

"We will pack tomorrow and leave early the next day," Thecla continued. "Put as much as possible on the wagon. Yaco, as before, will oversee the loading. We must walk in a closer group than previous travels. Be sure to keep the children inside the group. It's best to have the women, especially the mothers with children close to the center of the group, the men making a protective outer ring of the group.

"If there are any followers who wish to stay and not travel farther, feel free to let me know. Everyone is asked to make a free choice now." Thecla sat and most of the people talked among their groups and families. Dishes were cleared and the fire rekindled.

A man and his wife and two daughters approached Thecla. He began to talk by clearing his throat and timidly addressing her, "Dear minister Thecla."

"Please, no need for such formality, Hertko. What do you have to tell me?"

"We need to tell you we have chosen to stay behind. I want to keep my family safe and not venture into land that could result in their deaths."

"I understand and thank you for your openness. I will miss you all but I think you have made a reasonable decision. You may leave us as soon as you wish," Thecla said.

Jamel approached Thecla soon after Hertko's family moved away, "Thecla, I think the cripple, Tulc, should not accompany us. He will exhaust quickly and would not be able to defend himself if we are attacked."

"Have you spoken to him about this?"

"No, I wanted to know what you thought."

"I understand your concern. Do you wish to speak to him or should I?"

"No. I will talk to Yaco then speak to him if Yaco doesn't have any ideas."

"I think that is the proper way to deal with the situation," Thecla stated.

Thecla saw Jonas approach and remembered a warning she'd received from Zaortha and Jamel. "I still don't understand why we're walking into danger," Jonas said.

"I explained our mission is to spread The Word of the one, true God. We must go out not always to safe and secure places. Missionaries must be willing to tread new ground. If you are not up to it, stay in Laodicea and work with Epaphras to begin a new church."

"I think I'll do just that. Your trek to Sabatra is a suicide mission. You are willing to put all these people's lives in danger for your mission. It is shameful."

"Thank you for sharing your displeasure with me, Jonas. Now please leave us to rest before we begin our preparations to travel."

Jonas left quickly, grabbing his pack and headed for the city.

No one else approached Thecla and the camp quieted, everyone preferring to sleep before the coming day of hard work.

Two days later, the followers were assembled and prepared to make the journey. Spirits were high but muted. Everyone was unsure how this trek would develop. The wagon pulled by oxen started first, followed by Thecla, Zaortha, Jamel and the twenty some followers. Thecla noticed, with a sigh of relief, Tulc was not among the group. *Jamel and Yaco must have convinced him this trek would be too dangerous for him. I'll talk to Jamel this evening to find out the details.* The road northeast out of Laodicea was a sand track packed by wagon traffic leading to the Roman road.

They made better headway after joining the Roman road. The second day on the road began as any other day. They resumed their trek and stopped for a mid-day break to water the beasts at a spring after they collected the water needed for drinking and cooking. As they prepared to move out, several riders in dark robes surrounded the travelers.

"Where are you going?" the first masked rider asked.

"To Sabatra," Yaco answered.

"Not with that wagon and all that load," another said.

"We are not traders, we are missionaries," Thecla cut in.

"Who is this woman and why is she speaking to us?" The first bandit asked.

"She is our leader," Yaco stated.

"Led by a woman? What kind of man are you?" the second bandit asked, smirking.

"Enough talking, we'll take the wagon, the cart and all the supplies you're carrying. Get off that wagon or we'll take you off," the lead bandit said.

Yaco knew he had no choice. Another bandit already held Thecla's arms behind her back. Jamel and Zaortha also had been overtaken. The others were in shocked silence. At the edge of the group, several women pulled the children back toward the rocks by the spring to hide. The bandits, ten in all, brandished knives and swords to rob the followers. Yaco was killed and Jamel and some of the other men were beaten senseless. Two of the bandits raped Thecla and Zaortha and left them beaten bloody. The bandits beat many of the followers, too then left with the wagon and cart, including and the contents as well as any jewelry they'd stripped from the followers.

Thecla and Zaortha rose and, in tears, hobbled to the spring to clean up as best they could. Jamel and the other men finally regained consciousness at the ministrations of several followers. After everyone was treated and seated in a circle, they looked to Thecla. *I know they need me. I'm so hurt, so diminished in their eyes, in God's eyes. Oh, Paul, I need you now. I need your counsel and encouragement. How can I find the strength to continue?* Zaortha swallowed hard and reached for Thecla's arm, though she could not raise her eyes to look at the others, so overcome with shame, she was. "We must move on," Zaortha whispered.

"I know, but I'm withered inside" Thecla whispered back.

"Let me speak to the followers and we'll spend the night here," Zaortha whispered to Thecla.

"All right," Thecla said, still sobbing.

"Blessed followers, in God's name," Zaortha began, "we are being tested by the Almighty. Are we up to this test?" Some said 'yes' in muted tones, others nodded or shook their heads, 'no'. Zaortha continued, "Some are, some are not. We will spend the night here, eating what provisions were kept, utilizing the spring water to cleanse and make decisions tomorrow. We are without tents, so wrap using cloaks and other outerwear you have for sleeping."

"How is Thecla?" someone asked.

"She was gravely injured and will need time to recover," Zaortha answered.

"You were badly injured too. Why are you up and she isn't?" another follower asked.

"All are injured in degrees, not all injuries are the same. If you wish to help Thecla and your fellow followers, pray to God."

Zaortha sat next to Thecla and cried with her until one of the women offered to bring some bread and cheese to them.

They refused the food, neither having an appetite. Thecla asked Zaortha, "Please pray with me tonight."

"I'll do that, gladly."

After the others had bedded down, Zaortha and Thecla moved to a grassy strip near the spring to pray.

The next morning dawned and the encampment, such as it was, came slowly alive. Thecla, though not recovered, forced herself to lead. In pain, though in her body or heart and soul, she could not determine, Thecla addressed the followers in a soft voice the followers struggled to hear, "I am sorry you were all forced to endure the attack on our mission. I am not fit to lead this mission farther. We have lost Yaco and five other followers. I beg you to abandon the mission and we will retrace our steps back to Laodicea, from there return to your homes. We'll help each other as best we can. Continue to pray as you move. God bless you all." Thecla ended with a sob and sank to the ground.

The followers talked to each other in soft tones as they prepared to return home. Thecla recalled *this is not the first time a mission has been abandoned. Paul had to abandon them at least twice but not with such a loss of life, I don't think. What did I do wrong? I can't lead more people to their deaths. I can't lead; I won't lead. I'll retire to a cave to pray and repent.*

Thecla hobbled down the road assisted by Jamel and Zaortha. They were at the back of the followers—following the followers back to Laodicea. It was a broken, solemn march. They stopped when most could walk no farther. The trip back to Laodicea took three and one-half days. When the first of the group approached the city gates, the guards questioned them and heard the sad tale. Horses and carriages were sent out to assist the others. When all the people were within the city again, the city magistrate was called to come to them and learn the details of the horrific robbery. Jamel and Zaortha provided the most coherent description of the attack, with others adding details as they saw them. The city magistrate agreed all those not living in Laodicea would be provided rooms in a local inn. Carriages provided transportation for the seven people needing food and shelter.

Thecla and Zaortha shared a room, while Jamel slept in an adjoining room. After bathing and resting, they decided to find something to eat. Thecla was not hungry but Zaortha and Jamel encouraged her to try to eat a small portion. The meat stew seemed to be the pro-offered dish so Jamel ordered three portions. Thecla surprised her friends and herself by finishing her bowl of stew.

They were too tired to continue the evening together and retired to their beds for the night.

In the morning, all seven met to break their fast, Thecla, Zaortha, Jamel, Anna and Beta, and Tessa and Gracea; Anna and Betta were mother and daughter; Tessa and Gracea were also. Betta was ten summers and Gracea was eleven. Tessa and Anna were sisters; both women were widows. As they ate, they discussed plans for the future. Tessa and Anna said they had none, except to follow Thecla. Jamel and Zaortha said they'd planned for some time to be married and return to Lystra to further work on the churches there. Thecla agreed, having observed their closeness for some time and blessed them on their endeavors.

It was Thecla's turn and all looked to her. "I'm going to a cave in the mountains outside of Iconium to pray, fast and repent."

"We will accompany you to the cave," Anna said. Tessa nodded.

"That will be crowded," Thecla said, in surprise.

"We've seen some of those caves," Tessa said. "Some are quite large."

"Have you been there? Which mountains are you talking about?" Thecla asked.

"There is a wagon trail southeast of town then, if you branch off the trail to the right, walk two to three miles along the valley, you'll see the caves," Tessa said.

"Do others live there? I mean is it crowded?" Thecla asked.

"Oh no," Anna said. "There is a hermit, Zohres, living about four miles at the end of the valley but he is the only one we've met," Anna said.

"Why did you go there? Did you go alone?" Thecla asked.

"Oh, gracious no. We went with our husbands before the war where they were lost. You see, they were brothers and very close, serving in the same cohort. We left the children with our parents and went exploring in the mountains," Tessa explained and Anna nodded.

"I'd like to find a cave there. Are you both sure you want to join me? How do the girls feel about it?" Thecla asked.

"We really want to come too," Betta and Gracea said, at the same time.

"We want to live in the caves. We've heard so much about it, haven't we, Betta?" Gracea said. Betta agreed with a strong nod of her head and a big smile. Every one chuckled.

"That settles it," Anna said. "Let's go as soon as you are able."

Thecla glanced at Zaortha. Zaortha had a look on her face of 'Let's talk', which Thecla recognized immediately.

"All right," Thecla said, "let's meet for the evening meal and I will give my decision to you."

"That's fair; until this evening then," Anna said. They all said their goodbyes and left to their day's activities.

Thecla, Zaortha and Jamel met in Thecla's room to further discuss the situation. The women sat on the beds and Jamel sat cross-legged on the floor facing the beds.

"Thecla, I'm worried about your going to that cave in the mountains. So many things could happen to you. Are you sure you want to do this?" Zaortha asked.

"Zaortha, I'm worried about you and Jamel returning to Lystra. Don't you remember what a hostile city that was? We were expelled, that's why we went to Derbe and avoided it on the way back to Iconium," Thecla countered.

"Of course, we remember," Jamel said, entering the conversation. "Do you also remember Paul telling us a church was begun there? I don't know if it was completed and still meeting but Lystra is my home. Zaortha and I will be as safe there as anywhere."

"What about your answer to my question, which you seem to be side-stepping?" Zaortha asked.

"I suppose I have, Zaortha. Yes, I want to go to the cave. I feel quite safe with Anna, Tessa and their daughters. Zohres, the hermit, will be our neighbor; not a close neighbor but still someone else to have there," Thecla said.

"So be it," Zaortha and Jamel agreed, as they rose to take their leave.

Thecla recognized the abruptness of Zaortha and Jamel's leaving but she had blessed them on their endeavors and chose not to think about it; rather to concentrate on her new future in the cave. Anna, Tessa, Betta and Gracea arrived bearing food from the market and a hasty meal was prepared. After eating, they embarked on a serious conversation regarding their move to the cave. Thecla was the first to open the discussion.

"First, we need to return to Iconium then, I think, we should all make the journey first to inspect the caves and select the best one to make sure it is empty and suitable before bringing our belongings," Thecla said.

"That's a good idea and matches what we were going to suggest," Tessa said and Anna nodded in agreement.

"We can't be too careful at this point," Anna said.

"Should we hire a guide?" Thecla asked.

"Yes," Anna said. "We will find a guide with mules so we can take a cart or wagon.

"That is splendid," Thecla said.

"When will we leave?" Gracea asked.

"We will leave for Iconium tomorrow. We'll ask the innkeeper to help us find a cart or wagon to take us there. Then we'll search for the right guide with mules or asses," Anna said.

"Will we begin tomorrow at first light?" Betta asked, excitedly.

"Slow down," Tessa said. "Yes, we'll begin our trip tomorrow then begin looking for a guide but I'm not sure how quickly we can find the 'right one'.

"What is the 'right one' you're looking for?" Betta asked.

"The 'right one' must be reputable, affordable, have at least two to four mules or asses, a cart or wagon and be willing to escort five women into the wilderness," Anna said.

"Oh," Betta said, deflated and Gracea hung her head, recognizing the magnitude of the task.

"Please take your time to look for the 'right one'. It is an important task you are undertaking and must not be rushed. I thank you and bless you. I will pray for your success," Thecla said.

The women rose to clean after the meal and departed.

The Innkeeper agreed to find transportation for them to Iconium.

Three days after they arrived in Iconium, Anna and Tessa arrived at Thecla's living quarters. Thecla greeted them and asked them to be seated, offering them tea.

"We have found a suitable guide," Anna began.

"That is wonderful news, do tell me more," Thecla said.

"The guide, named Ascus, has twenty years' experience in the surrounding mountains, a herd of animals and is quite willing to escort all of us. He said he'll bring his two sons for additional security. He will charge us nothing because he is one of your followers," Anna said.

Thecla was aghast and overcome. She wept openly and thanked God, while the two women joined her in thanksgiving. After they recovered, they continued their discussion.

"When will they be ready to leave?" Thecla asked.

"As soon as we are ready," Tessa said.

"All right, let's not tarry. I'm ready tomorrow morning," Thecla said.

"Fine. We'll tell him to be ready tomorrow morning and we'll prepare for a morning departure also," Anna said.

They said their farewells and agreed to meet at Thecla's abode at sunup tomorrow morning.

The sun was rising as the five women watched three men approach on a wagon pulled by two mules with two asses tied to the back of the wagon. Ascus introduced himself and his sons, explaining the women were to ride in the wagon and his sons would ride the asses. They loaded the wagon with provisions and were off before the sun reached its zenith.

They were several miles into the mountains, almost ready to turn off the main road into the valley when a loud scream of a wild animal tore the silence. The mules reacted instantly, causing Ascus to control the beasts with almost all his strength. The sons were experienced riders and calmed the asses without difficulty. After everyone was calmed and a mid-day repast was consumed, the party moved on and began the trek up the valley floor.

Late in the afternoon, Anna yelled, "There it is. That is the cave we were telling you about. Let's look it over more closely."

Ascus agreed and stopped to peer at the cave. He ordered his sons to go into the cave and check it for animals and any humans, including remains. They waited for the young men to report their findings. Finally, they reappeared to give their report.

"All is clear," they said. "No sign anyone or anything is or has been in it. It is big and quite well light, except in the back; usual for most caves," the older one reported.

"The mouth of the cave is quite large so you'd best make your sleeping quarters in the back with the fire toward the front," the younger son advised.

"It might be hard to defend against large animals or marauders," Ascus added. "I advise you to continue on and check out a few of the other caves close by."

"All right," Anna said.

They trudged on another mile or two when they stopped to look at another cave, large but with a much smaller mouth.

"I'm suggesting this one might be a possibility. Go up and look to see if it is empty as before," Ascus directed his sons.

It was growing late in the day and too late for them to return to Iconium. Again, Ascus' sons returned saying there was no evidence of life in the cave.

Thecla suggested, because of the late hour, they build a fire and spend the night in the cave. All agreed, deciding the women would take the back of the cave and the men would sleep at the opening. The evening meal consisted of bread, cheese and fruit brought by Thecla, Anna and Ascus.. The sons brought in the sleeping mats from the wagon and all settled for the night. The animals were tethered outside the cave. The men were awakened by a stomping and snorting by the animals as torchlight approached.

"What's going on?" one of the sons asked, groggily.

"Shhh, someone's out there," the other one said.

Ascus arose and quietly went out. He stepped in front of a man with the torch.

"Who are you?" the torch-man asked, after he recovered from his surprise.

"I am Ascus and we're investigating this cave for occupancy," Ascus said. "Who are you?"

"There are four animals and a wagon here, there must be several of you," torch-man said.

"You haven't told me who you are or why you're prowling around before first light."

"I'm Zohres, the hermit. I live some miles north of here. I'm on my way to Iconium to buy supplies. I make the trip rarely, never noticing animals outside a cave here."

"We will be returning to Iconium in a few hours. Do you wish to join us?"

"I will do that. I'll wait out here until you are ready to leave."

By now, everyone was awake and aware of the disturbance. The eastern sky was beginning to lighten but it was hard to notice from the mouth of the cave, which faced west.

Thecla approached the mouth of the cave to ascertain the meaning of the disturbance. She inquired of Ascus and received a detailed description of the early morning event. Immediately, Thecla wanted to meet Zohres. Ascus went out and called in Zohres.

"Thecla, meet Zohres, your neighbor some miles to the north," Ascus said.

Thecla smiled and greeted the grizzled man. "I am glad to meet you, Zohres. My four friends and I plan to make this cave our home and, of course, we're glad to meet a neighbor." She then turned back to the cave and called the other women forward, introducing each to Zohres, as they arrived.

Ascus was a bit surprised and hesitant about Thecla's willingness to introduce Zohres to all the women without knowing him better. Ascus said nothing to her about it at the time but decided to warn her about it when they returned to Iconium. They proceeded to build a fire, break their fast, load up and get ready to move out. Zohres walked alongside the wagon. The trip back was uneventful and they reached Iconium in late afternoon. Zohres said his farewell and left the group for where he did not mention.

Anna, Tessa and their daughters returned to their home. Thecla invited Ascus and his sons in for something to eat and drink. After everyone was settled, Ascus broached the subject of Thecla's openness to Zohres.

"You seemed to greet Zohres quite openly for never having met him before," Ascus said.

"Yes, as a missionary, I'm open to greeting all God's children with loving openness," Thecla said.

"But you don't know him. He might be a murderer in hiding," the older son said.

"That is true," Thecla said. "My belief in God helps me to open up to strangers. Without that openness, we could never convert those who have never heard The Word."

"Maybe he doesn't want to be converted. Maybe he means you harm or the young women," the younger son put in.

"And maybe he wants to hear The Word and doesn't know it yet," Thecla said.

Ascus looked at his sons. They recognized the look of a warning to quit the argument now. Ascus recognized the futility of continuing the argument and changed the subject. He inquired as to when the move would take place and how much would be moved. They agreed to meet with the other women to plan the move.

The next day dawned as any other. The meeting with Thecla and the women took place after the mid-day meal. Ascus joined them to discuss the move to the cave.

"We'll only take what we need, which includes sleeping mats, cookware and food staples," Thecla said.

"We have set out enough for at least three months," Anna said.

"Will we have a cart to pack?" Tessa asked.

"A wagon has been set aside for you," Ascus answered.

"Thank you, Ascus. That will be most helpful," Thecla said.

"We will also take some coverings and clothing," Anna added.

"Ascus, can we rely on you to bring us more supplies within the third month?" Thecla asked.

"Yes, by all means, Thecla. Life will not be easy for you. My sons and I will do what we can for you. Other church members will also help," Ascus said.

"You are an answer to our prayers. When will you be ready to move us?" Thecla asked.

"As soon as you are ready; tomorrow morning?" Ascus asked.

The women looked at each other. "Give us one more day then we'll be ready," Anna said. The others nodded.

"Day after tomorrow will be fine. Do you want me to bring the wagon here or another of your houses?" Ascus asked.

"Let's all meet at Anna's because she has the cookware, which is the largest part of the load," Thecla said.

"All right, that will work best for loading," Ascus said.

"It is agreed then that we'll meet at Anna's and bring clothes, bedding and any small things we deem necessary for life in the cave. We will make life as simple as possible because we want to spend much of our time in prayer and contemplation," Thecla said. She then blessed them and bade them farewell until the move.

Thecla packed two undergarments, an outer robe, eating utensils and two letters from Paul in a satchel. After looking carefully at her abode, she put the satchel over her shoulder, said a brief prayer, stepped out and closed the door; whether she intended it or not, she was leaving Iconium forever.

Thecla arrived at Anna's home shortly. They waited only a brief time before Ascus and his sons arrived with mules and a wagon. The men launched into loading immediately. Most of the clothing and small items fit into the pot, which was set in the center of the wagon. They placed the satchels and the sleeping mats on the remaining open areas of the wagon bed. Though no one was walking on this trip, it was no faster because the wagon slowed them. The Roman road was good but the wagon was heavily loaded and somewhat fragile.

When they arrived at the trail that branched off the road and led up the valley, Ascus decided a decision had to be made.

"The trail is not smooth enough for the weight of the wagon. My sons will walk ahead, removing stones and other debris from the path. This will take extra time but if we don't do this we'll be carrying everything to the cave."

"No, we can't do that," Thecla said. "We can each carry our satchels, which would lighten the load a little."

"That won't be necessary. I don't think it would make that much difference," Ascus said.

The party moved on up the valley at a slower pace than the Roman road. The track was uneven and, in some places, rocky. Ascus' sons cleared rocks from the pathway so the mules and wagon could proceed. In at least two places, rocks were so large the men had to use a mule to pull the rock away from the path. Most often, the wagon could move slightly off the track to avoid a rock.

They arrived at the cave as the sun dropped below the western mountains. Ascus suggested the group settle for the night and unload at first light in the morning. Thecla and the women agreed and helped the men unload the sleeping mats and enough provisions for a cold evening meal. After their repast and under a full moon, the two girls retrieved their flute and lyre from the wagon. The group sang, danced and told stories late into the night. When it was nearly time to stop, a figure half stumbled into their camp. Everyone stopped talking at once. They looked at the man as he approached.

"Zohres?" Ascus questioned. "Are you all right?"

"Yes and n-no, I, I can't go any f, f, farther," Zohres said, gasping for breath.

Ascus looked at him closer and helped him sit on a large, flat rock. He realized Zohres was bleeding.

"You are bleeding. What happened?" Ascus asked.

"T-t-tell y-you l-l-lat-ter," Zohres said, nearly falling off the stone.

One of Ascus' sons took hold of him and, with Ascus' help laid him on the ground.

Thecla joined them asking, "What is wrong with our visitor?"

"It's Zohres and he's bleeding," Ascus said. "He's lost a lot of blood; he's nearly unconscious."

"I'll get the women to help me get some bedding and try to look for the wound. We'll need light and hot water so we must build a fire," Thecla said, in her 'take charge' style.

Ascus agreed and directed his sons to gather wood and build a fire. He went to the wagon to assist the women in removing a pot for heating water and some of the extra bedding. Ascus related what Zohres had managed to tell him before Zohres stopped talking.

"That sounds as if he left Iconium and has been trying to get back to his cave," Thecla said.

"Sounds like bandits," Anna said, when she overheard the conversation

"That may be. It's unlikely anything else," agreed Ascus

"Or a wild animal," Tessa added.

"That's why we have to look at the wound to know exactly what we're dealing with," Thecla said.

"Looks like my boys have a fire going, let's get the water heating and look at that wound," Ascus said, as he turned away from the wagon.

Tessa took a vessel to the spring for water. Thecla followed Ascus to Zohres, lying on the ground. They'd built the fire as close to Zohres as possible. Thecla approached Zohres carefully, not wanting to alarm him but she found him unresponsive yet alive. She saw the blood-soaked sleeve and side of his shirt. Anna, Betta and Gracea arrived moments later.

"We'll begin by tearing away the sleeve and side of his shirt. With so much blood, I'm guessing the wound is large," Thecla said.

Suddenly, Betta said "Oh no, Mother. There are many wounds, scratches, some really deep. Oh yuck. I'm going to be sick."

"Hush, Betta, move away so we can see," Anna said.

"I see a clean slice and large claw marks. Thecla, it looks as if he was attacked once by a brigand and then by a large cat. What do you think?" Anna said, after looking at the wounds.

Thecla looked closely at the wounds and said, "I agree; a most unusual double injury. We will wash the wounds then sew the deepest tear before he gains consciousness."

"Betta and Gracea stay with Zohres while we collect the needle, thread and bandages. Tessa should bring the hot water soon," Thecla said.

Tessa, Thecla and Anna set to work on Zohres. When they finished it was daylight and the fire was low. Ascus and his sons approached the fire with more wood and rekindled it to cook the morning meal. The women reiterated to the men their care for Zohres. They decided he should stay in their cave until he was healed enough to walk back to his cave. They knew he'd object so each tried to prepare an argument to keep him. Thecla won by telling them she would preach The Word to him and keep him busy learning about the one, true God. The other women agreed to help. The men decided they would stay another day, at least until Zohres 'came around' to see what shape he was in and if the women needed more help.

Ascus suggested they move the wagon to the opening of the cave and unload the contents. When the wagon was unloaded he said, he and his sons would load Zohres on to the wagon and move him to the cave.

"Even if he wakes by that time, I doubt he'll be able to walk to the cave," Ascus said.

"No, I think not," Thecla agreed. "We'll fix a sleeping place for him. We've already set Betta and Gracea weaving a sleeping mat for him. It should be ready later today."

"I'll begin heating some broth for him. He'll need it when he awakens," Tessa said.

"That will be fine," Thecla said, "Anna and I will unpack our satchels and prepare more bandages for Zohres."

The sun was high by the time the men returned to Zohres. They noticed he was in a fevered state and mumbling gibberish. "We need to transport him to the cave so the women can care for him," Ascus said. They lifted Zohres on the sheet he was laying onto the bed of the cart. Ascus walked, leading the mules, while the sons walked on either side of the wagon to keep Zohres from tumbling out, as he was beginning to thrash about in his fevered state.

Anna and Thecla met the men and the wagon and, seeing and hearing Zohres knew at once what they had to do. "Take him to the back of the cave where it is dark, quiet and cool," Thecla said. "We will give him an herb blend to help him rest and heal. Tessa is a master of herbal medicine; her skill is needed now."

"My sons and I will stay tonight and, if it seems all right, we will leave in the morning. In the meantime, we will gather more wood and anything else you may need to begin living here. We'll show Tessa and Anna where the best wood is," Ascus said.

"We appreciate your help and Tessa has already found some herbs she needs to supplement those she brought," Thecla said.

The daylight waned and evening encroached on the valley. Zohres remained quiet after Tessa gave him sips of her powerful herb concoction. The men prepared a cooking fire site on the side of the cave opening, lit the fire and lit two torches to light the cave. Anna and Tessa prepared the evening meal while Thecla changed Zohras' bandages, checking for signs of infection. Betta and Gracea finished the mat by torchlight and took it to Thecla for Zohras.

"That is a fine sleeping mat for him. Help me move him onto it while he's sleeping," Thecla said.

"Won't we wake him?" Gracea asked.

"No," Thecla said. "He has been badly injured and needs to sleep to heal."

"What happened to him?" Betta asked. "He was fine but a little strange when we went into Iconium."

"Yes, he was fine then but he must have had trouble on his way home. He was hurt too badly when he got here so Ascus said he couldn't talk. You saw the wounds," Thecla said.

"Yes, they were terrible. His arm was torn to shreds and a big slice cut into his side. I nearly vomited when I saw it," Betta said.

"Yes, let's move him quickly then he can rest here where it is quiet," Thecla said.

They moved him in one smooth move by pulling the sheet on which he was sleeping on to the mat. With that task completed, they moved to the front of the cave for the evening meal. The evening was warm so each person chose a stone on which to sit to eat. After the meal was finished, Ascus posed a question.

"Now that you've worked inside the cave for a little while, is there something more we could do to help you settle in for the longer time?" Ascus asked.

"We were discussing the possibility of lashing some boards together from the wagon bed to make a table and moving some flat-topped stones or chunks of wood into the cave for chairs," the older son continued.

"That is most kind of you, but so much work here would keep you from your work in the city," Thecla said.

"That wouldn't be a problem," Ascus said. "We have other church members taking care of the animals. Let us know what you think you might need and we'll do our best to help you."

"We'll talk about it tonight and let you know in the morning if we come up with any other needs. We'll discuss such needs after we break our fast."

With that, Thecla blessed them and the men left the cave for their tent.

Three days later, as everyone was seated at their new table to break their fast, Betta called from the back of the cave in an excited voice, "Zohres is awake and wants some water. Come quick."

Everyone stood at once and rushed to Zohres. Tessa took a moment to grab a cup of water before joining the others. Ascus lit a torch and Thecla knelt beside Zohres.

"You are awake. How do you feel?" Thecla asked, in a soft voice.

"Wa-ter," Zohres croaked.

"Here is some water," Tessa said, handing the cup to Thecla.

Tecla placed her arm under Zohres' shoulders, encouraging him to sip. He took several sips. Then she laid him down again.

"So good," Zohres said.

"We are happy you are awake with no fever or rot," Thecla said.

"We'll bring you a little gruel if you feel ready," Tessa said.

"Mmmm," Zohres agreed.

The others moved to the front of the cave. Tessa took a few spoonfulls of gruel to Zohres while the others settled to eat. This morning meal was upbeat and Ascus stated it was a good omen for beginning their life in the cave. Thecla quickly corrected him saying, "No, Ascus, God has blessed Zohres and the rest of us. He is pleased with our decision to take up this simple existence. Now, we must spend a few moments in prayer of thanksgiving to the one, true, God." They joined Thecla in prayer, with bowed heads.

Rising from the table, Ascus said it was time he and his sons left for Iconium. The women agreed but Betta and Gracea looked somewhat crestfallen at the prospect.

"We appreciate all you've done for us and we'll keep you in our prayers," Thecla said.

"We wish you the best here and will return in two or three months with supplies and any word from the city," Ascus said.

With that, Ascus and his sons climbed onto the wagon and, with a final wave, lumbered down the path.

The women returned to the cave to clear the table and check once more on Zohres. Pleased that Zohres was sleeping comfortably, Thecla suggested they explore the surrounding area for food items, herbs and any evidence of wild animals or other potential harm. Tessa wanted to show them where she found some of the herbs to complement her store. Anna, Betta and Gracea were looking for berries, wild onions, wild carrots and anything else for food. Each carried a basket for collecting items. Thecla wished to stay behind with Zohres to contemplate and wait for their report.

About two hours later, the women returned to the cave. Betta and Gracea were excited to show Thecla the wild vegetables they collected, wild onions, carrots, celery and lettuce. Anna's basket was heaped with large raspberries and blackberries.

"God has blessed us and the forest is truly sumptuous," Thecla said.

"Yes, there is more we haven't picked yet," Betta said.

"There are currents, cherries, mushrooms and several kinds of nuts," Gracea said.

"We will gather the nuts when they're ripe," Betta said

"We should dry as much of the produce as we can gather for the winter months," Anna said.

"Yes, and Gracea and I need to spend more time gathering and searching for herbs. We will bring in as much as we can for drying," Tessa said.

"I'd like to accompany you and Gracea to learn more about herbs," Thecla said.

"You're certainly welcome to join us on any of our forays," Tessa said.

"How is Zohres?" Anna asked.

"He's still sleeping but I think we should change his bandages when he wakes," Thecla said.

"Yes, we'll do that," Tessa said, looking at Thecla, "I'll need you and Anna for that. It will probably be painful for him."

The women set to washing, peeling and preparing the vegetables for the evening meal. A few of the berries would be eaten after the evening meal but most would be kept for the morning, a welcome addition to their gruel.

Zohres awakened as the sun was setting. Betta called her mother as she was bid to do. "Mother, Zohres is awake and wants water," she called.

"We'll be right there as soon as I light a torch," Anna said.

Anna and Thecla arrived momentarily. After administering the water, Thecla said, "We'll need to change your bandages while you are awake."

"I expected that," Zohres said, with a brief twitch of the corner of his mouth that Thecla interpreted as an attempt at a smile.

Tessa arrived with her basket of bandages and salves. When she removed the bandages, all the women looked relieved. The bleeding had stopped some healing had begun and, most importantly, no foul odor. Tessa spread salves on the injuries, wrapped them and patted Zohres on the uninjured shoulder. "You are healthy, strong and will heal quickly, I think," Tessa said.

"Thank you," Zohres said. The women smiled not sure if he was thanking Tessa for her work, for her kind words or if he was just glad the re-bandaging was over.

"If you stay awake a little longer, we'll bring you some food," Tessa said.

"I'll try," he said, making a short laughing sound.

Zohres left a few days later and the women settled to their daily tasks. Thecla went to the back of the cave where she spent much of her time in prayer and contemplation. Tessa, Anna and their daughters collected food for meals and wood to burn for cooking, baking bread and warmth. Their days became weeks, which became months and finally years. Betta and Gracea had reached puberty and were becoming bored with cave life. Anna and Tessa knew they needed to return to the city in the near future to find mates for their daughters. They were reluctant to engage Thecla in conversation about this issue, though they knew it was imperative they do so.

Chapter 8. Thecla joins Paul

It was fall; the women had been in the cave for almost three years. The fruits were picked and drying. The wood was gathered and stacked. Preparations for the coming winter were well underway. Betta and Gracea had been attempting to convince their mothers to abandon cave-life and move back to the city. Tessa and Anna had discussed it and decided to talk to Thecla about it this winter. Neither woman looked forward to the discussion because each knew how deeply Thecla felt about her reclusive life of meditation and prayer. What would it take to change that and convince her to move back to society and onward? Onward to what, though?

One morning, as Betta looked up the road from the cave mouth, she saw a man leaning heavily on a walking stick, limping and barely able to take each step. She turned and called to Thecla, "Thecla, there is a man coming down the road and he looks like he's going to fall."

"Do you recognize him? Is it Zohres?" Thecla answered.

"No, it's not Zohres. This man is older and can barely walk," Betta repeated.

"All right, I'll be right out," Thecla said.

Thecla arrived at the cave mouth to look at the visitor approaching laboriously down the road. Thecla could not see him well so she said, "I can't really see who he is. I'll walk toward him until I can see better."

Thecla began to walk toward the man and suddenly began to run to him. Betta was watching Thecla and realized Thecla must have recognized the man. Betta called her mother, aunt and Gracea from the garden to come quickly because they had company. By the time the women arrived in the cave, Thecla and the man were approaching the cave. Thecla called to Betta, "Betta, please come and help us get in and find a place to sit."

Betta and Gracea appeared almost instantly and brought a short log for a seat. Thecla was talking, almost nonstop to the man, who nodded often but said nothing. He looked as if he were barely breathing. Thecla helped the man to sit on the log and said, "Betta, please get some water for this man." Then she directed Gracea to get Anna and Tessa.

When all the women were together and the man seemed to be somewhat revived, Thecla said, "We have a special visitor today. We are honored to be visited by my mentor and leader of the mission here. This is Paul."

The women gasped at the mention of Paul. They stood immobilized for several moments, until Thecla said, "Let's get Paul and all of us something to eat then we'll decide what needs to be done next." The women scurried off to bring the table to Paul and the meal materialized in moments.

"Paul, will you please bless us all?" Thecla asked.

Paul, though weak, did his best to bless them saying, "May God bless us all here in this cave who so graciously welcomed your servant. Your divine providence has led me to them and I am grateful." He could say no more, clearly exhausted.

After the meal, Thecla briefly went to a place in the cave to prepare a place for Paul, the same place that had been occupied by Zohres several years before. Thecla asked Paul if he were able to come to the back of the cave for a place to rest. He was and rose to walk with her assistance to the sleeping place she had prepared for him. He reclined on the mat and was asleep before Thecla finished covering him.

"Paul will sleep today, tonight and maybe into tomorrow. We must be sure he has water available at all times," Thecla told the women, as she helped them move the table and log seats back to their accustomed places.

"Has he been injured in any way?" Tessa asked.

"I don't think so. He didn't mention any problems when I met him on the road," Thecla said.

"I ask because I thought I saw a bruise on his forehead, almost in his hair," Tessa said.

"Yes, I saw it too," Anna said.

"I didn't notice. I was so glad to see him and surprised," Thecla said. "I'll ask him when he awakens."

Late morning of the next day, Thecla was summoned by Betta to come to Paul's mat-side. "You called," Thecla said, as she arrived.

"Yes," Betta said. "Paul was mumbling about people throwing stones."

"That's what Tessa and your mother thought yesterday. I'll look at his forehead."

Sure enough, just on the forehead almost immediately into the hair was a large bruise, swollen to a ball. "He has been injured, perhaps by a stone. I'll ask him as soon as he awakens," Thecla said. "Please keep a watch for him to awaken. If he doesn't awaken by mid-day, I'll wake him."

"All right," Betta said. "I'll work on my weaving and watch."

"Very well," Thecla said and moved to her meditating space.

As mid-day came, Paul had not awakened. Betta was concerned and called Thecla, "Thecla, I think it's time to awaken Paul."

"Yes, Betta, you are quite right. Has he made any indication of waking on his own?" asked Thecla.

"No, just some mumbling and groaning."

"All right, I'll try to wake him. Please, find the other women and bring them here. Be sure Tessa brings her medicine basket." Betta nodded and hurried away.

Thecla commenced to try to awaken Paul with gentle touches and soft word, "Paul. Please try to wake up." She repeated this statement several times with increasing shoulder pressure. His only response was groans. Thecla's worry increased as she realized his injury was more severe than any of them had suspected. *He should have been treated last night. How could I have missed the bruise? I was so happy to see him. I hope Tessa hurries. How could I have made such a mistake?*

Tessa finally arrived, carrying her medicine basket and the other women close behind her.

"Tessa, I can't get Paul to awaken. Can you please see what you can do? I shouldn't have missed his bruise. Please do something," Thecla begged, sounding to be on the verge of hysteria.

"Shhh, Thecla. It's not your fault. Please be calm and I'll see what I can do," Tessa said, setting her basket on the cave floor, preparing to get to work.

She began to nudge Paul and speak to him in kind but authoritative words, "Wake up, Paul. It's time to wake up."

"Ummmmm." Paul groaned.

Tessa repeated this action and statement several more times and Paul groaned in response each time.

Tessa reached into her basket and withdrew a small brown bottle. She removed the stopper from the bottle mouth and passed the open bottle beneath Paul's nose. Paul did not react. Tessa performed the action again, this time Paul opened his eyes and reached up to bat whatever passed under his nose.

"Terrible smell," Paul said.

"So glad you're awake," Thecla said, rushing to him.

"My head hurts," Paul said.

"You have a huge bruise in the front of your head. What happened?"

"Not now. Water,"

Acquiescing, realizing Paul was in more pain than she'd first thought, she called to Tessa, "Tessa, please come back with your basket." Then to Betta, "Betta, please bring some water for Paul."

Tessa arrived almost immediately. "Paul is in pain from the bump on his head. Please look him over carefully for more bruises," Thecla said.

Tessa set to examining Paul's head and neck. She found four more bruises, three on his head and a large one on his neck at the base of his skull. Gracea came instead and helped Paul sip the water. After he finished, Paul lay back and went to sleep almost immediately.

Tessa addressed the women, "Paul has suffered a worse attack than we thought. He didn't mention it last night because that is Paul's way. He doesn't want to complain. I've found four bruises, the one we saw last night, two more on the sides of his head and one on his neck at the base of his skull." She stopped and looked at the others.

"What can we do?" asked Anna.

"Is it too late?" asked Betta.

"No," Thecla said, "it's never too late to help someone in need." The women saw the look of self-imposed guilt on her face and heard it in her quivering voice.

"We will do what we can to make him as comfortable as possible. We'll put cold compresses on his bruises." *Though it should have been done last night*, Tessa thought. "Someone must stay with him at all times. If he wakes, he should be encouraged to drink water or eat a bit of gruel," Tessa continued.

Turning to Thecla, who was quietly crying as she sat next to Paul, Tessa said, "Please don't place the blame on your shoulders. Anna and I thought we saw something and didn't react when we should have. There is no going back. We must do what we can now. We'll begin by placing cold compresses on the bruises to reduce swelling. We must be here to talk to him when he awakens."

"I tried to talk to him just now when he was awake but he didn't want to talk," Thecla sobbed.

"Yes, of course, he is weak and not ready to engage in conversation. That will come."

"I'll stay here with him today and tonight. I'll pray for him as I wait," Thecla said.

Gracea brought a fresh cup of water and the women left Thecla and Paul in solitude.

The next morning, Tessa came to check on Paul and Thecla. She found Thecla's eyes blurry with sleep. "I fell asleep for a time," Thecla confessed.

"That's not a surprise and it's not a problem. If Paul had awakened you would have known. He'd have probably asked for water. I'll change the compresses and keep watch, you should get some more sleep," Tessa said.

Thecla went to her enclosure at the back of the cave and Tessa settled to keep watch.

Paul roused several times, begging for water. Tessa and the others noted how long it was taking Paul to recover. They encouraged Paul to eat some gruel each time he awoke. This went on for nearly a week until he said he wanted to sit up. He seemed ready to talk and Thecla was summoned by Betta.

"Paul, we've waited so long for you to recover. What have you to tell us about your decision to journey here?" Thecla asked.

"Thecla, I'd heard you'd retired to a cave outside of the city. The person who comes here with supplies came to my teachings. Then several youths started a disturbance while I was teaching. They threw stones, some small, some quite large. I ducked out of the area but they followed me. I could not run but they finally gave up. My head hurt and my vision was blurred but I kept walking. I found the path the supply man told me about and after a while you came toward me," Paul said.

"Thank you, Paul, for the description of your difficulty. Please rest now and we'll bring you some food in a short while," Thecla said.

Thecla hurried to the front of the cave to tell the women what she'd learned from Paul.

"It sounds as if Iconium isn't a safe place to be right now," Anna said.

"There is almost always a segment of youths ready to incite violence against preaching," Tessa said.

"There is always a threat against preaching, not necessarily by youths only." Thecla said.

"Hopefully, the governor will take an interest in the event and punish those responsible," Anna said.

"Unless the youths were children of high ranking council members," Tessa said.

"Well, we can't solve the problem here, so let's get some food for Paul to keep his recovery on track," Thecla said.

"I'll check on Paul, Betta and Gracea can take his food to him," Tessa said.

Anna, Betta and Gracea moved to prepare the food, while Tessa and Thecla went to Paul.

"I'm actually hungry," Paul stated, when the women arrived.

"That's a very good sign for your recovery, Paul," Tessa said.

"My head has stopped hurting and my vision is clear," Paul stated.

"Your bruises are getting lighter colored and the swelling is gone down; all good signs," Tessa said.

"Your food is on its way. After you eat, perhaps, you'd like to try to stand and walk a bit," Thecla said.

"Yes, I want to try that. I need to move around a little," Paul said, with a smile.

Betta and Gracea came to Paul, bearing a bowl of gruel with berries and bread.

"A veritable feast," Paul exclaimed.

The girls laughed, Paul blessed them and the food then Betta and Gracea settled to watch him and listen to him as he began to tell them about the wonders of God. Thecla, Anna and Tessa heard him and joined the girls to listen as Paul instructed between bites. About an hour after he'd finished eating, Paul finished preaching. The women rose, removed the dishes and Thecla encouraged Paul to rest a bit before standing. He was grateful for the rest and was asleep before Thecla left his side.

Later that afternoon, Thecla asked Paul if he were ready to stand and, perhaps, walk. He was and Thecla and Tessa helped him stand. They watched him closely for signs of weakness or dizziness. Seeing none, they helped him walk to the front of the cave.

"Let me sit and enjoy the sunshine and the fresh air," Paul begged.

"Excellent suggestion, Paul," Thecla said. Betta rolled a piece of wood that served as a chair at the table for Paul.

He sat until the sun sank below the horizon and night encroached. Betta handed a lit torch to Thecla then Thecla assisted Paul to walk to his sleeping mat.

Two more weeks passed as Paul gradually recovered his strength and will to explore the surrounding area. *I think he's getting bored caged in a cave with all the women. He needs to visit someone new. Perhaps I should suggest he walk to Zohres' cave. Zohres has heard me speak of Paul many times. I know he'd be interested to meet Paul. Betta and Gracea know the way to his cave. They could walk with Paul and introduce him to Zohres,* thought Thecla.

This thought kept coming back to Thecla until she convinced herself to explore it with Tessa and Anna.

"That's my idea," said Thecla, after she'd recounted her idea to the women. "What do you think?"

"I think you are right. Paul needs some place safe to go. He needs to meet someone; someone who is non-threatening and more than willing to listen and, perhaps, debate some of Paul's ideas. Zohres is a thinker; we experienced his interest and questions." Tessa said.

"I think having Betta and Gracea show him the way and introducing Paul to Zohres is also a good idea," Anna said. "They're almost as bored as Paul."

"Then it is decided. I'll bring the idea to Paul to see his reaction. If he is willing, please discuss it with Betta and Gracea. Wait for Paul's reaction, though," Thecla said.

Tessa and Anna agreed.

The next day, Thecla decided to take her idea to Paul.

Paul had just finished breaking his fast when Thecla arrived at the table.

"Paul," she began, "would you like to visit a hermit about three miles from here? We cared for him after his accident and I converted him and baptized him. He had many questions and ideas I'm sure you would enjoy hearing and discussing. Betta and Gracea know him from when he was here and can introduce you to him. What do you think?"

"Thecla, that is a gracious suggestion and I would welcome spending some time with Zohres. Being a hermit, are you sure he'd welcome a visitor?"

"Yes, we got to know Zohres quite well while he healed. He's a hermit only because he ran afoul of the Romans, so now he's just staying out of their way," Thecla explained.

"I see," said Paul. "He may be interested in what I have to say and I'd certainly be interested in what he has to say."

"All right, I'll finish plans and let you know when we can accomplish this."

By the end of the week, Thecla's plans were complete. Betta and Gracea were in high spirits for the upcoming visit. They'd ridden on the supply wagon so they knew exactly which cave was Zorhes'. *Why don't we wait for the supply wagon then we could ride and Paul wouldn't have to walk?* Betta wondered. *I'll ask Mother, maybe she hasn't thought of that.* A few minutes later, Anna walked close to the table where Betta was preparing the evening meal.

"Mother, I have an idea," Betta said.

"Is that so?" Anna asked.

"Yes, why don't we wait for the supply wagon that should be here any day then we could ride with Ascus to Zohres' cave."

"That's a good idea. I'll check with Paul and see if he'd like to ride in the wagon to Zohres'."

"I'll ask Gracea. I'm sure she'll be all right with the idea," Betta said.

"I thought you'd probably hatched that idea with Gracea's help in the beginning."

"No, Mother, this one was all my idea."

"Do you need any help with the dinner preparation?" asked Anna.

"No, thanks, Mother, we'll eat on time."

"All right, I'll have a word with Paul. Call when you are ready."

Betta nodded and Anna walked outside to talk to Paul.

The sun was setting behind the western mountains, when Betta called that the evening meal was ready. This was to be a special meal. Paul had snared three rabbits and was roasting them over a fire. Betta had completed a vegetable dish of wild carrots, onions and celery in a honey and spices dressing. Tessa and Gracea had made fresh bread and honey cakes for after the meal. Betta called Paul to bring in the rabbits, everything was ready.

Everyone sat at the table and Paul said a blessing. Betta and Gracea closed one eye each, keeping one eye open to watch for a hint of starting to eat. They'd not had meat for many weeks. The smell of the rabbits was so tantalizing that Paul's prayer seemed to go on and on. `

The rabbits will be cold if he doesn't hurry, Betta thought.

My stomach is growling. I'm so hungry. Hurry, Paul. Gracea thought.

Finally, Paul concluded the blessing and everyone settled to eat.

The evening meal finished, Anna asked Betta to join her near the fire, which was low now. Betta joined her, with a questioning look. Anna began the conversation, "Betta, Paul said going to visit Zohres with the supply wagon is a good idea. He said he'd probably stay with Zohres for a time in that they will have much to discuss. He was concerned about you and Gracea walking back here alone."

"I didn't realize he planned to stay with Zohres for a time."

"Yes, I'm sure they'll have much to discuss and Zohres will welcome the visit."

"I thought Zohres was a hermit and didn't like people."

"What gave you that idea, Betta?"

"Hermits usually want to be alone."

"There are several different reasons for hermits. Zohres had problems with the governor and would have been imprisoned if he'd stayed in Iconium."

"Is he hiding?"

"No, I don't think so. If he stays out of sight and the Romans don't see him, he'll be all right."

"It sounds like he's hiding."

"I suppose it does but he isn't being hunted. The Romans are ignoring the whole affair."

"What caused the problem to start with?"

"I'm not really sure and we must not say anything more. We don't gossip."

"I know, Mother, but I'd like to know."

"You must ask yourself why you want to know. Will it make a difference to you or do you need this information."

"All right, Mother. No, I don't need the information. I just wanted to know so I could tell Gracea."

"Yes, and that is exactly the definition of gossip. That is why we'll speak no more of Zohres' situation."

"Does Paul know about 'Zohres' situation'?"

"Yes, he does. Please don't talk to him about it."

"All right, Mother. No gossip from me."

"Thank you, Betta." Anna hugged her and retreated inside the cave. Betta made sure the fire was extinguished before she went into the cave, also.

Two days later, Ascus brought the supply wagon for his fall delivery of supplies. He unloaded salted and dried meats, flour, salt, some non-native vegetables and fruits for Anna; medical herbs and supplies for Tessa; scrolls for Thecla and trinkets for Betta and Gracea. "Something to make the pretty girls prettier," Ascus said. Gracea and Betta blushed, giggled and thanked him.

The women went to work immediately storing the food supplies and deciding which foods to use for the meal that evening. Thecla wanted to try a recipe she'd learned from Daphne, with whom she had stayed while healing from a broken ankle. Tessa and Anna also had recipes in mind to try. The evening meal was to be special, with two guests, Paul and Ascus and all the supplies they needed. Paul offered a blessing that became a sermon. Nearly an hour later, when he finished, Anna and Thecla lit torches.

The evening meal was consumed by torchlight. The meal was not hot, the meat was dried and the fruits and vegetables were used fresh. The new tastes and combinations were enjoyable to everyone, especially to Betta and Gracea, who both had more helpings; an unusual request at normal meals. After the meal, Paul performed another blessing which lasted even longer. By the end of his sermon, Thecla, Anna, Tessa and Ascus seemed renewed, Betta's and Gracea's heads were drooping and their eyes were nearly closed. The girls went to their beds, the adults stayed to engage Paul in a question and answer conversation, lasting long into the night.

After Ascus repositioned the packages in the wagon, making room for Betta and Gracea, the travelers were off to visit Zohres. The girls were interested in the blooming plants of late summer and early fall. Some of the trees on the mountainsides were beginning to change color.

"Won't be long 'till winter," Ascus said, pointing to the mountains.

"Nights are already cooling faster," Paul noted.

"Can we stop at the creek to see if we can catch any fish?" Betta asked.

"We can do that on the way back, if Paul decides to stay," Ascus said.

"Why would you decide not to stay, Paul?" Gracea asked.

"Well, Gracea, there might be several reasons. First of all, Zohres is a hermit, he may not want visitors. Second, he may not want a visiting preacher and teacher to abide with him for a time. Also, he may not be well and not feel up to having a visitor. As you see, there may be many reason, so we will stop by his cave and ask," Paul said.

"If you can't stay, why won't we be able to stop and fish in the creek?" Betta asked.

"Because it will probably be getting late when we get underway again. Dark comes earlier this time of year," Ascus said.

"Oh," said Betta, disappointed.

Paul sensed her disappointment and knowing she wanted to take fish home for the evening meal, he said, "Don't be too disappointed, Betta; I think I'll be staying with Zohres for the rest of the winter."

"Oh, Paul, I hope so. I know you are looking forward to long discussions with him," Betta said.

"Yes, I am. Thecla has told me much about his recovery with all of you. I'm sure we will have many long, fruitful discussions," Paul agreed.

They rode on in silence until Ascus stopped the wagon in front of a foot path up to a cave. "We can all get off the wagon and walk up to the cave," Ascus said. "This is Zohres' cave. He'll be standing in the cave mouth waiting for us."

By the time they were half way up the path, Zohres was standing at the mouth of the cave welcoming them.

"Ascus, I'm glad to see you and the supplies. The hand cart is right by the side of the cave," Zohres said. Next, he acknowledged Betta and Gracea. "Anna and Tessa's beautiful daughters, how you have grown since I saw you last."

"Zohres, we are glad to see you again. We brought a visitor." Betta motioned to Paul. "This is Paul. He is a friend to us all. Thecla is his devoted follower and we all love to hear him teach," Betta said, as she had been instructed by Thecla and Anna.

Zohres turned to Paul, smiling and looking into his eyes, said, "I welcome you to my cave. It isn't much but it is home."

"God has provided a home for you and I'll bless it," Paul said.

"Do come into the cave. You are all welcome," said Zohres. The girls, however, sensed Paul wanted to speak to Zohres alone, said "We'll go and give Ascus a hand with the packages."

Nearly an hour later, all the supplies were unloaded and stored in the cave.

"Come in and have a refreshment before you leave again," Zohres said.

"For just a bit," Ascus said

Zohres poured small cups of berry juice for the girls and a cup of black coffee for Ascus.

They passed the time of day, discussing what news Ascus and Paul could bring to Zohres, especially political. Betta and Gracea finished their juice and, bored, went out of the cave and down to the mule, where they eased him to the side of the road where he could munch the tall grass.

Finally, Ascus came down the path toward the wagon and said, "Girls, Paul is going to be staying with Zohres, so we can get back to your cave before dark."

"Does that mean we can stop to fish for a little while?" Betta asked.

"Yes, we certainly can," Ascus replied, hoping that question would not come up again.

Betta and Gracea jumped from the wagon as soon as Ascus stopped at the stream. He brought the poles to them as they were busily digging for worms. They adeptly put the worms on the hooks and started fishing. Ascus could see these girls had learned to fish and were quite comfortable with the process.

Within an hour they had a sack of fish and were ready to go home. "We'll have these for our meal tonight," Gracea said, excited.

"I wonder if Zohres comes down here to fish," Ascus said, thinking aloud.

"Oh, yes, he's the one who showed it to our mothers," Betta said.

"All right, we best be on our way," Ascus said, as he helped the girls into the wagon.

They arrived home in late afternoon. Betta and Gracea had cleaned the fish so the fish were ready to be cooked. They joined together to cooperatively haul the sack of fish to the cave, while Ascus saw to caring for the mules and wagon.

"Mom," the girls called in unison, "we've brought fish for the meal tonight," Betta finished

They proudly presented their contribution to the evening meal.

"This is wonderful, girls," Anna said, in greeting.

"You both are being very helpful," Tessa agreed.

"We will get them on the fire. Along with our fresh bread and olives, we'll have a fine meal," Thecla said, as she joined the group, upon hearing the happy voices.

"Paul decided to stay with Zohres for a while," Betta said.

"Yes, I thought he would. I'm sure Zohres was glad to finally meet him," Thecla said.

"They started talking and were still talking when we left," Gracea said.

"They'll do much more talking in the weeks to come," Thecla said.

With that, the women proceeded to build a fire and cook the fish for the evening meal.

Ascus came into the cave where Tessa asked him to join her and Anna at the fire. The three began a discussion, using soft voices no one could overhear from the cave. Thecla knew the subject of the discussion because Anna and Tessa had discussed the plan to talk to Ascus about the pledging of their daughters in marriage to his sons. Thecla kept Betta and Gracea busy in the cave preparing the rest of the meal and setting the table. The girls did wonder what their mothers were discussing with Ascus and Thecla told them, truthfully, they were discussing a return to Iconium. Because they wanted to return to the city, they were happy to hear of that discussion.

In a short time, Anna and Tessa brought the fish to the table, saying it was time to eat. Ascus extinguished the fire and joined them at the table. Betta was the first to start a conversation with the question that was in her and Gracea's minds for several weeks, "Were you talking about going back to the city? Are we going?"

Anna glanced first at Ascus then Tessa before she nodded slightly, "Yes, we discussed it and, yes we will be going back."

The girls were jubilant. They raised their voices in a cheer and hugged each other before taking control and returning to their manners at the table of which they had been taught.

"Each of you will talk alone with your mother before bed-time tonight. Now, let's enjoy the bounty of the stream and I'll give a blessing," Thecla said.

Thecla invoked a blessing on all at the table, Zohres and Paul; thanksgiving for the fish and for Ascus and his sons. She'd learned from Paul to add a short teaching about the help God gives us each day to satisfy our needs. In turn, we must be thankful for that help and attribute praise to God for his generosity.

After the blessing, the dinner proceeded and the fish disappeared quickly. Ascus was grateful to the women for the fine meal and headed out to the wagon to prepare his bed for the night. After the table was cleared, the mothers and daughters went to the back portions of the cave for their discussions. By the time they were finished, bed-time was upon them. Torches had to be lit for them to see their way to their beds.

Of course, Betta and Gracea were too excited to be ready for immediate sleep. They remained as quiet as they could until they could hear the soft breathing of the women on the other side of the cave. Then the whispering began.

"I'm so happy I'm going to marry Ikild," Gracea breathed in a whisper.

"Yes, and I'm going to marry Gibbus," Betta said, a little louder.

"Shhhh, not so loud," Gracea admonished.

"I'm sorry, I'm just so excited," whispered Betta.

"We'll be able to live near each other because Ikild and Gibbus will inherit Ascus' business." Gracea said.

"That will be so great and no more living in a cave," Betta said.

They took a minute or two to stifle a giggle before recovering.

"I'd be so glad to get into the city, I'd marry a beggar," Betta whispered, which caused another smothered round of giggles.

"Can't do that, you might end up back in a cave," Gracea said, when she recovered. After more suppressed giggling and the sound of one of the women awakening, the girls chose to roll over and try to get to sleep.

The next morning, Ascus left after eating a chunk of bread and some meat left for him on the table. He washed it down with water and rode away on the wagon as it was becoming light. When Anna and Tessa awoke, they found the food was gone and knew Ascus had left. Thecla was next to rise and come to the table. The women said a brief prayer for Ascus and his sons then settled to break their fast.

"We'll let the girls sleep for a while. It took them a while to settle last night," Anna said.

Tessa and Thecla nodded agreement. "I heard some suppressed giggles," Tessa said.

"I heard one whisper something then get shushed," Thecla said with a smile.

"They were both excited by the news of their wedding arrangements," Anna said.

"Yes, and they want to get back to the city," Tessa said.

"They've tired of cave life. It was exciting while it was new, now they've grown and are looking to the future. The cave doesn't hold anything for them. It represents a barrier to their future. It is best for them to return to the city," Thecla said.

"The three plus years we've been here has seen them grow and mature into young women," Anna said, whimsically.

"It seemed to happen so fast," Tessa said, voice cracking slightly.

Taking each woman's hand, Thecla said, "Let us say a silent prayer to God for Betta and Gracea." They bowed their heads, eyes closed for a few minutes.

At this point, Betta and Gracea approached the table without a word. They knew their mothers and Thecla were deep in prayer. They tiptoed out of the cave to commiserate.

The winter passed and Ascus was due any day for the women and Paul to move back to Iconium.

"Watch the road for Ascus' arrival. He should be here soon," Anna told Betta and Gracea.

"He'll have to go to Zohres' cave to drop supplies and pick up Paul, won't he?" Betta asked.

"Yes, that's the plan. Now, let us know of his approach," Anna said.

Betta and Gracea left the cave to watch the road.

"He's coming," Betta and Gracea called as they ran into the cave.

"Wonderful," Tessa said. "Let's begin to prepare the evening meal."

Thecla joined them and all pitched in to begin meal preparation as Ascus appeared at the mouth of the cave.

"Hello, I'm here to take you back to the city," Ascus called.

"Yes, we've been waiting for you. All is ready," Thecla said.

"I'll make my mules comfortable and be back in a few moments," Ascus said.

"The evening meal will be ready when you return," Tessa said.

The women prepared the table and all was ready for the meal when Ascus' shadow appeared at the mouth of the cave. "Please sit, Ascus, and join us for the blessing before we eat," Thecla said.

Thecla finished the blessing and they consumed the evening meal. "I'll go to Zohres' cave at first light tomorrow to drop supplies," Ascus said.

"And bring Paul back?" Thecla asked.

The other women smiled and Ascus replied, "Yes, if he's ready."

"I do hope he'll be ready," Thecla replied, sternly.

"So do I," Ascus said, as if to appease Thecla.

The next morning, Ascus left early for Zohres' cave. The women chose to spend the time in final preparation for the trip to Iconium.

"All must be packed and taken to the city. We don't want to come back for forgotten items," Anna said.

"I'll take as many herbs and other medicines as I can," Tessa said.

"We've been packed for a long time now," Gracea said, while Betta nodded vigorously.

"Check again and make sure," Anna said.

Thecla came to the front of the cave, satchel in hand. "I'm ready," she said.

It was early afternoon when Thecla saw Ascus' wagon approaching. Sure enough, Paul and Zohres were sitting next to him on the driver's bench. She hurried back to the inner part of the cave and called, "They're coming and Zohres is here too."

As the wagon approached, the women brought their packages to the cave mouth. Betta and Gracea were so excited they could barely contain themselves. Anna and Tessa were more reserved out of consideration for Thecla. Ascus brought the wagon to a stop and, jumping down from the wagon seat, said, "You're all ready to go?"

"Yes," Thecla said, "we're packed and ready to go. We can be in Iconium before dark. We packed some food for us to share on the way."

"All right, we'll load those packages and be on our way," Ascus agreed.

The women brought their packages to the wagon. Ascus handed them to Paul and Zohres for even placement on the bed of the wagon, including the large cooking pot and leaving space for the women to sit. When all was loaded and everyone was ready, Ascus urged the mule team to start and the wagon clattered down the path.

They arrived in Iconium as the sun was low in the west. The trip had been uneventful but everyone was tired and ready for rest. They went to an inn to stay for the night. There they could wash up, eat dinner and sleep. Tomorrow, Tessa and Anna planned to check on their house, which had been rented.

The next morning, Tessa and Anna rose early and made their way to the house they'd rented before going to the cave. When they arrived, they found a note attached to the door, which said: **We must leave. Hope you arrive soon.** It did not look as if it were hanging there long, maybe just a day or two. Anna produced a key and they entered. All the furnishings and house were in good order and would be useful for everyone to join them. As soon as this was determined, the women returned to the inn to collect everyone and move their belongings to the house.

Everyone repacked their satchels and followed Anna and Tessa to the house. Upon arrival, the men were shown to a room with two beds. Thecla was shown to a bedroom, while Anna and Tessa shared a room as did Betta and Gracea. They took seats in the large anterior room to listen to Paul and Zohres tell of their experiences in Zohres' cave during the last winter. Betta and Gracea were absorbed in the tale told by Zohres about a huge brown bear, which chose Zohres' cave for a winter home. The women were more comfortable listening to Paul tell of Zohres' final conversion. By the time the stories were finished, evening was upon them and the women went to the kitchen to prepare the evening meal, while Paul and Zohres retired to the patio to discuss their plan to move on.

Thecla came to the patio to announce the evening meal was ready.

"Thecla, we need to talk to you about our plan to move on, if you are interested," Paul said.

"Yes, I certainly am but can it wait until after the meal?" she asked.

"Yes, of course," Paul answered and they entered the house to the anterior room, where they'd first arrived Although now, a trestle table was set up and the chairs were pulled to it.

Paul was asked to bless the food and all present. A lively discussion ensued regarding the possibility of Paul, Zohres and Thecla traveling to Jerusalem.

"I thought you'd already been there," Anna stated.

"Yes, I have but Thecla and Zohres have not. That's not all I want to do, I want to go to Rome, eventually."

"That will take several years. Are you up to that?" Tessa asked, looking at Thecla.

"Yes, I will follow where Paul leads. I want to spend the rest of my life listening to his teachings."

"I, too, want to hear more from Paul and, maybe, lead a church, if Paul so ordains," Zohres stated.

"That is part of the plan, Zohres," Paul said. "We'll try to find a place fitting for you and a congregation accepting of you."

"That should not be too difficult," Thecla said. "Zohres has learned from the best and is a personable man."

"Thank you, Thecla, but I don't have experience teaching as you both do," Zohres said.

"That is a mark of humility," Paul said. "We'll give you that experience during our travels."

The conversation continued as they discussed sea and land routes, what to expect at various stop-overs and the ever-present Romans. Anna suggested they stay in Iconium a while to revitalize the churches here, while securing funds to get to Syria. Paul and Thecla saw the wisdom of such a suggestion and they all gratefully accepted.

The next morning saw Paul, Thecla and Zohres breaking their fast and hurrying off to find the heads of the local churches.

Paul, walking close to Thecla asked, just above a whisper, "Do you want to visit your mother?"

"No," Thecla said. "She literally drove me out of the house on my last visit. I don't think she'd be ready to see me again." Paul noticed Thecla look away, hiding a tear, he supposed.

"We'll stop first at Tatin's house then on to Charis and Delva's, if they are still among us," Paul said.

They arrived at Tatin's house. Tatin saw them coming and hurried out to meet them.

"Welcome, Paul and Thecla; and who is your guest?" Tatin inquired.

"Tatin, meet our new church member, Zohres," Paul said and, turning to Zohres said "Zohres, meet the head of our churches in Iconium, Tatin."

"So happy to be here," Zohres said, shyly.

"Come inside. I want to hear how you all have been and all about your travels, Paul and, especially about your stay in the cave, Thecla. I also want to hear more about you, Zohres. I'll pass along some news about our Governor that may interest you," Tatin said, as he ushered them into his abode.

Tatin's lodging had grown to a comfortable living space, not ornate but satisfactory for hosting church members for services and discussions. Each took a chair and Tatin sat in his cushioned chair. His wife, Mariam, brought a tray of cheese, grapes and goblets of wine for the guests. Paul and Thecla recounted their experiences since they'd seen Tatin last. Zohres described his problems with the governor, which had led him to life as a hermit in a cave then his conversion by Thecla and the strengthening of his faith during Paul's visit to his cave.

"This is all so interesting and uplifting," Tatin said. "Please plan to visit our next service. I think the congregation will find your experiences of great value."

"We are most pleased to bring our humble experiences to the Iconium congregation," Paul said and Thecla nodded in acclimation.

Tatin then looked to Zohres and said, "Zohres, would you consider giving a description of your conversion and the 'strengthening' you received from Paul?"

Zohres finished his wine with a large swallow and said, "Thank you for the invitation but I am not versed in speaking to a crowd. I'm not sure how effective I would be."

Paul reacted immediately. "Zohres, we'll help you prepare. You have much to offer. We'll help you organize your ideas."

"That will help me. So, with that, I accept your invitation," Zohres said to Tatin, who nodded accent.

"Now, I must tell you about the new governor, Ambrosius. He is open to our church and has been no problem, so far. Of course, he's a Roman, so we will have to exercise some caution when planning outdoor activities that may draw crowds, some of which may disapprove of our church. Sometimes bringing our existence out in the open can result in a backlash on the Governor, causing a tightening of control. That, possibly, could put an unnecessary burden on church members," explained Tatin.

"That sounds promising, at least," said Thecla.

"Yes, there has to be a caveat at this time, though," Tatin said.

"Yes, it's wise to tread softly at this point and watch 'which way the wind is blowing', to borrow a nautical euphemism," Paul said.

On another note, Paul began, "We plan to leave Iconium next spring and head to Syrian Antioch. I've not been back there for some time, so I want to visit the churches. Thecla has never been there, so I want her to visit there, too. Zohres can gain much and, perhaps, have his own church."

Paul and Thecla continued to outline their plan to visit Syria and beyond. Of course, it was light on details in some places because they'd not finished the plan. Also, parts of the plan depended on their reception in Antioch and the availability of suitable ships, places to stay and the amount of money raised.

"That is an ambitious plan, Paul, but I know you are capable of achieving it. How can we best help you?" Tatin asked.

"We're hoping to collect enough money to fund passage for the three of us on a ship bound for Syrian Antioch," said Paul.

"We'll talk to some of the wealthier church members after your presentations. After they've heard you, talked to you and thought about it, some of them will be most generous; another reason why we don't want to antagonize the Governor," Tatin said.

"You are so right," Paul agreed.

"Please stay with us for the evening meal," Tatin said.

"That is most generous of you. Thank you," Paul said.

"Until then, Paul and Thecla, please lead us in prayer," Tatin suggested.

It was after dark when Paul, Thecla and Zohres returned to Anna's home. Exhausted, they took to their beds for the night.

For many weeks after their presentations, Paul, Thecla and Zohres met with congregation members on informal, one-on-one discussions. They met after church services, on invitations to members' homes, in the marketplace and even the government office. Church members had many questions and needed much information before they were willing to contribute to Paul and Thecla's mission.

One day, Thecla decided to visit Daphne, who had helped her when she'd been injured after leaving her fuming mother, several years ago. Daphne welcomed her with hugs and kisses, asking her about her ministry.

"I haven't talked to you in ages. How has your ministry progressed?" Daphne asked.

"That is a long story," Thecla said. "I'll tell you about it if you have time to listen. It could take several hours."

"I'm ready to listen. You can stay as long as it takes; then, longer, while I tell you all about my life."

"I definitely want to hear about your life, too," Thecla said.

Thecla launched into a description of her ministerial activities, including as many details as she could remember. She provided the most detail about her time in the cave. Daphne was spellbound through the descriptions Thecla provided. Daphne stopped her to enquire further of Zaortha and Jamal, whom she remembered from past acquaintance. Daphne also asked more about Anna and Tessa, whom she thought she'd met at a few church services.

"I don't remember having seen Betta or Gracea," Daphne interjected.

"You'd remember them if you'd ever met them. They will be married soon, at least Gracea will be. Her marriage contract is arranged. Betta is close behind in age, so she will marry soon. That was the main reason Tessa and Anna wanted to move back to town, because their daughters were reaching marriageable age," Thecla elaborated.

"I can understand that. While you continue your story, let's begin evening meal preparation."

"That will work fine, Daphne. I remember your kitchen well."

"Do you remember my husband, Orel?"

"Yes, I do."

Their discussion progressed, Thecla bringing Daphne up-to-date on her life since Thecla's last visit. It seemed so long ago for both women. Daphne was fascinated, especially with Thecla's life in the cave.

"You were brave to stay in that cave with only other women," Daphne commented, after the description.

"Oh, I don't think it was a matter of bravery," Thecla said with a short chuckle. "We were well hidden and no wild animals or humans were about. It was a quiet time for reflection and meditation. Then Paul showed up, injured and needed nursing care, just as Zorhes had done. All in all, we really weren't alone all that long."

"I suppose not, although I would have been uncomfortable."

"Life in a cave is not for everybody. I am not sure I would have done it alone, either."

They sat for the evening meal with Orel and Daphne urged Thecla to recount her stay in the cave again for him. After the meal, they retired for the night. Thecla had agreed to spend the night and return to her lodging in the morning.

Thecla, Paul and Zohres visited the congregations several times in the following weeks where they received several large and many smaller donations. At this time, Paul decided they had enough money for passage on a ship to Syria. A congregation member, Daniil, a worker at the docks in Perga agreed to help gain passage when the travel time for safer passage arrived. This gave the three missionaries time to preach and teach their way to Perga. Paul and Thecla were able to give Zohres enough practice so they could tell he would be as good a teacher as they were. By the time they boarded the ship to Antioch, Syria, Zohres, and his mentors were confident in his ability to preach and teach.

Chapter 9. The Missionaries travel to Syria

The day was cloudless and the breeze off the water was pleasing. Thecla, Paul and Zohres were eager to start their trip. Before they could find Daniil, they heard a booming voice, "I'm over here. Ready to go?"

"Yes we are," called Paul.

As they hurried toward the voice, a man leapt to the dock from a mid-sized ship.

"If you folks are ready to leave, come aboard and we'll start as soon as I clear passage out of the bay."

"All right," Paul replied. "Is that a new requirement, to get passage out of the port?"

"Yes, just started a few months ago," he replied, before hurrying away.

The three missionary travelers walked the gangplank to board the ship and find places to rest until the captain arrived. The rest was brief; Daniil with a taller bearded man right behind him turned and introduced the bearded man as Captain Jomas. Assuring the three they were 'in good hands', Daniil left the ship.

Captain Jomas turned to the three, welcomed them and gave them instructions as to where to stash their packs and satchels. Paul and Zohres would go below with the other crew members, a common method for male travelers. Thecla, though, was directed to a 'cubbyhole' of sorts, adjacent to the captain's quarters. The small room was only large enough to hold her bags and a small cot for sleeping. She thanked him, saying she required nothing more.

The sun was high when they left port. By the time they finally reached the open water of the Mediterranean, the sails billowed with a fine wind and the ship seemed to skip merrily on the water. The three missionaries soon met on deck and found a place to sit to discuss their next missionary venture.

"There will be no stops along the way, so our plan is for Antioch," Paul intoned.

"Yes, Paul, you have been there before. What is your plan?"

"I'll visit the churches already started, make sure they are functioning, preach if requested and try to gain support to go to Sidon then on to Rome," Paul replied.

"You've definitely decided to go to Rome then," Thecla said, much more a statement than a question.

"Yes, I must go to Rome. I feel called there, I'm not sure why," he said, lapsing into a quiet mode Thecla knew not to interrupt.

Zohres broke the silence with a question, "I'm thinking of talking to some of the sailors about our faith. What do you suggest?"

"That is a good idea so long as you only talk to the ones who want to hear your message. We don't want the crew to anger because that will, in turn, anger the captain and we can't afford that," Thecla said.

"Yes, I understand. I'll be careful. I've already been approached by two of them, when they asked about our trip. I told them we are missionaries and they wanted to know more but they had to go back to the oars."

"That's promising. My only words are 'Be careful'," Thecla said. *My concern with him is he's so very anxious to use his new learned technique to teach and preach he'll overdo it and anger those who seem interested. Does he know the finer points of contact; how to tell the difference between casual interest and wanting to explore the depths of faith? Should I try to bring Paul out of his reverie and ask him to watch Zohres? Maybe Zohres must learn this on his own. Maybe I'm worrying too much and Zohres will be all right.*

Thecla remained in her spot. Zohres had gone below, where Paul had discouraged her from going. She slipped into her own reverie as she tried to imagine what Syria would offer and how Paul's churches had fared. *Paul told me there were several large, beautiful temples to locally worshiped gods. Antioch had a large marketplace where goods from the west and east were sold. That is where he found his first converts and his churches started. I wonder if we can find more there now or have all those interested joined one of the existing churches. I doubt that. Even places where established churches are functioning well, there always seem to be more interested in the Word. When I go to the market, I'll concentrate on the booths which sell women's clothing, jewelry and household items. Women often are discouraged from joining groups where men appear to be listening as a group. Of course they should not think that but, too often, they're shooed away by men, usually their husbands. I want to speak to those women, in a group, if that is what must be...*

Thecla continued in that vein of thought until she heard the gong of the dinner bell. Paul reacted quickly, saying, "I'll get us some food. Where is Zohres?"

"He went below to speak with some sailors who he thought were interested in our message. I guess he hasn't returned."

"All right, I'll check on him first then I'll get the food."

Thecla didn't have to wait long for Paul's return. "He's been tied to a post down there and they've been hurling curses and fish guts at him."

"I told him to be careful. He insisted two crew members said they were interested in our message."

"It might have been a lure to get him down there or he might have gone on too long or caused them to take offense without realizing it."

"Perhaps he's not as ready to preach and teach on his own as we thought. He might have mistaken interest and not noticed the sidelong glances the crewmen gave each other, a clear but subtle clue they were up to no good."

"Very true, I'll speak to the captain to see if we can close this issue without further consequence. I'll bring our food as soon as this is resolved."

Thecla settled in to wait. *I hope all goes well for Zohres and he's learned a lesson. Paul will surely help him understand more about selecting well-meaning listeners. It takes practice and experience. Much can go wrong, as Paul and I have experienced. Our good Lord knows how many times we were driven out of cities by people who didn't want to hear our message and didn't want others to hear it, either. Will it help to tell Zohres about that, though? Maybe he has learned something today. I'm sure Paul will discuss it with him. I need to be the voice of support without criticism. Zohres will be a good teacher and preacher, we've heard him. I don't want Zohres to be discouraged by this incident. He just needs to learn from it. It's all part of being a minister...*

Paul and Zohres arrived at that moment with a bowl of stew for Thecla's dinner. Of course, being mariners, the cook had made a delicious smelling fish stew. All three set to eating, without speaking. When they finished the stew, Paul opened the conversation. "The captain was concerned and accompanied me down below to try to find what caused this problem. He had already thought of one sailor and pinpointed him immediately. Apparently he had been a troublemaker on previous trips, though he vowed to be better. The captain banished him to be above and work the sails with two other men, while another took the culprit's place at the oars."

"I see. It sounds as if the captain is a good crew leader."

It was Zohres' turn to speak. Looking sheepish, he confessed, "I mistook their interest in the Truth for just an excuse to have a little fun. I will be more careful in my future encounters with people who show interest. I will, in conversation, try to determine what they want to know and why. Have they heard previous ministers and, if so, what was their message. What sparked their interest in our faith? What have they heard in the past? If they'd heard nothing, I'll inquire as to why they want to hear it now. If the answer sounds contrived, I'll end the conversation as politely as possible."

It sounds as if Paul and he had a serious talk on the way back from below. I'll not say more now, just a few words of encouragement. "That's good, Zohres," said Thecla. "It sounds like you have the right of it."

At this time, they all decided to get some sleep and prepare for landing in Syria in the next few days.

The trip went well and relaxed for the rest of the time. Favorable winds and clear weather put them into the Orontes River port and the trip by cart to Antioch, Syria. The day was clear as the three missionaries left the cart. "We'll follow you, Paul, since you've been here before and know your way around," Thecla said, with Zohres nodding assent.

"All right," Paul said. "We'll go immediately to the first church and see if the leader is about. Hopefully, he'll be willing to take us in or find a member who will."

They trudged along the street leading away from the cart stop. The first church, also the leader's home was an adobe-like house, built of stone, low and unassuming. It looked more as a long shed than a house. "This is the one I remember best. Let's see if Ronal is about," Paul said.

Thecla and Zohres agreed to wait while Paul looked for the church leader. Several minutes later Paul returned with a middle aged man and introduced them to the man named Ronal. *He seems somewhat shy. I'm surprised he's a church leader. He doesn't seem to be one who would go out and spread the word. I'll just have to wait to see if he relaxes and I can learn more about him,* Zohres thought.

Ronal talked exclusively to Paul, seeming to ignore Thecla and Zohres. Paul made an effort to include Zohres in the conversation, moving nearer to him and causing Ronal to follow. Thecla knew she was being sidelined because she was a woman; an unwed woman travelling with two men. This would cause eyebrows to be raised in most cities at the time, which didn't bother her because she knew her heart was pure and so did her

Lord and Savior. Someday, though, in the back of her mind, she hoped the treatment of women would change.

Ronal said he could find room for Paul and Zohres and a woman of the church, Beatrice, would be willing to have Thecla in her home. Beatrice lived not far from Ronal so the group walked the several blocks to their lodgings. Ronal stopped first at Beatrice's home where he introduced Thecla to Beatrice. When all was settled there, he, Paul and Zohres walked another block to Ronal's house. The afternoon was edging toward evening as everyone sat in their respective lodgings for the evening meal and discussions of what might be next.

The next day, Beatrice and Thecla decided to go to the market. Paul and Zohres accompanied Ronal to call on a few of the church members nearby. Paul wanted to see some of the members, new and ones he'd baptized. Zohres was anxious to see the area, meet more members and, perhaps, glean a bit more information on how to form and institutionalize a church. He knew some but wanted to learn as much as possible from Paul and Ronal. He'd found Ronal to be an interesting fellow, much more likeable than he'd first surmised.

Beatrice and Thecla were becoming fast friends from the start. Thecla found Beatrice to be outgoing and friendly without spending great effort to know every detail of her life. Each was willing to wait for the other to open their past experiences as time and opportunity lent itself, the making of a true friendship. As they entered the marketplace, Thecla suggested they visit jewelry and women's clothing booths, figuring to find women who might be willing to hear the Word.

Several women were open to discussion and listening. Beatrice and Thecla suggested to the group to move to a quiet corner for further discussion. After about an hour the women were invited to the church for services and the group disbanded. Feeling as if they'd accomplished a worthwhile morning, they continued to shop and returned to Beatrice's home.

Paul, Zohres and Ronal went to the area of the house reserved for church services and discussed some minor renovations Ronal was hoping to make in the next year. Funds were always hard to come by and Rome seemed to be ever more vigilant of their activities. Paul was aware of Rome's tightening control in the outer areas, because, he reasoned, they had determined they were losing control at home; therefore, they were certain the entire empire was in danger. "It is only a matter of time," Ronal was saying, in a low voice, just above a whisper, "until they come and close us down. We'll have to move underground, maybe meet in small groups at members' homes again."

"That is unfortunate," Paul said. "We can't stop spreading the Word."

"No, we can't," agreed Ronal. "We'll have to change tactics and speak to individuals who wish to hear us in a small, known group."

"No more large groups as we had in Iconium?" asked Zohres.

"Not here," Ronal said. "The governor is a Roman, or at least tightly connected to Rome. That's how he was appointed. He thinks he'll be rewarded if he stamps out Christianity."

"We can't change that way of thinking, just have to do what is required for everyone's safety," admitted Paul.

"That doesn't sound like you, Paul," Zohres commented.

"It's not our safety that concerns me, it's our followers, the church members," Paul retorted.

"Yes, that concerns me too; that's why I'm leaning toward meeting in selected homes in smaller groups, if it seems to be getting worse," Ronal said.

"How will you know which homes are safest?" Zohres asked.

"I don't right now, I'd have to confer with other members who help me and know the community and individual church members. I used to know them all but we've grown larger and I haven't been able to keep up with all the new arrivals," Ronal said. Then he suggested, "Let's go back to my home, see if Beatrice and Thecla wish to join us for the evening meal."

Paul, Zohres and Ronal met Beatrice and Thecla as they arrived home and the women arrived after their shopping experience. It was only after everyone was inside the house and comfortable that Ronal and Beatrice disclosed they were fourth degree cousins and planned to marry. This was welcome news to the visitors and much joking and well-wishing ensued. Buoyed by the response, Ronal announced he would have a servant open an expensive cask of wine he had purchased some time ago. Ronal had two servants, a man and a woman who he introduced as Kena and Patel. Kena took control of the kitchen upon arrival and Patel was an all-round helper wherever needed. After the servants left, Thecla asked Ronal, "I didn't think you'd have servants. Isn't that unusual in your community?"

"Yes, I suppose you need an explanation. Patel and Kena escaped from a slave vessel that arrived a few years ago. They escaped, running at night through the dark streets, avoiding the Roman guards. They appeared at the back door, I talked to them while they begged me to take them in as servants. I said I didn't need servants but they said that was the only way they would not be found. They would stay out of sight and I'd be in no danger. I agreed, somewhat skeptical but it has worked well so far," Ronal said.

"So you've been able to do the Lord's work, right under the Romans' noses," Zohres commented.

"It does seem that way, at least so far," Ronal agreed, smiling in self-satisfaction.

"But, we can't take anything for granted," Beatrice said. "Kena doesn't go to the market. I do all the shopping for the households. Ronal goes out if anything outside is needed to be done. You see, Patel and Kena have chosen this life instead of slavery. Ronal provides a comfortable place to live, food and clothing and pays them an allowance, which they are saving for the future, if they're ever allowed to go out again."

"That's the way to treat people as God's people," Thecla said. "We should always treat others as we would wish to be treated."

"Yes, we see Patel and Kena as our brother and sister and try to treat them as such," Beatrice said.

At this point, Kena announced the evening meal was ready and all should join at the table. True to Beatrice's statement, Kena and Patel were seated at the table with Beatrice, Ronal and the three guests. Conversation during dinner was light, consisting, primarily of the local events, the marketplace and the church.

Paul talked about his plan to go to Sidon to visit the church there and, perhaps, go on to Jerusalem. "I want to visit the church in Sidon to see how they're faring. It was small and not too promising when I left. Perhaps, it needs more teaching."

"Perhaps, that would be a place where I could help," interjected Zohres.

"Yes, I was thinking that could be a place for you to exhibit your skills and, perhaps, work indefinitely," Paul said.

"I appreciate your faith in me. I welcome a place where I can spread the Word," Zohres said.

Ronal expressed a warning to the visitors. "I bid you take caution when traveling to and visiting Sidon. The Romans are active there. The church, if it survived, may be underground. The Roman armed force is arresting citizens, especially Christians, as enemies of the Empire."

"We will take heed," Paul said. "We are used to being run out of cities and dodging unfriendly forces."

"The Romans have increased their pressure here, more so than other parts of the Empire, so I've heard," countered Ronal.

"Why might that be the case?" asked Thecla.

"Apparently, there is much wickedness in the Imperial court and, they think, it's coming from here all the way to Alexandria. So, they have tightened surveillance of community gatherings, especially Christian gatherings. There are other Jewish-Christian 'look-alikes' in many communities, which are possible problems, too," Ronal answered.

"We will not travel the main roads most of the way and Zohres and Thecla will dress and act as my slaves as we transverse the roads, stopping at villages to stay the night," Paul offered.

"Yes, do your best to not attract attention and appear to be locals moving about," said Beatrice.

"It may work, but may God be with you. These are dangerous times, so be cautious," Ronal said.

The dinner ended and Beatrice and Thecla went to Beatrice's home. Paul and Zohres spent more time conferring with Ronal as they discussed leaving for Sidon the next day.

Beatrice and Thecla, with satchel in hand arrived at Ronal's house early the next morning. Kena was preparing the morning meal, while Paul and Zohres were packing their few belongings, with Ronal's assistance. "Please sit at table for the morning meal," Kena said.

Everyone sat and Paul began the morning prayer, "Bless us, oh Lord, for this bountiful food and bless those who have provided for us on this visit. We beg for safe keeping of our fellow members here in Antioch and throughout this worldly empire. We also beg for our safety on our travels to Sidon that we may spread your Word to secure everlasting salvation for all believers."

The morning meal was consumed in somber reflection after the prayer; each lost in his or her own thoughts. Paul, Zohres and Thecla rose to bid farewell and thanks to Ronal and Beatrice for their hospitality. Ronal and Beatrice wished them safe travels, Ronal with worried, lowered eyes and Beatrice hugging Thecla with tears glistening in her eyes.

Outside, the three travelers loaded their bags onto the cart. Paul took the reins of the mule, Thecla climbed in the back of the cart, while Zohres, as any male slave would, followed on foot. Eventually, Thecla would follow on foot, Zohres would take the reins and Paul would ride in the cart. Paul insisted on taking his turn as a "slave", allowing Zohres to be the "slave owner". Thecla knew, as a woman, she could not be a "slave-owner"; if she could have been, she would have to be moneyed beyond measure and would not have been able to play that role, nor would she have wanted it. That role was beyond her calling as an evangelist. As Paul had discussed with Ronal and the others at the evening meal, they took back roads and stopped at numerous villages along the way.

The missionaries arrived in Sidon twenty-five days after they left Antioch, tired and dust-covered. They stopped at an inn to obtain two rooms for the night, where they could bathe, get a warm meal and rest. When all was accomplished, Paul told Zohres they'd go out tomorrow to find the whereabouts of the church he'd left some two years ago. "Thecla will stay here until we are sure it is a safe place for her to teach," Paul said.

"Have you told Thecla that?" Zohres asked.

"No, I'll tell her tomorrow morning," Paul said.

"You must know how she'll react to that," Zohres said, with a twitch at the corner of his mouth.

"She won't like it but it may not be safe for her."

"That may be but Thecla is not known to be worried about her safety when it comes to spreading the Word."

"I know but I worry about her sometimes..." Zohres nodded, knowing nothing more needed to be said.

At the morning meal the next morning, Paul launched into details of the day, "Thecla, Zohres and I will go out to try to find the church I started two years ago. Please stay here until we return for you."

"What? Why am I not going out with you and Zohres now?" asked Thecla, incensed. Zohres was studying his meal intensely.

"Remember how Ronal warned us about the Roman cohort here. We don't want any trouble or calling attention to ourselves. A woman walking with two men may cause jeering and attention," Paul reasoned.

"I don't remember Ronal speaking about a whole Roman cohort, just some Romans. They're everywhere. Why are they suddenly so important?" asked Thecla, vehemently.

"Yes, they are everywhere but Ronal said they are looking for trouble, especially from Christians. Why is staying here for a while such a problem?" asked Paul.

"You know I can take care of myself, I have my knife in my belt."

"That wouldn't be enough if several Romans grab us. Please just stay here for the morning and we'll return and tell you what we found."

Realizing this argument was going nowhere, Thecla relented and agreed she would go to her room and pray for them.

Paul and Zohres left then to try to find the church, relieved Thecla agreed to stay behind.

Outside, when their eyes adjusted to the bright sunshine, Paul said, "Let's stay on this street leading toward the docks, it looks vaguely familiar. We shouldn't go all the way to the docks; the meeting place won't be there, besides it could be trouble."

"I understand," Zohres said. "It might be dangerous to ask anyone, too."

"Yes, we'll just have to keep looking. Look for an unassuming structure that may look like a shed, perhaps, overgrown with bushes or weeds."

About a half hour later, they saw such a shed under a large tree, with vines covering most of the building.

"Might there be anyone in there at this time of day?" Zohres asked.

"I doubt it. Let's watch it for a while to see if anyone comes by," Paul answered.

They sat under the tree where they could see the shed but a distance from the street. They retrieved food from their robe pockets to alleviate their hunger. No one came near the shed; making Paul more convinced this was the place.

Just as they rose to leave, two Roman soldiers advanced to them and grabbed their arms, twisting them behind their backs, shouting orders in Latin. Though Paul and Zohres understood them, the rough treatment resulted in hollering and loud talking. Zohres struggled mightily, Paul resisted more by talking. Zohres' struggle took him toward Paul and his captor. As Zohres made one final shove of his captor, they stumbled into Paul and his captor which meant all four of them were thrashing about on the ground. One of the soldiers was able to pull his sword out of the scabbard. He struggled to get his footing as the others fought. He got up, threatening to behead them both right there. Zohres was close enough to the Roman to grab his leg and, caused him to fall, the sword dropping out of reach.

Suddenly, a woman's commanding voice sounded, "Stop it right now. Get to your feet and show respect." Paul recognized the voice immediately. *How did she get here? Why?*

Zohres thought he recognized the voice too. *Thecla?*

The two Roman soldiers finally found their feet. All the men were bloody and filthy.

"Pickup that sword and leave," Thecla told the soldiers. Still in shock and bleeding, they hurried away. She stood, pointing her knife at them.

"Thecla, we're glad you came," Paul said.

"How did you find us?" Zohres asked.

"Someone came into the inn shouting about a disturbance down by the docks, I surmised it may be you two out looking for a church, perhaps getting into trouble," Thecla said, *as men are prone to do*, she thought but didn't put into words.

"You stopped the fight single-handed with your commanding voice. I didn't know you could sound that way," Paul said.

"I've learned over time, it works," Thecla said, *sometimes*, she wanted to add but didn't.

"I think we best go back to the inn. We think the church may be in that shed over there covered in vines," Paul told Thecla, pointing in the direction of the shed.

"Yes, that may be it. I think each of us should take turns watching for someone to come to it" she said.

"I agree," Zohres said. "I'll take the first watch."

"Until dark this evening?" Paul asked.

"Yes," Zohres answered.

"I think it's best if we all go back to the inn now and start our watch tomorrow." Thecla said. No one argued and they returned to the inn to clean up and rest.

Two days later, Zohres observed two men enter the shed. He decided to follow them. He approached the shed and rapped on the door. "Secret code," he heard a man holler.

"I don't know it," he called as quietly as he could. "I am with the teacher Paul."

A few seconds later, he heard shuffling as someone approached and opened the door.

Through the small opening, Zohres saw two dark eyes and a mouth, "What do you want?"

"I'm with the teacher, Paul. We were looking for the church he started here. He wants to visit and speak to the congregation at your next service."

"How did you know to find us?"

"Paul sent me here because he remembered vaguely where the church he founded was located."

"Did you ask anyone about the whereabouts of the church?"

"No, we were warned when we were in Antioch about the Roman guard."

"Come in then." He opened the door enough for Zohres to slide in sideways and immediately put the bar down to lock the door.

The men introduced themselves and began to talk again. This time, the second man said "We heard about a disturbance close by the other day, two men and two Roman soldiers and a woman showed up and it stopped quickly."

"Yes," Zohres said. "That was Paul and me watching this place to see if anyone came by. He was hoping to talk to whomever is the church leader."

"That could have ended much differently for you and us. We were not here at the time but could have been. Neither of us is the church leader but our next service is tomorrow mid-day, if there are no more incidents and no one else is found skulking around," the man said, with a slight smile.

"The service will begin at midday and last about two hours," the first man said. "We are a small community; many are too frightened of the Romans to attend. That is why we meet here. No one wants a meeting in their home."

"I shall tell Paul I met you and he will want to come to the service. By the way, the woman who broke up the disturbance was Thecla, Paul's follower and an evangelist. I, too, follow Paul and am a fledgling minister."

"Welcome to all three of you. We look forward to seeing you at the service tomorrow. The secret code is one short rap and one hard rap."

"Thank you. I must leave now. We'll return midday tomorrow."

The first man opened the door a crack to peek out, saw the area was free of Romans and any other passersby, signaling to Zohres it was clear for his departure. Without any more words, he departed, heard the bar descend and hurried away.

He arrived back at the inn met Paul and Thecla seated at a table, preparing to eat an early evening meal; early, because Paul was readying himself for the next shift of observation of the shed.

"I found them," Zohres said, as he slid into a seat. "Two men came to the shed and entered. I followed them, knocked on the door but didn't know the secret code. I told them I was with you and they decided to open the door a crack to check me out. Then they let me in, introduced themselves and said neither was the leader but he would be at the service tomorrow. The service is at mid-day tomorrow and we're all invited to attend."

"That's wonderful news, Zohres," said Paul.

"They are quite nervous about the Romans," Zohres said and placed his order with the inn attendant, who was waiting patiently.

"I'm sure they are. I'm surprised they answered your knock," Thecla said.

"I was prepared for them not to answer. I gave them a little more detail when I got inside," Zohres said.

"Thank you, Zohres. We'll gladly attend the service tomorrow. Glad you got the secret code, we may need it," Thecla said.

"We'll talk more about this upstairs after eating," Paul said.

They finished the meal and went upstairs to Paul's room to plan for attendance at the service the next day.

The day dawned bright and cool, with a steady breeze off the water. Thecla rose early to attend to her regular ministrations. She heard Paul and Zohres in another room doing the same. They would be leaving in the later morning for the service so they planned to stroll by the docks to pass the time.

Walking to the docks, the three talked of their impending address to the congregation.

"Paul, what approach do you suggest?" asked Thecla.

""I want to welcome them then begin with a prayer, as we usually do. From there, we need to remind them of God's love and ask if there are questions or events, which are uppermost on their minds," Paul said.

"Are we going to have a discussion group and not a teaching time?" asked Zohres.

"Yes, I think that is best, in this case," Paul answered. "I think the Romans may be key concern of the Christians', at this time."

"What information or counsel can we give them?" asked Zohres.

"We can listen to their statements and point out to them, Jesus walked this same line," Thecla said.

"That's right," Paul agreed. "We will remind them they are blessed because they believe in God. 'Blessed are those who are persecuted for righteousness' sake, for theirs is the kingdom of heaven'."

"Yes, we strive to give them something to hold on to, when their lives seem near to being out of control," summed Thecla.

As they approached the docks, a ship captain, who recognized Paul said, "What brings ya' here? Ya' certainly didn't come here to greet the Romans, did ya'?" he asked, jokingly.

"No we didn't," answered Paul. "Are there new Romans here?"

"Yeah, ships 've been comin' into the port for several days now," the captain said.

"From Rome?" asked Paul.

"Naugh, from Caesarea," was the answer. "Place is swarmin' with 'em, better watch your step."

"Thanks for the warning," Paul rejoined.

After this exchange Paul motioned for Zohres and Thecla to draw close, out of earshot of the dock employees. "There are many Romans here now, apparently from Caesarea. I'm not sure what that means but we should be aware of it," Paul said.

"Let's go back to the service so we can mingle with the congregants as they arrive," suggested Thecla.

Paul and Zohres nodded agreement and they walked, silently, all in their own thoughts, to the service. *What does it mean, all these new Roman soldiers converging on Sidon? I hope they don't interrupt the service. What can we do if they come in? Will they arrest us? Drive the people out? Kill some or all?* Thecla thought about these scenarios as she walked. The news had stilled their enthusiasm for the bright, sunny day; instead, it filled them with a measure of dread.

As they neared the shed, which was now open to the arriving church members, they quickened their steps. Several members recognized Paul and began a discussion. Paul introduced Zohres and he joined the discussion. Thecla introduced herself to several of the women and they, too, became immersed in conversation. A little later, the church leader called everyone inside to begin the service.

After the church members were seated, the church leader introduced Paul, Thecla and Zohres. Paul rose and began the service with a prayer. "Our Lord, Jesus, walks among us even though we cannot see Him. We feel His presence when we see the dawn of a warm, sunny day; when we partake of sustenance with our family and/or friends, when we gather for a service, when we sleep at night. We especially feel His presence when we see the arrival of more Roman soldiers. Then we know he is calling on us to be brave, beg for His help and re-pledge our devotion to Him. Let us this day, ask the Almighty to sanctify us and give us hope and salvation." The congregants gave their assent, standing a little taller and with eyes averted upward.

Paul had just concluded the prayer and readying to begin a discussion when there was a loud sound of hobnailed sandals on the rocks outside the shed. Moments later, a loud voice in Latin said, "We have come to disrupt and dissolve this Christian gathering." Immediately, six Roman soldiers took Paul and the church leader quickly grasping their arms and twisted them behind, while affixing chains to their wrists. The church members were driven out, including Thecla and Zohres. Thecla tried to go back into the shed but was barred strongly by two soldiers. Thecla begged the soldier to let her back inside, "I need to go back inside. I need to know Paul is all right."

"You don't need to go back. He's all right. We'll take care of him," the soldier said, as he held her from moving forward.

"Why are you doing this? We haven't caused any trouble."

"Oh, but you have. We can't have all these fake religions popping up in the empire. It causes disruption."

"You're causing disruption. We were quietly listening to Paul."

"You won't be quiet long. Now, move away from here. Go back to your home. Be gone," he shouted, as he shoved her, causing her to fall.

Zohres left the small gathering of church members who stood a distance away watching Thecla and the soldiers. He helped her stand and started to walk away when the soldier said, "Get her out of here and yourself, too. We want no more of these gatherings."

Zohres helped Thecla limp back to the inn where they all had rooms. So shocked and dismayed, neither spoke until they were in her room.

"Zohres, I'm worried about Paul. What will happen to him?"

"I'm worried too. They seemed to grab him first and most brutally. I think they've been waiting for him."

"I'm glad you were waiting a little further away and you didn't try to go back inside."

"No, I wanted to but I was consoling a church member who was terrified and caused a soldier to strike her."

"This is a terrible time. I need to know what's going to happen to Paul."

"I'll go out to see if I can find anything, you rest here and stay out of sight."

Zohres left the inn, not sure which direction to take but decided to walk to the docks. He stopped at an inn that catered to sailors. They served food and wine and other alcoholic drinks. He ordered some food and a cup of wine, sat and listened to the talk of other tables close by. Sure enough, he overheard mention of the church disturbance. "Yeah, they arrested one and they're gonna haul 'im off to Caesarea. They been watchin' for 'im for a long time."

"What was his name again?"

"Paul, I think I heard."

"Wonder what they'll do with 'im?

"Don't know, they might ship 'im back to Rome."

"Possibility."

Zohres had heard enough and all he needed to hear. He decided to take the information back to Thecla. As he walked, he turned the information over in his mind. *Taking him to Caesarea...probably have a sham trial and ship him back to Rome. That's what the governors always do; send 'trouble makers' back to Rome so they don't have to make the final decision. Of course, Paul was not a trouble maker but, in Caesarea, who will know or care?*

Zohres arrived at the inn and knocked on Thecla's door.

"Thecla, I have information for you." He heard the bolt being lifted and the door open.

Come in Thecla motioned, with a sweep of her hand. After shutting and bolting the door, she asked "What have you heard?"

Zohres, lowering his voice to just above a whisper, repeated the conversation between the sailors he'd overheard.

Thecla became immediately distraught. "What can we do? We have to stop them."

"No, Thecla. We can't stop them. Sadly, there is nothing we can do."

"There must be something. He must be still here, somewhere."

"Even if he's still here. We can't help him now."

"We can find the Roman camp and beg for his release."

"Thecla, take a few minutes to think about what you're saying. You know better. You know how the Romans work. They've been watching Paul for some years now, they consider him a trouble maker—a threat to the Empire."

"But he's none of that. Don't you see?"

"Of course, we know that. The Romans don't care about what we say."

"Then I'll go to Rome and find him there."

"He'll be in a prison. You'll never find him."

"We need to leave here and go back to Antioch and visit the friends we left when we came here."

"Yes, but that's a long trip. It will take weeks to get back there walking; yet we do need to speak with Ronal and Beatrice again. She is helpful. Ronal may have some suggestions, also."

"Quite true. Patel and Kena are good people too."

"And so they are. How should we travel?"

"I saw many carts and wagons hauling merchandise and several riders on the back of the wagons. We could probably ride on one of those."

"Yes, we have money Paul left us. We can use that if the wagon master asks for payment."

"We need to pack our satchels and be on the road tomorrow morning. We have to leave this Roman infested town."

"All right, I'll pack my things and be ready to leave early tomorrow morning."

Zohres returned to his room; Thecla continued her prayers and contemplation until the evening meal.

Zohres knocked on Thecla's door shortly after dawn the next morning. She unbolted the door and whispered, "I'm ready." Each carrying a bag, they descended the stairs and took a seat where the morning meal was served. They consumed slices of meat, eggs and bread; Zohres ordered extra bread and six slices of meat for the trip. They planned to walk and find a willing merchant, with whom to ride to Antioch.

It was late in the day, several days later, when they reached Ronal's house. Zohres knocked on Ronal's door but they heard nothing. Zohres continued to knock several more times before they heard mumbling and the bolt being lifted. "Who is it?" asked Ronal from behind the door, opened only a crack.

"It's Zohres and Thecla," Zohres said. "Please let us in. We can explain."

"Please come in," Ronal said, sounding much more awake. "Where is Paul?"

"That's what we want to tell you," Zohres said.

"Wait a minute. I'll get Beatrice. Please have a seat, I'll be right back," Ronal said.

The seats looked inviting after their long trip on a produce wagon. Zohres and Thecla settled on the padded chairs, exhaling in relief. Several minutes later, Ronal and Beatrice entered the room. Beatrice brought two cups of water and offered them to Thecla and Paul—each, accepting a cup, gladly.

"Now, please tell us why Paul is not with you," Ronal said.

Thecla began to tell them what they'd been doing, with Zohres adding details now and again. When she got to the part of Paul's arrest, Thecla became emotional and could not continue. Beatrice held her and Zohres picked up the story, ending with their arrival at Ronal's house.

Everyone sat quiet for several minutes. Thecla stopped sobbing and gained control. Beatrice finally stood and said, "This is terrible news. We can't solve the problem tonight. Please take the rooms you stayed in before and we'll talk more about it when we're rested and can see the matter with clearer minds."

"Excellent suggestion, Beatrice. Yes, take the rooms down the hall and join us for the morning meal. We will talk more then," Ronal said.

Bags in hand, Thecla and Zohres made their way to the rooms where they were to sleep. It took little time for the house to go dark and quiet, again.

Morning found all four people breaking their fast. Beatrice asked Zohres and Thecla, "Have you thought of any recourse?"

"I must find where they're taking Paul. I will follow where ever they take him," Thecla said, in a voice solid with affirmation.

"I want to stay in Sidon and work with the churches there," declared Zohres.

"You plan to return to Sidon?" Ronal asked.

"Thecla, you have chosen a difficult path to tread. We will help as much as we can but discovering what the Romans will do with Paul is not an easy task," Beatrice said.

"Yes, I realize that," Thecla said, "and I don't mean to lean on you for determining the truth. We'll go back to Sidon and maybe find Paul."

"No, you'll not be leaning on us but there is only so much you can accomplish, safely," Ronal said. "Zohres can go to the docks to listen and inquire of a few friends who might have seen or overheard Romans talking. That, I think, is the first and best place to hear any news."

"That makes sense. I'll go with him," Thecla said.

"Oh, no, Thecla. That is not a place you should go. Besides, they'd be more likely to share information, if a woman were not present," Ronal said.

"Why is that the case? I want to hear about Paul. What if he is there?" Thecla stated.

"Seaman don't talk when women are around. That's just the way they are. They haven't changed in hundreds of years," Ronal explained.

"All right then, we'll see what we can find out," Thecla said, in a bit of a huff.

Ronal said he would find a wagon and mule for them to traverse back to Sidon.

The sun had passed its zenith, when Ronal arrived home to give Thecla the information he'd learned. "Thecla, I have some information for you," Ronal called.

Thecla came rushing down the hall, "What have you found?" she asked, breathlessly.

"Please have a seat," Ronal said, as he called Beatrice to listen, also.

"I found a mule and wagon for your trip to Sidon. The driver will return with wines I've ordered."

"Thank you and God bless you, Ronal," Thecla said.

"Be sure to look for Thiam and Rose when you get to Sidon. The church leader will know how to find them," Beatrice said.

When Zohres arrived, Thecla told him the news. They agreed to leave tomorrow morning when the wagon arrived.

The next morning, shortly after sun rise, the wagon arrived. Thecla and Zohres boarded the wagon, waved farewell to Ronal and Beatrice and the wagon rolled off.

Four days later, they arrived in Sidon. Zohres asked the driver to deliver them to the inn he pointed out; the one they'd stayed in when they'd arrived with Paul. They checked in and were assigned the same rooms they'd had before.

"I am glad we went back to visit Ronal and Beatrice. They were helpful and generous," Thecla said.

"Yes, but we should have stayed here and not made such a hasty trip, even though we were able to get a ride most of the way," Zohres recounted.

"Yes, that is behind us. Now, we must get as much information as we can about Paul."

"I'll go to the docks tomorrow morning to listen and find anyone who has any information."

"All right, I'll wait here for you."

"I'll meet you tomorrow morning, before I leave for the docks."

After they broke their fast, Zohres left for the docks and Thecla went to her room to pray and contemplate.

Several hours had passed when there was a loud knock on her door.

"Who is it?" Thecla asked, tentatively.

"Zohres. Please open."

He heard the bolt rise and the door open. He entered and Thecla lowered the bolt again.

"I heard much," Zohres began,

"What did you hear," Thecla asked, before he could continue.

"I overheard a group of sailors talking about a Roman prisoner being taken to Caesarea."

"Did they mention his name?" Thecla asked.

"No, but I'm quite certain it was Paul they were talking about."

"Can you find out when they'll leave? Was Paul there?" Thecla asked.

"No Paul was not at the docks. I believe it was Paul; who else would be transferring to Caesarea?"

"There may be other prisoners."

"Yes, but this prisoner was detained after a disturbance at a church service a few days ago. It all seems to fit."

"You didn't say that."

"You didn't give me a chance," Zorhes said, testily. "I'll go back to the docks in a couple of hours, when there'll be more information. Don't want to be hanging around and seem too interested."

"That's wise. Sorry, I'm just so worried about Paul." Thecla said.

"Yes, I am worried, too."

After another visit to the docks, Zohres had managed to speak to the captain of the ship bound for Caesarea. He returned as fast as possible with news for Thecla.

After knocking at her door again and gaining entrance, he began to relay the information he'd gathered, "The Romans will take Paul to Caesarea,"

"What can we do?" Thecla asked, as tears glistened in her eyes.

"Nothing more, at this time," Zohres said.

"Let's find Thiam and Rose. Ronal and Beatrice said they might give us shelter until we get more information. They can give you details about working on gathering more converts, also," Thecla said.

"Indeed. I'd almost forgotten that, being so interested in finding word of Paul," Zohres said.

Thecla and Zohres spent the next few days, looking for Thiam and Rose through the church leaders. When they found Thiam and Rose, help and shelter were given immediately. Thiam and Rose welcomed Thecla and Zohres, pleased to hear Beatrice and Ronal were well and had recommended them. Thiam and Rose showed Thecla and Zohres their rooms, Thiam and Rose settled the visitors with a cup of wine to discuss, further, the disturbance at the church and Paul's arrest. Thecla and Zohres didn't learn any new facts because they'd experienced the disturbance, first-hand. They did learn more about the arrest, though. Paul was taken to a Roman holding facility outside of town where he was beaten and threatened. This word came to Thiam and Rose through a worker at the facility, who was also a church member.

Zohres' detail from the captain was authenticated by Thiam, who related Paul's impending forced trip, by ship, to Caesarea to be tried by the Governor.

"How long will all that take?" Thecla asked.

Thiam shrugged, "It's hard to say, maybe months, maybe years."

"Can we go to Caesarea?" Thecla asked.

"It would not be advisable," Thiam said. "It would not be in Paul's best interest, either. It is best to wait here for further word."

"But how will we know if he's sent to Rome?" Thecla asked.

"They'd surely come through this port, no ship will go directly to Rome from Caesarea, without passing through this port," Thiam said.

"All right," Thecla said, resignedly.

Chapter 10. Thecla and Paul in Rome

Two years later, Thecla finished her time of prayer and meditation, when Thiam burst through the door. He grabbed a stool and sat. Finally catching his breath, he said, "Thecla, please sit."

"What is it?" she asked.

"Paul is here," Thiam said.

"Paul, here, in Sidon?" Thecla asked, incredulously.

"Yes, he's on his way to Rome but a centurion of the Augustan cohort named Julius is allowing him to visit friends for a little recovery time."

"Is he ill?" worried Thecla.

"Perhaps, somewhat emaciated after all this time in prison."

"Where is he now?"

"They'll disembark and be here in an hour or two."

"We must have something for him to eat."

"Yes, please; I'll tell Rose, she'll be ready to work with you."

It was evening before Paul finally arrived at Thiam's door. Julius said he had other prisoners with whom to deal and would be back to check on Paul tomorrow morning. Paul must stay in Thiam's house and Thiam would be held accountable. Thiam agreed and Julius departed.

Paul shuffled to a seat and took it with a groan.

"We're ready for the evening meal, Paul. I'm so glad you are here to join us," Thecla said.

"Welcome, Paul. Please join us this fine evening," Rose said.

Paul looked sallow and so weak, he could barely sit upright. He smiled gratefully, though, and took a meager helping of fruits, cheese and bread. Thiam poured wine for everyone then sat and began the evening prayer. The prayer finished, they consumed their meal. No one talked because they wished for Paul to have time to eat. His weakness caused him to eat slowly.

After Paul finished eating, Thecla asked "Paul, can you tell us a little about how you got here and where you are heading?"

"Yes, I can tell a little but I might trail off, as my thinking is diminished now," he said. Then he began, "When it was decided we would sail for Italy, they proceeded to deliver me and some other prisoners to a centurion of the Augustan cohort named Julius. Embarking in an Adramyttian ship, which was about to sail to the regions along the coast of Asia, we put out to sea accompanied by Aristarchus, a Macedonian of Thessalonica. The next day we put in here. Julius wants me to recover; it wouldn't do for me to die before I get to Rome." Paul's sense of humor shone through his weakness.

Thecla smiled and asked, "Why did it take so long?"

"There were multiple trials in different courts. I'll explain it all tomorrow," Paul said, as he began to sink lower in his chair.

"Come, Paul, we must take you to your room. We'll talk more when you are ready," Rose said. Thiam stood and he and Zohres helped Paul settle in his room.

When they returned, Thiam said, "Paul is in bad shape. He may have at least one broken bone. We'll see to that tomorrow."

"I doubt he'll be up and around for several days," Rose observed.

"I agree, Rose. I wonder how patient the Romans will be," Thecla said.

"I suspect not very patient. Though Paul tried to jest, I think there was a large measure of truth to his last statement," Thiam said.

The next morning dawned bright and cloudless. The house was quiet with only small sounds of Rose in the kitchen, preparing the morning meal. Thecla joined Rose in the kitchen. Zohres and Thiam came to the table before being called to break their fast.

"Thiam or Zohres please check on Paul," Rose asked.

Both men stood at that request and walked toward Paul's room.

"It's quiet," Thiam whispered.

"Yes, he may be still sleeping," whispered Zohres.

Thiam tapped lightly on Paul's door. No response. He tapped again, louder. Nothing.

"Paul?" Zohres called. No response.

"Let's go in," Thiam said. Zohres nodded in agreement.

Thiam opened the door, both men entered. They found Paul, seeming to be asleep.

"Paul, wake up," Zohres said, nudging him softly. No response. After trying again multiple times, Zohres leaned to listen for Paul's heartbeat or breathing. It was a faint sound but Paul was alive.

"He's unconscious, I think," Zohres stated.

"Let's eat the morning meal and check back," Thiam said.

Both men left the room, closing the door behind them.

After taking seats at the table, Zohres said, "Paul may be worse than we thought. He seems to be unconscious. We couldn't wake him, though I heard a heartbeat"

"What can we do to help him?" Thecla asked, in a worried voice.

"Nothing at the moment," Thiam said. "After we finish eating, we'll go back to him and feel for broken bones, if we find any we'll set them while he's unconscious. You and Rose should check him for fever and any other obvious signs."

Nodding in agreement, they finished eating and prepared to work with Paul.

Two hours later, they'd finished setting Paul's broken arm and wrist, cleaning him and checking for fever. They also found several skull indentations, which were probably healed skull fractures. He still had several bruises in various states of healing.

"There is nothing more we can do now until he wakes. It may be at least another day," Thiam said.

"That it may be," Zohres said. "I'll go to the church to see if they need more help."

"I'll go with you. I'm sure they'll want to hear about Paul. If there's two of us, they may be more inclined to stop their work and listen," Thiam said.

"Don't you think they'd listen to me?" Zohres asked, feeling offended.

"No, it's not that at all," Thiam said, placing his hand in Zohres' shoulder. "I will stand watch outside the door, so all the others can remain inside to hear your news."

"Ah, yes, I remember now how you have to be careful of intrusion by the Romans," Zohres said.

"Yes, exactly," Thiam said as they donned their plain, brown cloaks to go to the church.

At the church, both men were admitted readily. Thiam took his place outside the door behind some vines while Zohres lead a short prayer and gave his news about Paul. The six church members listened quietly, asking few questions after Zohres finished. No one was surprised, only somewhat awed by the news of his being allowed to heal. *So un-Roman,* was the thought. The church leader lifted the bar and Zohres stepped outside, motioned for Thiam and left without a word.

Two days later, Thecla found Paul awake when she entered his room. His eyes were open and he was staring at the ceiling. She did not wish to disturb him because he might have been praying. Thecla walked around the foot of the bed, when he suddenly croaked "Wa-ter."

"Oh, Paul," she said, "I'll get you some."

In a few seconds she returned with a cup about half-full of water. "Here you are. Please sip it slowly," she said, as she held the cup to his lips.

"Ahhh," he said, as his head dropped back to the pillow. "Bless you," he said, as he closed his eyes and proceeded to go back to sleep.

Thecla wasn't sure he knew who brought the water but it didn't matter. Her mood was elevated just by having heard his voice. *Now, he's sure to recover,* thought Thecla. *My prayers are being answered. Surely, the Romans will think kindly of him after such long, dreadful treatment. I'll pray they think he's suffered enough and allow him freedom. I'll ask Thiam, Rose and Zohres to pray, along with me. Maybe we can ask the entire congregation to pray for his freedom, too.*

"You're asking God for the impossible, Thecla," Thiam said, in response to her request for prayer, later that day.

"Oh, Thiam, where is your faith in God?" Thecla said. She was so caught in the need to beg for help for Paul, she didn't mean to be questioning Thiam's faith.

"Thecla, my faith in God is true and strong. I just feel we must do everything we can for Paul and trust God will watch over him. You know, if He chooses to call Paul home, He will do it," Thiam said.

"Yes, what you say is true but we could still ask God to consider freeing him from the Romans," Thecla countered.

"Yes, we can do that but how God chooses to free him might not be how we wish it to be," Thiam said, gently putting his arm around her shoulder as she dissolved into tears. "Though it will be hard for us to accept, if God calls Paul to his heavenly home, we must rejoice in God's benevolent wisdom." *Not feel sorry for ourselves,* he thought.

At the end of the week, Julius decided Paul had recovered enough to resume travel to Rome. Thiam answered the routine knock on the door, knowing it was likely Julius. "Hello, Julius," Thiam greeted.

"Hello, Thiam. I'm here to take Paul and the other prisoners to the docks to resume our voyage to Rome," Julius said.

"I think it's a little too soon. Paul is not ready to resume travel; he's just begun to eat normally."

"That's a good sign. He's bandaged and wearing a splint on his arm for healing. That's all we need."

"He'll weaken again on ship food and, maybe, be re-injured if tossed about in a storm."

"That could apply to all of us, Thiam. We're leaving with the tide, so hand him over."

"This is against my better judgment, as Paul's friend."

"So noted," Julius said, with a smile, part sneer.

Thiam knew there was no point in arguing with a Roman and, if he continued, it could go bad for Paul. "All right," Thiam said. "I'll bring Paul to the door."

Several minutes later, Thiam arrived at the door with Paul. "God bless you and your household," Paul said, looking at Thiam. Then turning to Julius, he said "Let us be gone. It is God's will I go to Rome as a prisoner."

The sun was low in the sky when Zohres and Thecla arrived at Thiam's home. They'd spent the day conferring with church members.

"Where is Paul?" Thecla asked, when she didn't see him in his usual chair.

"Thecla, Julius came this morning to take him and the other prisoners to the docks. They've left for Rome," Thiam said.

"What?" Zohres said.

"No." Thecla said, at the same time. "He wasn't ready. How can he make that trip? He's hardly able to walk."

"I know, Thecla. I tried to reason with Julius but his mind or somebody's mind was made up. You know, there's no arguing with Romans," Thiam said.

"It's wrong but you are right, Thiam. To try to change Julius' mind could further endanger Paul," Zohres said.

"Yes, Zohres, that's why I stopped arguing and turned Paul over to Julius. Paul blessed everyone in the household before he left. He showed no fear, accepting God's will," Thiam said.

"Why would they take him so quickly? I thought he was here to recover. That's what they said," Thecla exploded.

"Yes, Thecla, that's what they said; but they were Romans speaking. They change their minds in a whim, just to please a senior officer. One can never be sure," Thiam said in a calm voice hoping it would affect Thecla with calmness.

"We need to go to the docks to find out what their route will be and what ship they're on," Thecla said, trying a new tack.

"They've left hours ago. It will be hard to find any sailor with reliable information."

"They don't pay attention to Romans unless the Romans want to get a ship for Rome or some other destination," Thiam said.

"That's what we need to know. Did they use a ship from this port or the one they came on from Caesarea, the Adramyttian ship, Paul called it. We need to know the way they'll go to Rome," Thecla maintained.

"Thecla, let's have a cup of wine, slow down and give this situation more thought," Thiam suggested.

"I agree, Thiam," Zohres said. "I'm concerned for Paul and am anxious to know more but our sources are limited…to a few drunken sailors," he added after a brief pause.

They continued to talk about Paul's destiny and each ones dire prediction. Rose joined the group, as she had overheard the early heated discussion upon Zohres' and Thecla's arrival. Rose sat quietly, wringing her hands, occasionally, in obvious concern. As the hour grew later and darkness settled on Sidon, Rose brought plates of bread and cheese for all to share. The discussion finally came to a close when Thiam and Zohres agreed to go to the docks tomorrow morning to seek information. They bade Thecla to stay with Rose and await their return. With that agreement, the household members shuffled to their rooms for the night.

In the morning, Thecla and Rose prepared the morning meal. Thecla was buoyed with the expectation of the men's success in finding information about Paul. When they sat to eat, Thecla lead them in prayer for the success of their search for information about Paul and Paul's safety. After the meal, the men left for the docks, Rose took up her stitching and Thecla went to her room to pray and meditate.

In late afternoon, Zohres and Thiam returned with a modicum of news. Thecla met them as they entered, begging to hear what they had gleaned at the docks. "Do you have news? What is your news? Will Paul be all right? What ship is he on?" breathless, Thecla couldn't ask the questions any faster.

"Slow down, Thecla, let us sit with a cup of wine, to relate what we heard," Thiam said.

Rose heard Thiam's answer and entered the room, almost instantly, with a tray of four cups of wine. When seated, Thiam and Zohres each took a large swallow of wine and wiped their mouths with the backs of their hands. The women stared with questioning looks, which shouted *what has become of Paul?*

"Here is what we heard from some of the sailors. Paul and five other prisoners, in chains, were loaded on a merchant vessel, too small to go all the way to Rome. A captain said they'd probably hug the coast and likely go as far as Myra. Another sailor said it will be a dangerous voyage this time of year, especially from Myra to Cnidus, if they go that way," Thiam related.

"That scares me. Paul is in such danger. We all must pray for him," Thecla said, with a tremor in her voice.

With those words, they all bowed their heads and joined hands while Thecla led them in prayer, "Oh, my almighty God, please bless and care for your beloved minister, Paul. He is a captive of the pagan Romans, who wish harm to him. He has served you with every fiber of his being. He has spread your Holy Word to countless people throughout our known world. He has taught, preached and baptized, bringing those people to salvation. Please don't desert him and us who care for him in this hour of need. We beg you, oh Lord."

A moment of silence then the four people stayed sitting; the women softly sobbing while the men sat with eyes closed, in meditation.

Thecla stood first. She said, "We must eat our evening meal then go to our rooms for more prayer and meditation. Sleeping tonight, may not be possible for me."

"I will assist you, Thecla," Rose said. "Sleep will escape me, too."

Zohres and Thiam began a low level conversation rehearsing what they'd heard at the docks. After some minutes of contemplating the discussion, they decided nothing more could be done. Zohres suggested he and Thiam should talk to the church leaders tomorrow. The meal was served and discussions were brief and solemn. No one felt the need or the desire to express their private thoughts or concerns.

Days passed into weeks, which flowed into months. It was nearly a year since Paul had been taken to Rome. Thecla rose one mid-summer morning and announced she was going to the docks. "That's not a good idea for you to go alone, Thecla," Thiam said.

"Yes, you and Zohres have both told me that but I need to find a ship that will take me to Rome," Thecla said, as she started down the hall to her room.

Thiam and Rose were not surprised. He thought, *Rose and I noticed her talking to sailors when they came to the church. We supposed she was asking them about going to Rome. She knew we'd try to talk her out of it, so she's going to take matters in her hands, as she's done for many years. We can't treat her as a child, holding her hand, protecting her. We've tried several times to explain to her the dangers of going to the docks alone. Rose even sat with her, talking woman to woman. Why won't she listen? What can we do? If only Paul were here…*

Thiam sat to talk to Rose once again. "Rose, Thecla says she's going to the docks. What can we do?"

"Thiam, we can do nothing. She is a determined woman, well aware of the risks. She is set to follow Paul to Rome, regardless of the risk."

"I'll follow her, at a distance; that way, I could protect her if she runs into trouble."

"I don't think that's a good idea. Even if you appeared in time to help her, she'd not appreciate it. You and I both know

Thecla well enough to know she'd begin preaching to the offenders, so strong is her faith."

"Yes, that's what worries me. I fear her faith has blinded her."

"No, I think she is relying on the power of prayer. We, too, must believe and pray for her."

"As you say, Rose, we will pray for her."

Thecla left the house, unimpeded to journey to the docks.

"It's decided then, you are leaving on the *Euraquilo*, taking the same path as Paul," Thiam said, as they sat for the evening meal.

"Yes, we'll leave on the morning tide, following the coastline to Myra then another ship on to Rome, if the winds are good," Thecla said.

"You know your ship has the name of one of those winds?" Rose asked.

"Yes, but I don't believe in omens," Thecla said.

"That's fine because it would frighten many passengers," Thiam said.

"Many passengers may not have heard the true Word," Thecla countered.

"We will keep you in our prayers and have the congregation pray, also," Thiam said.

"Then I will be safe," Thecla concluded.

Ten days later, the *Euraquilo* docked in Myra. This was the end of the line for her vessel. Now, Thecla must find a ship bound for Rome. Myra was a port servicing Egyptian grain vessels under the ownership of the Government of the Empire. Rome was in continuous need of grain for food. Famines struck on a semi-routine basis, making grain transport a priority for the Empire. Thecla spent many hours of the day, visiting shipping offices in search of a ship transporting grain to Rome. She was summarily turned away or a few times, men were boorish and obscene. At these times, she walked to a bench and prayed for those men and for help and guidance from God.

She had just finished one of those prayer breaks when a young ship captain approached her. Wary at first, she looked up at him, wincing when he laid a hand on her shoulder.

"I mean you no harm," he said quickly. "I overheard your interaction with the last dock man. I am Captain Spurgus and I sail a grain vessel to Rome. My last sail to Rome will leave in two days. I am offering you a place on that vessel."

"You, Captain Spurgus, are an answer to my prayer. I am Thecla. I have endured much rudeness and animosity from these men. I will accept your offer of passage, most thankfully," said Thecla, somewhat in awe.

"You will be safe on my vessel, with a cabin adjacent to mine. No sailor will dare interrupt your peace.'

"Thank you. I'll spend my days in prayer and meditation, for I'm planning to visit a holy man, Paul, now in Rome."

"Yes," he said, "I know of this man. He and several prisoners were taken to Rome last year. We don't usually haul prisoners."

"I am amazed you've heard of him. I follow him and preach and baptize with him."

"You are welcome on my ship. Be here in two days' time."

"I will. God bless you."

Two days later, Thecla arrived at the dock, where she stood watching the bustling sailors make final preparation for the voyage. She spied Captain Spurgus making his way toward her, stopping now and then to speak to a crew member. He approached her, smiling, "Good morning, I see you are ready to board."

"Yes, this is a much anticipated voyage. I appreciate your willingness to allow me to board your ship," she said, with the sidelong look at the crew busy loading bags.

"Yes, come along. You will be safe on this ship. The whole crew was told of your embarkation and the importance of your safety."

"You are deserving of mine and God's blessings for your kindness and help." *He must be blessed by You, my God, sent specifically by You to help me through this travel. So few men can show a lone, unescorted woman true respect. Oh my Lord, you have provided the help I sought. I thank you and I love you with all my heart, my mind and my soul. Please continue to help me through this journey so I may again follow your beloved minister, Paul.*

Standing by the rail next to her small cabin, Thecla watched as Myra disappeared into the haze of the shoreline. The heat of late August was ameliorated by the steady breeze off the water. A loneliness, unknown to Thecla, began to settle on her. Tears rolled down her cheeks as she tried to blink them away. *Oh Paul, what are they doing to you? I am coming to you, to hear your voice, your words of faith and love of the holy Word. I want to hear, again, the story of your conversion. Tell me, yet again, the Words you heard from Jesus. Do you still hear them in your imprisonment? I miss you; I miss following you in the crowd of believers. I miss my followers, too. I'm on this ship heading to Rome. I'm coming as soon as I can to be with you. I'm praying you're not being tortured and you have some faithful followers with you.*

Drying her eyes and doing her best to recover her composure, Thecla made her way back to her cabin. Just as she took her seat, a knock came on the door.

"Who is it?" she called.

"The captain," Captain Spurgus said.

"Oh, come in," Thecla said, unbolting the door.

"Hello, I'm glad you're keeping the door bolted," he said. "That's not why I'm making this visit, though."

"Is there some problem?"

"Oh, no. I saw you at the rail. You seemed to be crying. What is the matter? May I be of help?"

"No, I meant for no one to see me in a brief moment of loss of composure."

"Is that what you call it? I could have sworn you were crying. Please feel free to talk to me if something is not right with you."

Thecla felt relieved, instantly, almost as if Paul were speaking to her. "I had just become aware of an overpowering feeling of loneliness; something I've never felt before. I wish it hadn't come while I was outside where I could be seen."

"Yes, I understand. That is why I waited for you to return to your cabin before I approached you. You may not believe this but I, too, have bouts of intense loneliness."

"Oh, Captain, that is difficult to believe. You are surrounded by a large crew, some undoubtedly are friends."

"No, it's not the number of people; it's the one particular person, who is gone, my wife."

"Your wife is gone? Did she leave or did she die?"

"She died, eight months ago. She died in childbirth. Both she and the baby, my son, died." He turned his head so Thecla couldn't see but she thought he was hiding tears that started to fill his eyes.

"You are lonely, I can see that. Please feel free to talk to me when you have the time. I'd like to tell you more about Paul."

"I've heard snippets about him from other seaman. I'd like to visit you from time to time and hear about him and his message. We're heading into some treacherous waters so please remain in this cabin and try to remain calm."

"Yes, I'll do that and I look forward to your future visits."

Captain Spurgus closed the door, Thecla replaced the bolt. *I wonder what he's heard of Paul. His wife was the love of his life, certainly and his lost child was a blow; yet he manages to hide such difficult, emotional feelings. Perhaps, I can help lift his burden by sharing the Word of God with him, through our discussions about Paul. I will pray for guidance on this profound task.*

Suddenly the ship started rocking, slowly at first. Then the rocking motion was a tossing so strong Thecla was forced to lie on the cot and grasp the edges to stay off the floor. She began to feel nauseous and dizzy. Then she remembered the captain saying they'd be entering some treacherous waters. *We must be in the waters he mentioned. Oh, Lord, help us through these waters and see us safe in calmer waters,* she prayed over and over. She felt a swirling motion, which added to her sick feelings. She vomited but only dry heaves because it had been so long since she'd eaten—

her stomach was empty. This discomfort lasted through the night. Thecla prayed between brief naps.

At last, morning light shown through the small window and the tossing and swirling stopped. Thecla tried to rise but felt weak and her legs shook so she dared not walk to the door. She remained sitting on the cot until her head cleared and she finally felt stable enough to open the door and, perhaps, seek some food. A small tray, just a slab of wood, held a cup of water and a bowl of gruel. Pleased, she took it into her cabin and consumed it, readily. Thecla surmised she had the captain to thank for the food.

Three days later, Thecla heard much loud talking outside her cabin. She lifted the bar, opened the door and saw the crew preparing to enter a dock. The ship yard looked large, with several sailing vessels at dock. She heard someone shout "Fair Havens, Crete". Captain Spurgus walked by at that moment, seeing Thecla, he said, "We'll be stopping here briefly then we go out to sea until we reach Malta. From there it will just be three more stops until we get to the port closest to Rome. We're past the worst part and if the winds hold, we should not have any more rough seas. Are you all right?"

"Yes, I made it through the tumultuous night. Did you leave the food outside my door?"

"Yes, I did. It was the least I could do. You were being a brave passenger," he said.

"Thank you for the food. I prayed all during that night."

"Then your prayers were answered. We had only one perilous incident. You probably felt the swirling."

"Yes, I was quite sick by that time."

"Most of us were, to some degree. I must complete my rounds. We'll be off on the next tide."

True to his word, the ship left Fair Havens the next morning, early.

The next day, just after mid-day, Captain Spurgus knocked on her door. "Captain Spurgus," he called before she could ask. Thecla unbolted the door and admitted him. "Would you like to come to my cabin? There's more room and would be more comfortable."

"Yes, that would be fine," Thecla said.

Upon entering his cabin, she was astonished at the size of the room and the furnishings. "You have a nice cabin, Captain," Thecla said.

"Yes, I do most of my work here, checking maps and charts, completing logs and various tasks to keep the records current," he said. "Then I must keep watch on the pilot and other sailors, oarsmen, supplies, cooks, many chores."

"You are, indeed, a busy man. Do you ever have time just to think?"

"I've tried to minimize that time because my thoughts always darken."

"Yes, you told me a little about your thoughts. Do you wish to tell me more?

"I've never had someone to talk to, who really cared about my inner thoughts."

"Have you no family?"

"No, I have no siblings and my parents are both long dead."

"I will listen then. What do you most wish to tell me?"

"I want to talk about my beautiful wife, Nadin. She had flowing, wavy black hair and black eyes, in a way similar to yours."

That may be why he's decided to talk to me. Be careful and listen carefully, thought Thecla.

"All right, tell me about Nadin. What was she like as a person?"

"Nadin was a delicate person, confident but quiet. She kept to herself, not spending much time out of the house, except for shopping. I thought she might be afraid of crowds but she claimed she wasn't, just wanted to spend as much time as possible with me or in our home. Our love story began when we were young, too young to marry. We lived near each other in Alexandria. We invented stories, her about the children she would have; mine were sea stories about the places I would travel. We finally approached marriage age. I sought her hand. Her father and mother approved immediately. The wedding took place and Nadin became pregnant within a few months. I sailed to Rome and before I got back, six months later, Nadin was dead and so was the baby."

He finally felt comfortable to break into full weeping. Thecla reached for his hand. He held her hand as he shook in weeping. Finally, through tears he looked at her and said "I never got to say 'Farewell' or hold my son."

"That is most painful," Thecla said. "Would you like to offer a prayer for their souls?"

"Would that help?"

"If you think it will. Join me, I'll lead the prayer."

"I'm willing to try."

They joined hands and Thecla began, "Oh, Heavenly Father, please hear our prayer in supplication for Captain Spurgus' peace of mind. He is a hard working seaman who has lost his dear wife, Nadin and their infant son. Please shower your blessings and graces on Captain Spurgus to help him through these difficult times. Please release him from the burden of guilt he bears for having been gone when his wife and son were called. Though we do not know why you chose that time to take them, we have faith you took them to a beautiful, peaceful place they deserved. Please continue to shed grace unto us and hold Captain Spurgus' hand and tread with him so he may lean on you in times of need. Bless us all."

"That was a beautiful prayer. I feel better already. It was a healing prayer."

"Yes, prayer can be healing. It's not magic, though. There will still be tough times. Please recall the words as best you can to derive some hope again. Of course, you will meet them when you arrive in your heavenly home."

"How can I be sure to get there?"

"We'll talk more about these things as your time permits. I will share enough of Paul's message with you, to help you think about baptism and salvation."

"I am most grateful to you."

Thecla left his cabin and walked to the rail to partake of the sunshine and contemplate Captain Spurgus' desire to hear Paul's message. *How will I begin speaking to him? Should I find out first what he has heard about Paul and, especially, what has he heard of Paul's message? From there I can work to show him the power of God, the power of faith and where we stand in the eyes of God. If he wants to continue and we have time, we'll talk of Paul's conversion and his missionary trips. I'll also help him learn to pray. I'll try to answer his questions along the way. I must go back to the cabin now to pray and contemplate this impending task.* She entered her cabin, dropped the bolt and stayed inside for the night.

Docking in Malta was much different from docking in Crete. The islanders welcomed the ship, inviting Captain Spurgus and five of his top crewmembers and the passenger, Thecla. They debarked and walked a short distance to an estate, belonging to Publius, the chief official of the island. He welcomed them to his home and showed generous hospitality for three days. During their first dinner, Paul's name came up when Thecla said, "I'm going to Rome. I am a follower of Paul."

"Yes," Publius said, "Paul was on a ship that docked here last year. He was a prisoner, along with five others. My father was sick in bed, suffering from fever and dysentery. Paul went in to see him and, after prayer, placed his hands on him and healed him. We all prayed in grateful ardor. When this had happened and the word got out, the rest of the sick on the island came and were cured."

"That is an amazing story but Paul is a blessed man and chosen by God to spread his Word in many forms," Thecla said.

"We found that. He chose to spread the Word through healing then he proceeded to teach. All quite interesting and many are now believers," Publius said.

"Have they opened a church?" Thecla asked.

"Yes, some have started regular services as Paul directed. He baptized many. He and the prisoners were here for three months," Publius said.

"Would you introduce me to the church leader?" asked Thecla.

"Yes, we can do that tomorrow morning," Publius agreed.

Thecla, realizing she may have been monopolizing the host, turned to her meal and Publius went on to talk to the captain and his crew.

After a restful night in a "real" bed, instead of the cot in the ship's cabin, Thecla rose and joined the other guests who were breaking their fast.

"Thecla, I've arranged for Soma, part of the house staff, to escort you to meet the church leader," Publius said, soon after Thecla was seated.

"That will be a most interesting visit," Thecla said.

A dark haired olive-skinned young woman came in and stood behind Publius. "Thecla, meet Soma," Publius said.

Thecla first bowed in gratitude to Publius then a slight nod of her head, as a way of showing respect and expressing thanks to Soma. Soma smiled and expressed her wish for Thecla to finish eating and they'd be off.

Thecla joined Soma, as the men left to engage in ship repairs for the next several days.

"Publius suggested we begin by finding the church leader, Suleiman. He will be able to give you information about the beginnings of the church," Soma said, as they began to walk toward the city..

"I find this visit exhilarating because Paul was part of that beginning wasn't he?"

"He definitely was. Did you know Paul?"

"Oh, yes, I've followed Paul. I followed him in Iconium, Pisidian Antioch, Syrian Antioch and Sidon, until his capture. I am a minister because of him."

"What does that mean, exactly?"

"Paul anointed me to be a minister to preach, teach, baptize and start churches."

"I didn't know women could do those things."

"Traditionally, women did not. Paul said God instructed him to anoint me a minister."

"You must be excited to be the first woman evangelist."

"Yes, I was excited but overwhelmed and deeply in need of more teaching and observing Paul's preaching and teaching. I had many questions for him and much to learn.

"He was an amazing guest. People came from around the island when they heard he'd cured Publius' father."

"I would have loved to be here when that happened. Paul is a powerful man when he teaches and preaches."

"Yes, people were in awe when he preached, as well as when he cured the sick and infirm."

"I have seen him do those things when he visited other cities. I think that is why the Romans tracked him and arrested him."

"Yes, he was a prisoner when he came here. Julius, the centurion in charge of the prisoners was a good man. He gave Paul his freedom to heal the sick, to preach and teach, to baptize and start a church. Secretly, I think Julius believed in Paul's message but could not bring himself to shed the Roman mantel."

"That is a precious thought. I'll pray for Julius and beg God to give Julius the grace to follow his belief."

"Oh, Thecla, that would be wonderful if Julius becomes brave enough to follow Paul."

"I'll be going to Rome in a few weeks; maybe I can find information about Julius. I could ask Paul about him."

Moments later on the edge of the village; "Here we are at Suleiman's house. I'll knock to see if he is home."

"Who is it?" called a man's voice.

"It is Soma, with Thecla, a close follower of Paul," Soma replied.

The bolt slid open and Suleiman stood in the doorway. "A close follower of Paul?"

"Yes, I am Thecla, an anointed minister by Paul's word," Thecla said.

"Thecla, you are most welcome and thanks to Soma for bringing you," Suleiman said. "Please, both of you come inside."

When all three were seated, Suleiman asked Thecla, "Please tell us of your time following Paula and your anointing."

"It's a rather long story. Do you want it all?" Thecla asked.

"As much as you care to tell," Suleiman said, as Soma nodded.

"All right, when you've heard enough, let me know," Thecla said.

She began her story when she first heard Paul teach, from there she commenced her story, finishing as the sun was lowering in the west and light in the house was growing dim.

"It will be getting dark soon. We must be going, for we have a ways to walk," Soma said.

"I so appreciate your visit. I can harness my mule and take you home by cart," Suleiman offered.

"Oh no," both women said simultaneously. "I am accustomed to walking," Thecla said. Soma readily agreed, saying "I, too, walk to the village often. I enjoy the walk."

"That is fine then," Suleiman said, "Please join us for our next service here, in two days."

"We look forward to it," Soma said.

They walked as fast as possible to arrive home before dark. They talked little, both lost in their own thoughts. Soma thought about Thecla's story and Thecla thought of Suleiman and his hospitable offer of the ride home and the invitation to the church service at his home.

The next morning, as they broke their fast, Soma and Thecla learned the extent of the repairs needed on the ship. It was greater than either thought, according to the discussion of Publius and the crew. They projected it would take three weeks to make the repairs. Captain Spurgus appeared distraught. "We can't wait more than two weeks. We are already behind schedule and the weather is going to get worse, not better in the seas we still must navigate," he said.

"That is true," Publius said. "We'll do our best to make the repairs as quickly as possible but pitch can't be rushed."

"That I know," Spurgus said. "Please do the best you can."

Two weeks and a day later, Thecla boarded the ship and they left port on the morning tide. She arranged her things again and made herself as comfortable as possible in the tight space. The odor of pitch was noticeable, pleasant at first then becoming an irritant to eyes and nose. At that point, she ventured out to view the sea and take the fresh air. The sails were full and the ship skimmed the water. Then she looked to the south and saw a dark cloud mass rising, a storm was coming, she was sure. Only a moment latter, Captain Spurgus said "There'll be a storm tonight." Thecla jumped, noticeably startled.

"Sorry, I thought you heard me approach," the captain said.

"No, I did not but that's all right. I had just noticed the storm clouds," Thecla said.

"Yes, it is coming fast as these storms tend to do. Be sure to get into your cabin and settle in as best you can. The ship will rock for a while."

"Yes, I realize that. Do the best you can and God be with you."

"I will and say a prayer for us."

"I certainly will," Thecla said and the captain was gone.

How would Paul handle this? Thecla thought, as she entered her cabin, bolting the door. She'd heard about his shipwreck experience from Suleiman's church members. *Paul would pray and ask for God's help. He would listen for word from God. I am not able to receive word directly from God, in the same way. I'm not chosen as Paul was. That doesn't matter, though. God loves me as much as He loves Paul. He doesn't play favorites. When I need Him, He listens and helps.*

Later, the sky darkened and Thecla heard rolls of thunder, each roll seeming closer. *The storm is upon us,* she thought. Instead of just thinking about Paul's shipwreck, she began to pray in earnest for their ship. She prayed through the night, as the ship was tossed.

Morning came; though the winds calmed and the ship was none the worse, the rain pounded the deck. Through it all, there was a knock at her door. *Who could be out in this rain,* she thought, while saying, "Who is it?"

"Your captain," she heard.

"Please come in," Thecla said, as she hurried to lift the bolt.

The captain entered, bearing a bowl of porridge and a cup of water, covered by an oiled cloth. "I thought you might want to break your fast," he said.

"You are absolutely right, captain," she said, with a smile.

"The wind is calmer and we're moving fast. We'll be in Rhegium tomorrow then it's on to Ostia. There the grain will be unloaded and we can search for Paul."

"Are you going to help me find Paul?" Thecla asked, surprised.

"Yes, it isn't safe for you to go around Rome in search of Paul by yourself."

"I welcome your assistance. God bless you."

"I have an additional motive."

"And what is that?" she asked, with faint suspicion.

"I want to meet Paul and talk with him."

"I understand, you want to make sure our teachings are the same?"

"Oh no, I believe your teachings, it's just you've spoken so much and so highly of him, I wish to meet him myself."

"That is most kindly of you. Of course I want you to meet him. You will enjoy talking with him."

"All right, it's settled then. Wait for me when we dock at Ostia. As soon as I've checked our load in, we'll head for Rome."

"How far is it from Ostia to Rome?"

"Not far, an easy walk, about five or six miles."

"That will be fine."

"I must go now to prepare for our next port then prepare to sail and dock."

"We'll talk again after we dock in Ostia?"

"Yes, I'll meet you on the walk by the grain depot."

"Go with God, Spurgus."

Five days later, after smooth sailing, they docked in Ostia. The day was clear and a little chilly. Thecla walked down the gangplank after several sailors. She walked toward the only building, which looked to be busy with men coming and going out its doors. Spying a wooden bench within eyesight of the door, Thecla walked to it. There, she commenced waiting for Spurgus.

At least an hour went by before Thecla finally saw Spurgus emerge from the building. She walked toward him, realizing he hadn't seen her. "Spurgus, I'm right here," she said, coming up behind him.

"Where did you come from?" Spurgus asked, surprised.

"I was sitting on that bench over there," she said, pointing to the bench.

"Oh, I didn't look over there."

"That's all right, let's be off."

"Yes, the load is accounted for, so there is nothing left for me to do here," he said, tucking a parchment receipt into his robe.

On the road leading to Rome, they encountered heavy traffic, with carts pulled by mules, slaves carrying litters and groups walking in both directions. They found little time to talk as they dodged people and animals.

Finally, the city came into view. "I had no idea how large the city of Rome is," Thecla said, in awe.

"Yes, it is the largest in the known world." Spurgus said.

"Have you seen other cities in the known world?"

"Yes, Alexandria, that is a major city. Have you been there?"

"Oh, no, I heard Paul mention he'd like to go there."

"But he never made it there?"

"I don't think so. We should ask him when we meet him."

"First, we have to find him. I'll go to our grain office and ask where I might find the prisoners brought recently from Sidon."

"It hasn't been recent. He may have been here over a year by now."

"Yes, but this ship from Sidon had Roman prisoners on it and had been wrecked, grain lost and recorded. There must be some record of it."

"All right, that's as good a place to start as any; better than asking anybody on the street."

"Much better," Spurgus agreed, smiling.

Arriving at the Grain Office, Spurgus went inside, while Thecla sat on a bench by the door. Several men left the building; at last Spurgus returned, smiling. "Yes, they did have a record of the tragedy. The grain was lost, as were several sailors. The prisoners were logged into the roles of the prison and Paul was placed on House arrest."

"Did they record where the house is?"

"No, we have to go to the prison office to find that information."

"Well, let's go then."

The prison office was further up the hill. Spurgus, again, entered the prison office, while Thecla waited outside. Spurgus returned after a short time, "The house is not far away, just two streets over."

"That's fine. We will actually get to see Paul now," Thecla said, excitedly.

"We'll walk in that direction. Hopefully, he'll be there.

"Yes, I hope so too."

They walked over to the second street and began to inquire at houses. They went to the house pointed out to them by the slave at the last house where they'd stopped. When they arrived at that house, sure enough, the door slave said he'd get the resident. They heard shuffling and other noises as they waited. Then the door opened and a soldier came to face them. "Our prisoners are not allowed to receive guests," the soldier said.

"I have traveled from Sidon to see Paul," Thecla said.

"I don't care how far you've come," the soldier said.

"We visited the Gain Office, of which I captain the Imperial vessels for grain delivery. I brought her here as a special guest," Spurgus said.

"A special guest of a prisoner? I never heard of that," the soldier said.

"Paul is a special prisoner, ask Julius who was the centurion who brought him to Rome," Thecla said.

"Julius will be here tomorrow morning. Come here early and he may let you speak to this Paul," the soldier said.

"We'll be back tomorrow morning," Thecla said, disappointment clouding her eyes, as tears began to form. She turned away to hide the tears and the soldier returned to the house.

"We must find a place to stay tonight so we can arrive early tomorrow," Thecla said.

"There is a house not far from here where the owner lets out rooms. Maybe he has some available," Spurgus suggested.

"That would work well," Thecla agreed.

The next morning, after a light meal, they walked to the House where Paul stayed. As soon as Spurgus knocked on the door, a slave opened it. "We are here to call on Paul," Spurgus said.

"I'll get the Centurion to speak with you," the slave said and disappeared into the house.

Momentarily, the door opened and Julius stood before them. Thecla greeted him with a big smile, as he recognized her. "I remember you from Sidon but I don't remember your name," he said.

"I am Thecla and this is Spurgus, the Captain of the ship that brought me here," Thecla explained.

"That's right, I remember now, Thecla. You are a close follower of Paul," Julius said.

"Yes, is Paul here? Captain Spurgus also wants to meet him," Thecla said.

"Paul is a prisoner on house arrest and cannot have visitors," Julius said.

"Can you make an exception? We have come so far to see him and my health and well-being depend on my hearing his words," Thecla said.

"I have no doubt of that from what I saw in Sidon. Yes, I can and will make an exception," Julius said.

"We are grateful, Julius. Praise the Lord," Thecla said.

"Praise Him," Julius said, bowing his head as he said it. "I'll bring Paul out."

I wonder if Paul has baptized Julius. He bowed his head while praising the Lord. No pagan Roman would do that. I won't ask him, though: maybe Paul will explain or say something about it, Thecla thought.

Julius returned with Paul almost immediately. "Paul, you look healthy and happy," Thecla said, surprise in her voice.

"God bless you, Thecla. I did not expect this surprise," Paul said.

"I decided to follow you, when your ship left Sidon. It was too late in the sailing year, so I had to wait for the next year," Thecla said.

"Paul, I've made an exception for you to visit with these guests. You are all welcome to come inside. I must remain with you while you visit," Julius said.

When they were seated inside on couches, Thecla introduced Spurgus to Paul. Paul talked of his travels to Rome, the shipwreck, loss of nearly the entire crew, his arrest and his life in Caesarea. Thecla begged him to lead them in prayer. Paul, of course, was happy to do this:

"Let us first give praise of thanksgiving to the Almighty God for Thecla, Spurgus, Julius and this house. Please accept us as we are and we beg you to accept Spurgus as one of us, Your believers. You sent me a dream last night that a sailor would come to me, requesting Your Word. I am only too pleased to share Your Holy Word with Spurgus. Please give us the strength to complete this mission. We praise Your Holy Name and beg Your blessings."

Spurgus was aghast, "You dreamed I was coming?"

"Yes, God said 'a sailor would come this next day to hear My Word'," Paul said.

"Does God speak to you often?" Spurgus asked, with some doubt in his voice. He'd heard other charlatans making such claims.

"No, He does not. I only receive mental thoughts, never dreams. I only saw him once when I fell from my horse on the way to Damascus," Paul said.

"Please tell me about that and all of His Word," Spurgus said, relieved and convinced Paul was real and a true minister of God, as Thecla had said.

Paul and Spurgus continued to talk while Thecla listened and Julius left to check on his other prisoners.

Julius returned and said, "We must now end this teaching for today. Please set a time to meet again."

"Let us continue this discussion and teaching tomorrow morning," Paul said.

Spurgus agreed and Thecla and Spurgus left for their rooms.

After several more meetings, Spurgus announced he would have to leave to go back to Ostia to reconnect with the grain office and resume shipping. "Paul, can I please have baptism now, before I leave?" he asked.

"Yes, please meet us at the fountain in the park near here," Paul said.

"That is the place we perform all baptisms. It is close and few people are there," Julius said.

"That sounds perfect," Spurgus said.

Just after mid-day, Thecla, Spurgus, Julius and Paul walked to the fountain. Children were playing at the fountain but ran away as the adults approached.

Standing by the fountain, Paul began a prayer, "Bless us, oh Lord, as we prepare to admit this man, Spurgus, into Your church. We pray, he will live according to your commandments and Your Holy Word," withdrawing a cup from his robe, he proceeded. "I baptize you, Spurgus, with this water upon your head," and while pouring the water on Spurgus' head, he said, "in the name of the Father, the Son, and Holy Ghost. Live with God in your mind, in your heart and in your soul," Paul finished.

After the baptism, Spurgus felt relief and he joined the others in kissing and hugging to welcome him into the church. Julius and Paul walked back to the prison house, while Spurgus and Thecla returned to their abode.

"I must pack my few belongings and leave for Ostia in the morning," Spurgus said.

"I'm sorry to see you go, though I know you must," Thecla said.

"Thecla, you changed my life and brought me happiness. I know now and I believe my wife waits for me in heaven," Spurgus said, placing his hands on her shoulders.

"Yes, she does. Go with God and pray in times of happiness as well as times of difficulty. God appreciates thanksgiving as much as pleas for help."

"I will take to heart your words as well as Paul's. I will sail with a new mindset. I know God is with me no matter where I sail."

"Yes, be an instrument of peace and goodwill. God bless you always."

Spurgus removed his hands from her shoulders and she turned away, immediately, because tears were threatening to spill from her eyes. Thecla didn't realize Spurgus was fighting the eruption of tears, also. He walked to his room then, to avoid having Thecla see his tears.

Spurgus left in the morning at first light. He would try to get a lift from a farmer with his cart or wagon but he knew that was not dependable. The walk to Ostia would take a few hours.

Thecla walked again to Paul's prison house. Julius met her at the door. "I have bad news for you, Thecla. Paul must go back to prison and I will be re-assigned as soon as the army decides who needs a Centurion," Julius said.

Thecla was in a state of shock. "How could this happen? I thought everything was moving along as Rome wanted it," Thecla said, close to tears.

Julius took her in his arms, attempting to give her a shoulder to cry on. "There's nothing that can be done, Thecla, Caesar will have his way," Julius said.

"I know but why now? Everything was set up so well," Thecla said, as she began to sob.

Julius was prepared for her breakdown. He soothed her as best he could, patting her head and back and hugging her close. When she finally brought herself under control, Julius, with his arm around her shoulders, ushered her into the house and bade her sit on the couch while he brought Paul in to meet her.

Paul came in with Julius. Paul was looking subdued but, otherwise, unmoved.

"Paul, what do you think will happen?" Thecla asked, hoping to hear Paul had some inkling from God.

"I'll go back to prison as soon as the guards come to take me," Paul said.

"They'll be here within the hour, I think," Julius said. Looking at Thecla, he said, "It would be best if you were not here then."

"I want to be here to defend Paul and try to change their minds," Thecla said.

"There is no changing their minds. This is Rome, not an outlying area where guards are sometimes not loyal to anyone," Paul said and Julius shook his head in agreement.

"Their minds are not changeable. They have their orders and they will carry them out. They will beat you if you try to stop them, maybe kill you," Julius warned.

Thecla continued to defy Paul and Julius until there was a loud knock at the door.

"They're here," Julius said, as he walked to the door.

Opening it, three big prison guards stepped in, pushing Julius aside, saying "Where is he?"

"I am here," Paul said.

The guards moved to him, as he extended his arms behind him, the chains scraped with a cold, metallic clang as the guard tightened them.

"No, you can't take him," Thecla yelled, attempting to free herself from Julius' grasp.

"Shh, Thecla, it won't help him," Julius said, as he re-established his hold on her.

The prison guards ignored her as they marched Paul out of the house and down the street to the wagon meant for prisoners. The wagon had wooden bars on the sides and both ends. Two guards sat on the bench with the driver, with one in the back with Paul. Thecla saw them drive away. After they were gone, she dissolved in a flood of tears. Julius could do nothing to calm her so he decided to let her cry it out. Later in the day, Thecla calmed herself and sat on the couch. Julius came into the room and said, "Thecla, are you all right?"

"Yes, I'll be all right, I think," Thecla said.

"Do you have a place to stay?"

"Yes, the place where Spurgus and I were staying."

"Is it expensive?"

"I don't know, Spurgus was paying for it."

"But he's gone now. Did he leave you any money?"

"No and I never thought to ask him for any."

"I'll walk to the place with you and inquire how much has been paid."

"Oh, Julius you don't have to do that. I'll figure out something if he hasn't paid."

"No, I'll not have you sleeping in the street or in a doorway. Paul would not want that either."

"I understand. Certainly there must be church members close by. They are usually welcoming to another member."

"Yes, I know of a few. Let's go to the place you were staying first then we can decide what to do next."

"All right, we should go before dark."

"Yes, my replacement will be here in a few minutes."

Several minutes later, Julius came back to Thecla. "It took a little longer because I had to explain Paul's absence to him," Julius said.

"He was probably surprised," Thecla said.

"Surprised and unhappy. He enjoyed listening to Paul. I don't think he was baptized but maybe considering it."

"I could help him with teaching, if he desires to keep learning."

"That's right. I remember you're saying you are also a minister."

"Yes, chosen and anointed by Paul."

"I'll ask him if he's interested. Not now though, let's be off."

They found the rooms had been paid for but not paid beyond the last night. Thecla's small satchel was behind the desk and the attendant immediately handed it to her. Julius thanked the man and they exited the house.

"I know church members, Elon and Paula. They live near here and may be able to help," Julius said.

"All right, I'd like to meet them," Thecla agreed.

They set out to find Elon and Paula's house. The sun was low in the west, when Julius and Thecla arrived at Elon's house. Julius knocked on the door and they heard a soft voice ask who was there.

"Julius and a woman from the church."

The door opened and a small black haired woman stood in the doorway. "Hello, Julius. Is Paul all right?"

"Paula, this is Thecla a minister chosen and anointed by Paul. As for Paul, he was just today taken to Mamertine Prison."

"Oh, that is terrible news," Paula said, clasping her hand over her mouth.

"Is everything all right?" Elon asked, coming to the door.

"They took Paul to Mamertine Prison this morning," Julius said.

"What will happen now, Julius?" asked Elon.

"We won't know until we hear from the prison," Julius said.

"Is there any way to find out sooner?" Paula asked, recovering from the shock.

"I plan to go to the prison tomorrow morning to get answers," Thecla said.

"I'll go with her tomorrow morning," Julius said, surprised at Thecla's declaration.

"Please, come inside so we can talk privately," Elon said.

When everyone was seated and served a cup of wine, Julius delineated Paul's activities leading up to his removal to prison. He emphasized Thecla's arrival and Spurgus' baptism had nothing to do with Paul's sudden removal. *I think he's saying that for my benefit, to make me feel better. Paul was probably removed because Julius let us visit him at the house. According to the first soldier we met, visitation at the house was forbidden but Julius would be there the next day, shifting the blame to Julius, a Centurion,* thought Thecla.

The conversation finally shifted to Thecla's need for a room in which to stay until Paul's situation was understood. Elon and Paula readily agreed and Paula took Thecla's hand and they walked to the room in which she would stay.

"Do you think Paul's removal will reflect badly on you, Julius?" Elon asked, after the women had gone.

"That I don't know. I think they've been ready to re-assign me to a training facility for some time. I am a trained soldier, after all. I've been expecting to be re-assigned to a regiment. The Parthians, as you know, are our main problem right now," Julius said.

"Yes, we've heard of them for years now."

"It will boil up again sooner rather than later. I'm sure Caesar is planning to build a better Imperial Army to meet the next uprising."

"That's most likely true. Let us know how it affects you, Julius"

"I surely will, Elon."

The women arrived in the room arm-in-arm, smiling. They looked as though they'd been friends for life.

Feeling relaxed, Julius said, "I'll be going back to my room now. I'll return to go to the prison with Thecla tomorrow."

They all agreed and said their farewells until tomorrow.

Just after they'd finished breaking their fast, a knock sounded at the door.

"That's probably Julius," Paula said, as she went to the door.

"Welcome, Julius, come in," Paula said, as Julius entered.

"Is Thecla ready to visit the prison?" Julius asked, hoping she'd changed her mind.

"Julius, thanks for coming," Thecla said, "I'm ready to find out about Paul."

They exited the house and began walking. "We need to talk about this mission," Julius began.

"Yes, we do," Thecla returned, adamantly.

Julius knew from her response, there was no possibility of changing her mind. "We won't be able to change anything. What has happened has happened by Caesar's decree."

"I don't think Caesar decrees every prisoner's life," Thecla said.

"No, only the ones he takes an interest in."

"And why would he take an interest in Paul; one crippled man, preaching love and peace?"

"You've mentioned the word, 'preaching'. His preachings are about the one God, love and peace, when Caesar is about to go to war and is trying to get as many recruits as he can for the next Parthian war."

"So what damage can one man do?"

"Plenty, if the words become known to those who don't want to serve. Caesar considers that to be treason."

"That's ridiculous. Paul's not a traitor, he's a Roman citizen."

"That may be true, but treason is a problem, even for or especially for a Roman citizen."

"He is also of the Equestrian Class."

"That will make no difference in his sentence, only how it is performed."

"We'll ask to see him and find out why he's being held."

"Be prepared. We may not get much information."

"We'll see." Thecla said, as determined as ever.

They continued to walk in silence, each consumed in his and her thoughts.

Arriving at the door, Thecla wanted to knock. "I know you are anxious to talk to them but I'd better make the first introduction," Julius said.

After a second, louder rap on the door, a slave appeared. "What is your need?" he asked.

"We need information about a prisoner, Paul," Thecla blurted, before Julius could answer.

"I do not and cannot give out information about prisoners," he said.

"We understand that," Julius said. "Will you please allow us to talk to one who is in charge?"

"I will do that," the slave said.

Moments later, a guard, armed much as a soldier came to the door. "You are seeking information?" he asked.

"Yes, we're asking about the prisoner, Paul, who was brought here yesterday," Julius said.

"He is awaiting a hearing and judgement by Nero," the guard said.

"May we see him?" Thecla asked.

"No," was the guard's emphatic answer.

"Why not? He's done nothing wrong," Thecla stated.

"That is for Caesar to decide," the guard said.

"But Caesar doesn't know him as well. I've followed Paul for years," Thecla said, voice beginning to waver."

"That may be true, but Nero met him in Crete on one of Paul's trips, so he knows him," the guard countered.

"Can't I at least talk to Paul?" Thecla asked, almost begging.

The guard knew she was close to breaking and shouted, "No."

"That is unkind, Paul would want to talk to me," Thecla said, her voice catching in her throat.

"My work does not include being kind to prisoners. I will return to my work." Turning, the guard strutted through the doorway, dropping the bolt after shutting the door.

Thecla was in tears as they left the prison. Julius wasn't sure what to do so he put his arm around her shoulders and they started to walk back to Elon and Paula's place. Thecla sobbed all the way to her room. Paula didn't know exactly what happened but she knew they'd gone to the prison and she was sure it hadn't gone well, at least the way Thecla thought it would. "Thecla, dear, sit on the bed and tell me what happened as soon as you can," Paula said, in as soothing a voice as she could muster.

Thecla responded to Paula's soothing voice and hand rubbing her shoulders. Thecla finally stopped sobbing and looked at Paula, saying, "I'm sorry. I just fell apart when that guard shouted at me when I asked if I could see Paul. He just shouted 'No' as loud as he could."

"Yes, dear, the prison guards only know how to speak that way. They are brutes."

"I only wanted to tell Paul I'm praying for him."

"I know and Paul, being human, would want to hear that but, look at it this way. Paul knows you're here and knows you follow him. He realizes he is in your prayers as are you in his. Please take that to heart."

"Thank you, Paula. Those are beautiful words. I'll pray now for Paul. I'll come to the common room when I've finished,"

"That's fine. God bless you, Thecla."

Paula returned to the common room where Julius and Elon were discussing the situation at the prison. Paula heard Elon tell Julius, "I know of a few church members who are guards at the prison. I don't know if any of them are near Paul's cell block."

"That could be helpful. Perhaps, I could work something out with one of them, if they'd consider helping a fellow Christian," Julius said.

"It would probably be best if we waited for word of his meeting with Caesar and the decision Caesar will make."

"Yes, we need to proceed slowly. Keeping Thecla from jumping out there could be the biggest problem."

"Bless her, she's praying and calming. I think I've helped her to see this as a problem that requires calmness and a clear head," said Paula.

"Paula, your intervention is priceless. I could not calm her," Julius said.

"Actually, as we talked, she calmed herself and turned to prayer, which usually calms a troubled soul," Paula said.

Two years later, Paul was scheduled for his meeting with Nero. He had been in prison, teaching and preaching to the prisoners and guards. He'd baptized many prisoners who were facing death. At least three guards were converted and baptized. More guards were interested but wary of baptism because of their jobs. Paul understood this and included them in his prayers.

Julius had the names of two Christian guards at the prison where Paul was held, Jessic and Tomas. He had approached them over time and they were happy to give Thecla a pass to Paul's cell. The guards reported to Julius that Paul's execution was scheduled for Saturday, Juno 25 at sunrise. Thecla was advised of this and was determined to visit Paul the day before.

"I will go to Paul on the evening of Juno 24," Thecla said to Paula.

"That is a good idea. He will welcome your presence," Paula said.

"We'll talk about our missions and pray together for the spread of The Word."

"We'll join you here. Maybe most of our church will join us in prayer."

"Paula, that lifts my heart. I will try to not spill tears in Paul's presence. I've probably shed all the tears I had for him already."

"You are a strong woman. I'm sure you will be strong in his presence."

"God bless you, dearest Paula."

"God bless you too, my dear Thecla."

Exactly ten days later, as the day, Juno 24 was drawing to a close. Thecla was prepared to go to the prison. Julius arrived, looking nervous and apprehensive. "Are you ready to go, Thecla?" Julius asked.

Surprised that Julius was being so abrupt, she answered in her usual upbeat tone, "Yes, Julius, I've been ready to see Paul for a very long time."

"I know you have, I just want to get this over with. I'm more deeply affected than I thought I would be."

"Yes, we are all deeply affected. Paula and Elon will try to gather the church members here tonight for a prayer vigil."

"I plan to join them as soon as you are safely in the cell with Paul."

Outside as they walked toward the prison, Thecla said, "I am grateful to you for arranging this visit with Paul for me."

"Oh, Thecla, it's the least I could do for you. I only wish I could have arranged more visits for you."

"I know; there's only so much the guards could do. It would be a problem for them, Paul and me, if I'd been allowed to come in more times. Once is enough. I certainly don't want you or the guards to be in any trouble."

"I don't think we will. Jessic and Tomas know what they can and cannot do."

"Yes, they are wholesome men."

As they rounded the last corner near a side door of the prison, Jessic was standing beside the door. "Put your veil over your face so only your eyes are visible and tighten your cloak about you. You must be bent at the shoulders to look as a cleaning woman. I'll hand you a bucket when we get inside."

"All right," Julius said, "I'll meet you at this door tomorrow morning."

Jessic and Thecla nodded and went inside the prison. Jessic handed her a bucket and Thecla did her best to look to be an old washer woman. "You are doing fine," Jessic whispered, as they made their way down the long hallway. A few minutes later, a guard came down the hall toward them, smiled at Jessic and asked, "Need the old woman to clean a cell?"

"Yes, a prisoner vomited and shat all over the cell. He's facing crucifixion tomorrow."

"Ah, that would explain it." He chuckled and moved on.

Having rounded two more corners, they came to a cell with Tomas waiting nearby. "We're here, Thecla. Go inside with Tomas," Jessic whispered, as he turned and walked back the way they'd come.

Tomas quickly unlocked the cell and ushered Thecla inside. He had explained to Paul how Thecla would be brought in earlier in the day, so Paul was not surprised by her mode of dress.

Paul immediately blessed Tomas and whispered a short prayer for Jessic. Thomas left noiselessly and disappeared down the hall. Thecla was amazed at how quietly Tomas shut the cell door; usually the guards shut cell doors with a loud "clang". *This is a different task than the guards usually have. They seem to be enjoying this assignment, which they've taken on with the grace of God,* Thecla thought.

Though there was no place to hide in the cell, Thecla sat on the floor on her cloak, behind Paul's cot in the corner where the light did not reach. They did not talk for several minutes.

After they recovered, Paul said "This is where my mission ends."

"I will carry it forward, God willing," Thecla said.

"Let us end this mission in silent prayer," Paul said.

"God's will be done," Thecla enjoined.

Early in the morning, at first light, the guards came to take Paul for execution. He, without a word, accepted their tying his hands behind his back.

Thecla was not as accepting; but in her usual manner, screamed, "No, do not take him. He has done no wrong." She lashed out at the guard, screaming "No, No, No."

The guard grabbed her flailing arm as she tried to strike him, always screaming. She pulled away and tried to strike him again. He hit her harder this time and pulled his sword from its scabbard. With the flat of his sword blade, he hit her hard across the top of her head and pushed her to the ground. Her head hit the dirt floor with a loud thump.

"That'll shut her up. Let's go." The guards marched Paul to the execution site.

Jessic, the prison guard entered Paul's cell to find Thecla on the floor. He could not awaken her and found no breath being expelled from her nose. He carried her body to the side door of the prison where Julius awaited. When Jessic exited the door, he said to Julius, "I am quite sure she is dead. The guards must have found her and killed her."

Julius, overcome with grief, took Thecla's body in his arms and sat to weep.

"I must go back inside," Jessic said, as he placed a hand on Julius' shoulder and wiping a tear from his own eyes.

In time, Julius recovered, stood and carried the body to Elon and Paula. They too were overcome with grief. Elon was the first to recover and said, "I'll go to announce to the church members her death. I'm sure there will be another vigil."

A vigil was decided on that night. All church members attended. Julius was selected to give a prayer and brief statement about Thecla's life. He ended saying, "Thecla's mission ended with Paul's mission. She was, as God willed, the first woman evangelist. Thecla and Paul have been silenced forever but God's Word will continue to spread. This we pray."

Epilogue

The growth of the church during the second century was a time of great challenge, unrest and great excitement. The new Christian movement was expanding rapidly from its primarily Jewish boundaries and into pagan and gentile territories. A diverse mix of people from eclectic backgrounds were coming together to form the church. Discussions were evolving about the role of men, of women, of sexuality, the worthiness of marriage, divorce and singleness, wealth and self-control as tools for the expression of faith.

Many women during this era made controversial decisions drastically altering their lives when they encountered the power of the Holy Spirit and felt the calling to press into this radical movement. One of these women was named Thecla. Thecla was, genetically, an Egyptian woman from a wealthy family. Her story leaves us with a fascinating example of the life of a woman who rejected a life of comfort, marriage and the expected gender norms of her time to carve out her own ministry as a scholar, teacher, preacher, healer and missionary.

Thecla's story is one of many in the Apocryphal Acts which portray women giving up riches and sexual activity to follow the

Apostles. She was an aristocratic woman who, despite great opposition, upon hearing the preaching of Paul, renounced her family and fiancé to follow him. She eventually became a missionary and lived out her life teaching The Word of God.

Who then was this remarkable woman? A first century woman from Iconium, Thecla heard the Apostle Paul preach during his missionary journey to Asia Minor (Acts 13:51). A young woman from the upper class, she was engaged to an equally wealthy man, until, from her window, she heard Paul preach. After hearing Paul's gospel message, Thecla longed only to hear more. According to legend, Thecla refused to eat or sleep, and repeatedly attended Paul's sermons despite the disapproval of her family. Because Thecla became a Christian, her family was outraged, viewing her conversion as a betrayal of Rome and all Rome represented. Thecla rejected the status and comforts of her class to serve God, as an ascetic and missionary near Antioch. There she had a dynamic ministry of preaching, teaching, and healing. In fact, Basil and Gregory, two early church fathers, referred to Thecla's ministry in Syria, as a prominent center of teaching and healing. A team of archaeologists excavated her compound in 1908, describing its dimensions as approximately the size of a football field.

Thecla was a popular figure in early Christian art work, often pictured between two lions, kneeling down in submission to His Holiness. Thecla served as a pious model of women's ministry in the early church. Murals celebrating her legacy of teaching beside Paul suggest she had a prominent reputation as a teacher and leader.

In the Eastern Orthodox Church, the wide circulation of the *Acts of Paul and Thecla* is evidence of her veneration. She was called "apostle and protomartyr among women" and "equal-to-apostles in sanctity". She was widely cited as an ascetic role model for women. During the fourth and fifth centuries, Thecla was lauded in literature as an exemplary virgin and martyr by ascetic writers and theologians, such as Methodius of Olympus, Gregory of Nyssa and Gregory of Nazianzus. The Eastern Rites of the Eastern Orthodox Church commemorate her on 24 September in churches following the new Calendar and 7 October for those using the old or Julian calendar.

Her veneration flourished particularly at Seleucia Cilicia (where she was said to have lived to old age and be buried), Iconium (present day Konya), and Nicomedia. The society also appeared at least as early as the 4th century in Western Europe. Chamalières in France was believed to hold relics. The obscure saints, Tecla of Aquileia and of Trieste are modeled after her. In Bede's martyrology, Thecla is celebrated on 23 September, which was her feast day in the West, though in 1969, the Roman Catholic Church removed Thecla's feast day from the Calendar of Saints for lack of historic evidence. The Western Rite Parishes of the Orthodox Churches continue to celebrate her on 23 September (new Calendar Parishes) and 6 October (old Calendar Churches). The Western Rite Monastic Order of Saint Paul the First Hermit celebrates her feast day on 24 September.

Notes

[1]Berean Study Bible (Acts 15:36–41; Acts 18:23–28)
[2]Churchs - a body of believers not a church building. The believers met in a believer's home. Rarely, a congregation grew too large to be accommodated in a believer's home. In that case, well-to-do believers sometimes would contribute money to build a church building.
[3]https://www.cbeinternational.org/blogs/thecla-coworker-apostle-paul

Character List

From the Bible:
Paul
Thecla
Barnabas
Theoclia, Thecla's mother
Thamyris, suitor rejected by Thecla
Alexander, city magistrate of Pisidian Antioch; attempted sexual advances directed at Thecla

Fictional characters:
Leos – Thecla's older brother
Governor Castellius – governor who heard Theoclia's and Thamyris' complaint against Thecla
Daphne – Thecla' friend
Orel – Daphne's husband
Zaortha – Thecla's best friend and ministerial helper
Jamel – convert in Lystra and joined Paul's group, becoming Thecla's follower and close friend of Zaortha
Abril and Jonas – heads of the church in Iconium
Onesiphorus – friend of Paul and Barnabas in Iconium
Cestus and Amatol – minor city officials in Lystra
Governor Captilan – Governor of Lyconia
Charis and Delva – Paul's friends in Iconium
Tatin – Pisidian Antioch church leader
Tortus – minor city official in Misthia
Anna, Tessa – sisters from Iconium who lived with Thecla in the cave
Betta – Anna's daughter
Gracea – Tessa's daughter
Lexus – chief Misthia city council member
Epaphras – in charge of a new congregation in Laodicea
Jonas – a new, impatient follower, refused to follow Thecla to Sabatra

Hertko – head of a family who decided not to make the trek to
Sabatra
Yaco – wagon master and follower of Thecla
Zohres – hermit living in a cave outside Iconium
Ascus – driver of the supply wagon
Thaddeus and Janis – owners of a home in Derbe where Thecla,
Zaortha and Jamel stayed
Margot – Thaddeus and Janis' neighbor interested in Paul's
message
Captain Jomas –Captain of the ship from Perga to Syria
Ronal – church leader in Syrian Antioch
Beatrice – Ronal's fourth cousin and soon to be his wife.
Kena and Patel – Ronal's, servants and escapees from a slave
vessel
Thiam and Rose – church members at Sidon
Julius – a centurion of the Augustan cohort
Captain Spurgus – captain if a grain vessel of the Empire
Publius – the chief official of the island of Malta
Soma – woman from Publius' house selected to introduce Thecla
to the church leader on Malta
Suleiman – the church leader on Malta
Elon and Paula – Church members in Rome
Jessic and Tomas – Roman prison guards who had been
converted to Christianity

About the Author

Mary Jo Nickum is an award winning author. She has published a chapter book, two young adult novels and six reluctant reader books for high school science students.

She is a retired professional librarian and an English teacher. She lives with her husband, John, in the Phoenix, Arizona area.